I0535527

MINDSHOT

A novel by

JOE MENENDEZ

Copyright © 2012 by Joe Menendez

This is a work of fiction. Names, characters, places, and incidents either are the product of the author's imagination or are used fictitiously. Any resemblance to actual persons, living or dead, events, or locales is entirely coincidental.

All rights reserved.
ISBN: 0988379805
ISBN-13: 9780988379800
Narrow Bridge Films

Cover Design by Kyle Valentic

For my mother, for sharing her love of reading with me.

To the memory of my brother, with whom I made many Super 8 films (including sci-fi ones).

For my sister, for putting up with me our entire lives.

And most important, for my wife and daughter, who inspire me each and every day to be a better man.

PROLOGUE

These were not aliens.

Their immense, angular vessel descended from space, puncturing the daytime sky like a blinding flash-bulb rupture.

But these were not aliens.

Seeing their astral mother ship plummet down that fast was like a scene from any standard science fiction movie—especially when the craft halted to an abrupt stop, hovering above the fortified military base, brooding over it like looming death.

But these were not aliens.

When tall, hideous, androgynous humanoid brutes emerged from the strapping spaceship, revealing their oily, lanky, over-sized heads and deep black eyes, when they levitated off the ground and breached the base forcibly, everyone assumed this was some sort of apocalyptic invasion by hostile alien life forms.

But this was not an invasion, and these were not aliens.

Not even ten minutes earlier, things had been so quiet in the surveillance unit on the base that Colonel Craig Canoga was debating if he should sneak off and get in a workout. After all, this day had gone like the one before it and the one before that—and all the ones prior to those. The days came and went just as Colonel Canoga desired them to—uneventfully. Certainly, there was no reason to suspect anything like this would happen today. There had been no warnings about an inward-bound anomaly in space. No early detections of what was arriving.

Canoga was confident that all was indeed well.

So he figured—after dutifully checking in with the last of the various security stations—that he'd be able to clock at least thirty minutes on the treadmill down in the gym. His hand had just wrapped around the doorknob to the exit when a lance corporal sitting at a computer station behind him called out, "Sir. You need to see this."

Canoga sighed to himself. *Figures.*

He turned and headed back, as he was charged to do. After all, this base was highly classified and among the most secretive in the United States, so it was proper protocol to clear every anomalous blip that appeared on radar or satellite, no matter how small. It was always nothing—typically an off-course weather satellite or errant meteors—so Colonel Canoga strode over to the lance corporal expecting nothing more than that.

"This wasn't there during our last sweep ten minutes ago, sir." The lance corporal pointed to a monitor with an intricate satellite display of the galaxy. "It's just moved past the moon and is coming right at us."

On screen, a blinking blip moved fast, careening right toward Earth—a direct line, moments from impact.

"Put that on the big screen," Canoga ordered.

A moment later, the lance corporal patched into the largest central security monitor up on the sprawling surveillance wall, spread horizontally before all the gathered military personnel.

The blip continued to move at an astounding speed.

"Defense department drill?" Canoga's eyes narrowed as he leaned onto the lance corporal's desk to get a better look.

"No, sir. I checked." The lance corporal shook his head. "There's nothing going on today. That's not us."

"Could be the Chinese. Russians maybe."

"No, sir. It's not any of them either. In fact, they're tracking this is as well and were hoping we knew what it was," the lance corporal revealed. "Whatever that is, it didn't originate on Earth."

Canoga stood bolt upright and glared down at the twenty-three-year-old. The lance corporal looked up at him and whispered, "Sir, that's a goddamned UFO."

Canoga didn't believe that of course. He couldn't.

Even though they were only mere miles southwest of the infamous Roswell base, in all of his twenty-six years serving, he'd never heard of anyone actually *finding* little green men. It was a myth as far as Canoga was concerned. Aliens simply did not exist.

Yet, there was *indeed* something out there—coming right at Earth—and nobody knew what it was.

Canoga picked up a nearby phone, punched a few buttons, and waited. A moment later, he spoke.

"Ma'am, we have a situation." Colonel Canoga told whoever had just answered and then proceeded to debrief the person. The moment Canoga was through, the lance corporal pointed at the monitor.

"*Breach*! It's here, sir! Breach!" the lance corporal called out.

All heads turned to his monitor.

"Whatever that is, sir, it just crossed into our atmosphere! And, Christ! It's heading right toward this base!"

No longer satellite imagery, the monitor switched to long-lens security cameras, which were pointed skyward, and had now focused in on this strange vessel in the sky that was descending so fast, the camera was barely able to keep it framed.

Canoga returned to the phone, tension in his voice.

"Ma'am, we may be under attack. No, this is not a drill," Canoga reported and then listened. "Understood. Lock down the base, protect Dr. Logan. Roger that, ma'am."

Canoga hung up and raced off to carry out his orders, but not before he looked back one last time to the security monitors.

A massive alien vessel of some sort was now towering over the base. Canoga did not believe in aliens, never had, but that was probably about to change.

Because it seemed aliens had just landed.

However, none of this was as it seemed. Despite all the evidence to the contrary, these chilling, slender creatures that rumbled like a twisting maelstrom onto the military installation hidden deep in the New Mexican desert were simply not aliens.

Who they were, however, and why they were there this day would be shocking to all. For their arrival signaled the end of the human race as we know it.

CHAPTER ONE

Dr. Norman Logan's subterranean lab sits several steel-plated floors down below this military outpost, which, according to the United States government, officially doesn't exist.

This is why one has to pass through various levels of rigid security in order to reach Dr. Logan's highly restricted and sterile laboratory. After all, the US military's top-secret elite weapons, advanced technology, and armaments that nobody has heard of yet are being designed, developed, and built down here within the stainless-steel enclosures, bulletproof glass, and protective polycarbonate laminate white walls.

Usually, it is very quiet on this level. Only on those rare occasions when generals or presidents visit does this section of the base get any attention, which is why when the alarm sounds, Dr. Logan doesn't quite know how to react. At first, he thinks it is another drill, which frustrates him. Logan isn't yet used to the peculiarities of being an army scientist—too many years in the private sector. He is still getting acquainted with all these stern military protocols.

Don't they have anything better to do? Logan wonders, referring to the well-coiffed brass sitting in the cushy administration building aboveground.

Logan sighs and sets down the bizarre helmet in his hands—bizarre mostly because of the squid-like array of electrode tentacles that protrude from the inside base of the helmet.

The alarm is still blaring when his fellow scientist, Dr. Rosenberg, steps over, eating a sandwich.

"Was there a memo about a drill this week?" Rosenberg asks, chewing a mouthful of kale lettuce on Ezekiel bread.

"None that I saw, but maybe they didn't want us to know about it this time. You know, so we'd act like it was a *real* emergency," Logan responds dryly, knowing he now has to step away from his work, even though the presentation for it is tomorrow morning.

Then the floor rattles violently, as if impacted by a sizeable object on the roof of the building. The whole edifice roils with a deep, concussive jolt, and Dr. Logan loses his balance and stumbles forward, but he reflexively braces himself on the edge of his table. The deafening bang is followed by a reverberating, low-end rumble—an aftershock of sorts.

Logan and Rosenberg exchange looks. *What was that? An earthquake perhaps? Wow, maybe this is a real emergency,* Logan fears.

Then, another fervent quake follows—this one deeper and more ferocious than the first, sending items shimmying off tables. Glass shatters. Beakers and the like smash onto the linoleum. Logan immediately grabs hold of the bizarre helmet he was working on, just as it slides off his table. He pulls it close, protectively. This is his life's work after all.

Boom! Boom! Boom!

Three jolts now in succession. Something's happening out there, above them, and it's no earthquake.

Just then, six fully armed marines, led by Colonel Canoga, barge into the lab and immediately take defensive positions. Canoga barks orders back and forth. Tensions are high.

"Secure all the entrances! Lock it down. Nothing gets in. Move!" Colonel Canoga commands.

The other marines disperse expertly, readying their weapons as they go. The metallic sounds of bullets being chambered startle Logan and Rosenberg.

The colonel then fixes his burning gaze on the two scientists. "I need both of you to stay calm and to move back. We'll keep you safe."

But Logan can't move. "Keep us safe from what?"

Instead of responding, Colonel Canoga flicks on an LED security monitor situated at the entrance to the lab. As it powers up, he grumbles, "You're supposed to leave this on at all times."

Logan shrugs. "Sorry. It's just, there's never anything to see on there. Only people coming and going. Nothing ever happens."

"Well, there's something happening *now*," the colonel retorts.

3

Logan and Rosenberg lean toward the monitor, just as the image fades in, revealing a multitude of security panels, each holding a different exterior camera angle. At first, Logan can't understand what they're seeing. The images don't make sense. He then leans closer. All the cameras show a different angle of what appears to be...

A firefight. Yes, *a battle of some sort—outside the base.*

Tanks, artillery, Apache helicopters, all unleashing heavy ordinance on...

What is that?

It appears to be a huge—a very huge—sharp-cornered vessel. A type of vessel Logan's never seen before. And it's hovering over...

Oh my God!

"That's a...there's a spacecraft hovering over the base!" Logan blurts out in starts and stops.

The colonel nods and then adds, "Came out of nowhere. One second to the next. From outer space. We took no chances. Opened up on it right away. Fired everything we had. But nothing's working."

Logan watches as the greatest weapons of the greatest military in world history inflict no damage on this spacecraft.

Instead, something startling happens to every tank that approaches the vessel.

Each tank is *levitated* and hoisted into midair, and flipped vertical, cannons pointed downward. And every attack helicopter? Each one of those is abruptly suspended *in midair too*, as if the pause button was pressed.

"They just do *that*. They *freeze us* there...helpless."

Then the colonel drops the worst news yet.

"And now...now those *things* have made their way inside the base."

Logan looks away from the monitor and into Colonel Canoga's eyes. For the first time, he notices fear in them.

Fear? From this hardened marine?

The men and women guarding this secret base were specially chosen and trained to be here. They're elite killing machines. Nothing scares them. Nothing. Yet, now, fear opaques the colonel's eyes like cataracts.

"*Inside* the base?" Logan asks, hoping he heard the colonel wrong.

Just then, another jolt rocks the building from above. That one was closer—they all felt the concussion reverberate in their chests. And this time, they can see what caused it. All eyes return to the monitors.

There, flickering in unsaturated colors, are three lanky, spindly creatures. They're tall—maybe seven feet in height—moving, *hovering* just inches off the ground, gliding down the halls of the base.

Marines and soldiers arrive and attack them, firing hailstones of lead, point-blank—but their slugs stop in midair where they seem to freeze harmlessly for a moment and then fall to the ground, riddling the corridor with bullets that never once came close to hitting an alien. It's as if the monstrosities *anticipate* the moment the infantrymen are about to fire, and prevent impact.

Then, every soldier, grunt, paddle-foot, and buck-ass private is suddenly hoisted five feet in the air—just as the machines outside were—and all become seemingly frozen

5

there in place. Their weapons are ripped out of their hands and also left in midair, just out of reach. Yet, nobody is truly frozen. The troopers can move and squirm, but they can't break free of their midair perches.

The three creatures glide past them, moving on at will, deeper into the base.

"That can't be real. That can't be!" Logan mutters—mouth agape, breathing hard, eyes on the monitors.

"I assure you, sir, that's real," Canoga says quietly.

The three angular beasts move out of view. The colonel taps the keyboard and switches to other cameras. They watch as the aliens reach a sealed, steel-plated door. They raise their skeletal hands toward the door.

Boom!

A shock wave of energy blasts out from their palms, ripping the heavy doors clean off, hinges and all, as if they were thin, aluminum, coffee-can lids. This jolts the whole building once again. Now, Logan sees what's been causing the violent shakes.

But then, the alien trio stops abruptly.

The lanky brutes glance at each other. Logan can make out their eyes—wintry-black eyes—yet can't see a mouth on any of them. Despite this, they seem to be *communicating* with each other. Conferring even. A moment later, they release another shock wave from their palms, but downward this time, at the floor.

Logan and all the others instantly look up at the ceiling. The newest, most violent jolt came from directly over them. All eyes urgently return to the monitors and watch as the three entities levitate over the gaping hole they've just torn open in the hallway floor. A moment later, they descend into it and float down through the orifice.

The colonel figures it out immediately and says, "Jesus Christ. They're coming *down here*."

He taps a few keys, switches over to another set of security cameras, and watches as the still-descending trio reaches another floor where they release another shock wave. It cuts through the steel and concrete of the floor like a knife through brittle French bread. Again, all heads whip upward as the room quivers. No doubts, the sounds—and the creatures—are getting closer.

Back on the monitor, they watch the trio drop through the new hole and make their way to the floor below. They send down another new intense shock wave—never once slowing. Another overhead boom—they're really close now.

The colonel's seen enough; he moves away from the bank of monitors. "Doctors, I'd suggest you take cover."

Logan, still clutching the peculiar helmet, scrambles away with Rosenberg. Not sure where to go, they decide to duck into Logan's office, which has a window looking out onto the expanse of the lab. Rosenberg instantly locks the door behind them. Logan shoots him a look.

"Oh, good thinking. *That'll* keep 'em out."

Colonel Canoga redirects the marines to form a wide perimeter around the center of the lab, as he barks, "All right, men. They're not coming through the front door. They're coming in through the attic. Weapons upward. Fire at will."

The marines dutifully find and take up new positions in the lab, which, they'd be the first to admit, provides porous cover anywhere they crouch. But it's all they have. Once set, they hold their positions, keeping their M4 carbines trained on the ceiling.

And then, breathing heavily, they wait and they listen.

The powerful concussions get louder. Their breathing gets heavier. The blasts get louder. The alien trio is still coming.

The low-end, booming concussions topple over anything not bolted down in the lab. Soon, however, even items that are bolted down lurch from their foundations too. Kinetic mayhem this way comes. It's as if fifty locomotives attached to one thousand hellfire missiles are barreling down from the ceiling, full speed, descending toward them.

Finally, after what seems like hours, the laboratory ceiling is blown open by a blinding shockwave. A haze of smoke and debris conceals them at first, but then, *there they are*. Dust drifts away, as the elongated trio submerges from above and lands gracefully.

Their oddly peaceful appearance betrays the ferocity of their entrance.

Logan has been looking out the office window this whole time from his hidden vantage point, and he can't believe he's seeing this. It's amazing and terrifying—but amazing foremost.

Rosenberg is hiding under Logan's desk, trembling, almost hyperventilating, not daring to look. He manages to whisper, "W-w-what's happening, Logan?"

Before Logan can respond, the marines open up on the trio—unleashing a hailstorm of firepower. Logan ducks down immediately and doesn't dare stand again, lest an errant bullet find its way to him. The unrelenting cacophony of pounding gunfire and falling shells just outside Logan's office is deafening. The stark smell of scalding burnt metal fills the air.

And then, the shooting is abruptly cut short. Except for the ringing in Logan's ears, it's suddenly eerily quiet. He and Rosenberg exchange horrified looks.

What's just happened out there?

A moment later, they get their answer.

They hear the lock to Logan's door being jimmied, but whoever's working it can't seem to get it open. Logan looks at Rosenberg, who manages a smile, as if to say, *"See? Locking the door worked, ey?"*

But the smile fades instantly when the entire office wall and door explode inward. The dust disperses, and the creature trio coasts forward through the wafting granules. They loom tall over Logan and Rosenberg. Their alien eyes of onyx probe the scientists curiously, as if they are trying to identify them.

Finally, they lock in on Logan, eerily.

With that, Rosenberg is levitated out of the office, away from them—as if discarded. He panics, yelling as he goes. This is horrifying. But he's simply being moved off gently and placed next to the marines, who are all also floating in midair, but they're all alive. Not one was killed, yet they're unable to move. Their weapons are floating near them, out of reach uselessly. Evidently, disarming the US Marines was very easy for the alien trio.

Now Logan is all alone with the aliens, who gaze down on him. Oddly, he's still clinging to the bizarre helmet, but not for long. The helmet begins to rise out of his hands. Logan realizes they're somehow taking it from him—*telekinetically*. When they pry it free, Logan stands without hesitation and reaches for it, snatching the helmet back out of thin air—pulling it back close again. He does this instinctively, as a small boy would with a prized toy.

The moment he does so, he grimaces regretfully.

Why'd I do that? he wonders. *Did I just piss them off?*

Curiously, the trio doesn't seem to react. They just watch Logan, deadpan, and a moment later, they exchange looks. Logan can see that they definitely don't have mouths, yet seem to be communicating again, as if they are intrigued by Logan's instinct to clutch onto the helmet. They all turn back to Logan, and a moment later, the helmet begins to wiggle out of Logan's hands again. This time, he wisely lets it go.

No sense fighting with a superior species, he thinks.

The helmet levitates over to the trio, but they don't take hold of it. It just floats there in front of them, and they examine it inquisitively. Logan doesn't know what to make of these strange beings giving his prized invention the once-over.

Then, the helmet moves back to Logan, but not into his hands. Instead, it moves over his head and is gently lowered onto it, fitting perfectly.

Colonel Canoga, still hovering helplessly, has been watching all this and yells, "What the hell is going on, Dr. Logan?"

By this point, the helmet is secured onto Logan's head, and he knows exactly what they want. He looks from creature to creature to creature and exhales nervously.

"They want me to talk to them."

CHAPTER TWO

Logan straps on the helmet, making sure each electrode is placed on a specific section of his head, just as he designed it to function. He stands there for a moment, eyes locked on the alien trio.

He tells them, "I have to power it up. The helmet. I have to turn it on."

They don't respond.

Logan's not sure if they understand. "It's going to take a minute. The lab is...you know, out of order. It's going to take a minute to get it all operational again."

Then, the creatures do something interesting. They move aside and motion for Logan to proceed. They understand what he's saying. No doubts.

Logan nervously returns to his discombobulated workstation, knowing that every step he takes is being watched closely by the trio. He ticks over to the colonel, his marines, and Dr. Rosenberg—all still hovering at the far end of the lab helplessly, just where the three entities left them.

Logan arrives at his workstation. Equipment and materials are strewn everywhere, shot up to pieces. It's a mess. Logan turns back to the trio and attempts a joke. "You couldn't have come in less bull-in-a-China-shoppy?" He laughs awkwardly.

No reaction. Just stoic looks back from the trio.

"Jokes? Really? You're trying jokes on them now?" Rosenberg whispers through gritted teeth. "Don't piss 'em off, Logan. Please."

The trio exchange looks with each other again.

Is this how they communicate? It has to be, he reasons. Logan is fairly sure of it. He also presumes that's why they had him put on the helmet. So he can understand them. Once the helmet is powered up, Logan suspects he'll be somehow privy to their silent conversation.

The trio finishes conferring—soundlessly—and then turn back to Logan. They motion to his workstation again. Logan understands. A moment later, he begins to clean up the mess and reset his gear.

After a few silent minutes, the still-floating Colonel Canoga—who has been patiently watching Logan reconnect his intricate gear—finally asks, "What exactly does that helmet do?"

Logan is surprised by the question. But then he remembers that even though these brave marines are charged with protecting him, they may not know what he does down here. It's not their job to know. It's all highly classified. Logan glances at the alien trio. They don't seem to object to idle chatter, and besides, Logan gets the sense these beings already know what Logan does down here, so as he continues reorganizing the mess, he explains.

"This helmet allows the person wearing it to communicate with somebody else who is wearing a helmet of their own *with their mind*."

"Wait. You're talking about...mental telepathy?" the colonel inquires.

"I prefer the term *thought-transference*, but yes. Telepathy," Logan responds. "The concept has been around a long time—since the end of the nineteenth century. It's not a new concept, I know, but the way I intend to use it... *is new*."

Canoga then remembers something. "That's right, of course. I heard about this," he admits. "This is what tomorrow's presentation was all about, wasn't it? We were going to field test a new way to communicate with each other on the battlefield. Silently. Without speaking."

"I get the feeling that tomorrow's test isn't going to happen anymore, Colonel."

They all glance over to the alien trio, still watching them in deafening silence.

Logan goes on to admit that the way the military intended to use his device was one option. But his initial goal, long ago, was to create an alternate means of communication with just the mind, forgoing the spoken word. He had one simple and wholly social purpose for his invention—*to cure shyness*. After all, what we're *thinking* is often better expressed than what we end up saying. So why not give humans the ability to converse telepathically? To do that, Logan absorbed all the research and data already in existence on the subject. Over the years, he then started to devise his own massive data on top of the massive data that already existed to make mind-reading possible.

After college, Logan began marketing himself, conducting seminars on thought-transference, and became the world's renowned expert on all things telepathy, which is when he started toying with the concept of noninvasive headgear that could work as the conduit for mental telepathy. Which is what led him to the creation of the Mindshot.

"The Mindshot?" the colonel asks. Clearly, Colonel Canoga is skeptical.

"This." Logan taps the strange helmet on his head. "This is the Mindshot. It's a brain controlled interface. With this helmet, I can read your mind."

Logan then explains that he was twenty-eight years old when he built the first fully functional Mindshot prototype. The colonel, in turn, wants to know how it works.

"I won't bore you with the convoluted minutia of nanotechnology science and neuro-imaging, but it's actually remarkably simple," Logan tells him.

Rosenberg rolls his eyes and smiles. He'd long ago gotten over his resentment of Dr. Logan and his genius invention.

After all, until the day Logan had arrived, Rosenberg had been the base's resident scientific wunderkind, enjoying all the accolades and deference Logan did now. Rosenberg was even a lifelong military man from the get-go, having first enlisted and served in the navy to then cash in on the full ride the US Government provided for his education. After he'd received his doctorate in applied sciences, Rosenberg was immediately assigned to this base with the expressed purpose of designing and building weaponry of the future.

His was a brilliant mind to be sure, but as was soon discovered, Rosenberg was better at improving existing designs and never once came up with an original invention of his own. It was only a few years ago, when he'd first heard of the scientist claiming to have invented a device giving a person the ability to read minds. But Rosenberg dismissed it as rubbish and parlor tricks. Not serious science. So the day General Teapard told him this guy, Dr. Norman Logan, the inventor of something called the Mindshot, would be joining him to work on the base, taking over the laboratory to develop it, Rosenberg couldn't have been more antagonistic and rude. He dismissed Logan at every turn, belittled his work, and could hardly mask his disdain.

To make matters more annoying, the thirty-three-year-old Dr. Logan didn't even look like your typical nebbish scientist—with his matinee-idol good looks and Crest-clean smile.

This guy had it all, so Rosenberg resented Logan deeply back then.

The animosity ended the day Rosenberg put the helmet on, however, and saw it work for himself. That day, he became a believer and Logan's biggest supporter. Rosenberg felt the Mindshot was a game-changer. He knows how it works, so by rote, he repeats how for Colonel Canoga's benefit.

Rosenberg says, "Dr. Logan figured out, conclusively, what parts of the brain transmit direct thoughts. Then he designed intricate and proprietary state-of-the-art electrodes that would receive those thought transmissions, allowing you to hear them just as clear as if you were talking on the phone."

The colonel seems impressed. "Really?"

"Yep. Really," Logan says, flashing his perfect smile. "All you need are two people, each wearing a Mindshot, and Bob's your uncle—you can read each other's minds."

Logan holds up a second helmet now. Just like the one he's wearing. The only difference is this one was damaged when the trio dropped in right over Logan's workstation. Falling concrete and drywall has partially crushed the second helmet, disconnecting electrodes and denting the shell. Indignantly, Logan shoots them a look about this. But the alien trio remains quiet and simply gives Logan an eyeful back. His false bravado fades in an instant. Logan is not about to get into a staring contest with these three.

After a few more minutes, Logan finally connects the last tether—the one running from his helmet into the console on his workstation.

"Now, let's see what these three have to say."

Logan then presses the power button. The Mindshot he's wearing powers up. LED indicator lights shine brightly. Logan turns to the trio and freezes right away for some reason. He says nothing for several moments and just stares at them.

Finally, Dr. Rosenberg cocks his head. "Doesn't one of those things have to wear a helmet too?"

Logan's eyes are wide open in dismay, as if he is listening to something. The trio of aliens moves closer to him.

"They don't need to wear one," Logan says, not moving. "I can already hear them."

What Logan is hearing is perfect American English—urbane and erudite, but distinctly American. It isn't what he expected. Actually, he didn't know what to expect. Certainly not that he'd hear them speak without any of them having to wear the second helmet, but the fact that they are speaking with an American accent is very puzzling.

Dr. Logan, it's indeed a pleasure to meet you, says the creature in the center. It moves forward, establishing that it is the leader. It sounds distinctly male.

Canoga, Rosenberg, and the other marines watch—what is for them—a silent exchange. But it's not silent for Logan.

I'm sure you're wondering what this is all about, the leader continues.

Logan has to resist physically speaking, which of course is an instinctual reaction when being addressed, even if it's through the mind. Obviously, he's still getting used to the Mindshot himself.

Logan responds with just his mind. *Yes. A lot of people here are very frightened,* Logan says. While saying that, he never once utters a word.

Frightening all of you was certainly not our intention, but we knew it was unavoidable, says the leader. *I assure you, however, that no harm will come to anybody here.*

All right. I believe you, Logan says.

You do? The leader seems puzzled. *We're an unknown entity having arrived in a spacecraft. We're impervious to all your weapons. Yet you, Dr. Logan, believe we will not harm you?*

Just makes sense. You seized control of this base without once using lethal force, Logan answers. *Clearly, you could've killed everyone here. Easily. But you didn't. Instead you contained all your opposition without spilling a drop of their blood. So, yes, I believe you.*

The leader seems disappointed by Logan's response. *Oh, I see. I was hoping you were going to say you believed us because you knew who we were.*

That's odd, Logan thinks, momentarily forgetting that his thoughts are now his words.

What's odd about that, Doctor? the leader asks.

Logan smiles. They heard him wondering that. Of course, while wearing the Mindshot, Logan has to remember that there is no such thing as inner dialogue. They can hear *everything* he thinks. *Well, it's odd because I'm not sure why you'd think I'd know who you were.*

The colonel and Rosenberg continue to watch Logan and the alien engage in this uncanny silent conversation. They wish they could hear what's being said. All they can do is watch, as they stare silently.

Suddenly, the alien in the center inches closer to Logan, who then instinctively backs away a step. Logan seems confused by something he's just heard. Becomes more so by the second.

Logan suddenly blurts out loud, full volume, "No! That can't be true!"

Rosenberg and the colonel are startled.

Those are the first words they've heard Logan say in several minutes. They don't know what's happening. They can only watch as Logan continues to back away fearfully from the alien—the one that seems to be following Logan around the lab. No words are being spoken between them, but clearly, Logan is *hearing* something distressing, because second by second, he becomes more and more disturbed.

After a few more torturous minutes, Logan rips off the helmet—as if he can't bear to hear any more of it. He plops down onto one of the many Aeron chairs in the lab and rolls away from the alien, trying to catch his breath.

Whatever he's just heard has him spooked.

"What? What is it, Logan?" Rosenberg finally whispers.

But Logan doesn't respond. He only stares off into the middle distance, ashen.

Colonel Canoga doesn't like this. Something's wrong, clearly. But what? He ticks over to the center alien, who has now moved back, next to the other two. The trio resumes watching Logan patiently, yet unemotionally.

A moment later, Logan turns his glossy eyes to Canoga and says, "Gather your superiors, Colonel. Everyone needs to hear this."

CHAPTER THREE

One by one, each marine and soldier and guard suspended in levitation is lowered to the ground, safely and unharmed. Their weapons, however, are moved away, out of reach. Nobody knows to where. Point is, there are no more guns of any kind. No sense tempting anyone to use them. Every warrior on that base has now been reduced to nothing more than a guy or gal wearing battle fatigues. Not one of them has so much as a pocketknife. With that, they're all told to head outside the base—to the hovering mother ship—and wait.

Up close, the vehicle is awe-inspiring, with its hull made of a foreign-looking alloy. Its sleek aerodynamic design suggests it travels at speeds unimaginable. However, something about the rawboned spacecraft seems oddly organic—as if it were covered in scaled-flesh, like that of a dragon.

And the entire ship seems to be...*breathing*. Heaving. The vessel seems to be a living organism. What Logan learns later is that the carboniferous respirable material that encases the outer shell of the craft is, in fact, critical for traveling through space. That hull allows the immense module to constrict and expand; preventing it from being pulled and ripped apart during what can be a turbulent space flight to and from far distances.

The landing lights—they dazzle with alluring colors never before seen. The vessel is also whisper quiet, yet the cobalt-blue steam that wisps into the air from what seem to be exhaust ports tells everyone the craft is clearly idling.

The vessel is truly gorgeous. Yet, there's also something ominous about it, especially in its sheer immensity and magnitude, which dwarfs them all, reminding everyone gathered that a more advanced life form than they built and piloted this magnificent ship. Whoever constructed this could surely annihilate them at will. It's because of that unspoken disquietude that Logan can tell that General Anne Teapard—one of the few female five-star generals serving in the military—is not happy about having had her entire base disarmed, putting them at the mercy of these...*things*.

It doesn't take long for General Teapard to step outside from the admin unit with her entourage in tow, including Colonel Canoga, who surely had the unpleasant task of debriefing the general, informing her that the entire base was now under occupation. All the enlisted men and women snap to attention and salute as she passes, heading directly toward Logan, who waits for her just below the gargantuan vessel. Teapard sees that every person, enlisted and not, who works at the base has been gathered at the foot of the gigantic spacecraft, which still hovers overhead.

Teapard despised being summoned like this, like she was just some lowly private. By anyone. Even a superior alien species that arrived in a monstrous spaceship. Hell, she even grumbles when the president of the United States summons her, so Logan can't blame—or miss—her obvious agitation as she stops right in front of him.

"What the hell is going on here, Doctor?" she spews. "Tell me right now, before I kick these clammy bastards off my base."

They call her Patton in a skirt. Logan can see why.

"Actually, there won't be any need for that, General," Logan advises. "Would you like to hear it from them directly?"

"Hear what from them?" she snarls.

Logan steps aside and reveals that he's wheeled the lumbering Mindshot console outside to the mother ship. "Why they've come here," Logan says.

Teapard scoffs. "If you think me, or any of my men and women, are going to put that thing on when it hasn't even been field tested yet...Wait...Wasn't that test going to happen tomorrow?"

"It was." Logan ticks over to the colonel, who stands at attention behind the general. "But don't worry. I've been talking to them. So I'll wear the helmet and translate—well, repeat. They speak perfect English." Logan slips the helmet back on, powers it up, and faces the craft towering over them.

A moment later, a gateway-panel on the underbelly of the mother ship opens slowly, unlike any door anyone has ever seen open. It looks like a blossoming flower covered in reptilian skin.

All eyes go there. Watching. Now what? Are *they* coming out now? Are they coming out *from there*? But how? There's no gangway or ramp.

Then moments later, *they* emerge.

Not three, but *eighteen* of these lanky creatures—descending past what appears to be a gantry of sorts for the spaceship. They all look identical, not one different than the other. None of these creatures walk—they all *glide* as if they had no use for their smallish legs. In fact, Logan learns later, they don't. There's also no urgency as they drift down. They know nobody here is going anywhere, so they move slowly, as if milking this moment.

This is the first time most of these people have seen the aliens up close. Some weep instantly at the sight of them, and some tremble fearfully, but most just remain still, absolutely thunderstruck.

The leader—now wearing an ornate sash of some sort—sidles up next to Logan.

And then...silence.

Nobody is saying anything—at least not out loud.

I don't know where to start, Logan tells the leader.

Start at the beginning, the leader says.

Logan smiles. *The beginning. Of course.*

He turns to the gathered throng and proceeds to catch everyone up—taking them to the point he first powered up the Mindshot, telling them about the first words he heard from the visitors and then about the moment the leader identified himself.

After a deep breath, Logan says, "Ladies and Gentlemen, I'd like you to meet Peter. Peter *Logan*."

Same last name? What does *that* mean? The crowd buzzes in whispers.

"He's a direct descendant of mine."

The crowd's mumbles grow louder.

"Peter Logan is not an alien. None of these eighteen travelers are. No. *They are all human beings*."

Human beings?

And one of them is a direct descendant of Dr. Logan?

What does that mean?

How is that even possible?

"I wondered the same thing. At first," Logan admits loudly, over the din of muttering, which gets them all to pipe down.

He then gives more details: While everyone was assembling at the ship, Peter subjected himself to a simple DNA test down in the lab. All human beings have one double helix of DNA, made up of two strands coiled into a spiral—and so does Peter. He also has twenty-three pairs of chromosomes and a bevy of other human commonalities, confirming they are indeed human.

"Except they're humans from…*three thousand years in the future*," Logan reveals.

The collective murmurs grow louder now. Feverish. White noise, as people buzz in disbelief.

Logan makes eye contact with General Teapard. He's not sure what she's thinking, but she's locked in on him intensely as if she's trying to make sense of all this too.

Finally, somebody shouts from the crowd, "Humans? No, they're aliens! Look at them!"

Logan looks to Peter. They had both expected this reaction. After all, Peter looks every bit like what we've been programmed to accept as classic sci-fi movie aliens–hence, the understandable confusion. Time to clear it up. Peter nods, motioning for Logan to continue. He faces the crowd and raises his hands to get their attention. Finally, they quiet down enough so Logan can speak.

"In every sense, yes, they look like our *preconceived* ideas of aliens. But I assure you, they are not," says Logan. "Over the centuries, we humans eventually *evolve*. Into this."

Dead silence. Somewhere, a pin drops.

"In the next three thousand years, a dramatic chain of events in human evolution will be triggered, transforming our appearance and DNA dramatically. We will evolve from *Homo sapiens* to the next phase of mankind..." Logan points to Peter and the other seventeen. "We become *Homo telethians*."

Homo telethians? This is incomprehensible to most, if not all.

"*Homo telethians* have been working on perfecting time travel technology for a very long time and have dispatched many trial missions over the years prior to this one—hence the rash of UFO sightings in the last thirty to forty years. Which means aliens from another planet have never visited Earth," Logan reveals. "No, every UFO sighting ever recorded in history has always been us witnessing *ourselves—Homo telethians*. Future humans, if you will."

The audience is mesmerized, silent and staring. No more murmurs.

"So, the question you're all asking now is..." Logan continues. "How did we end up like this? No offense, Peter."

Peter does something inherently human—he shrugs and waves Logan off casually. Sheepishly, as if saying, "No offense taken." A very common human gesture. Peter doing *that* turned some skeptics into believers. But not all.

"And more importantly, *why* did we end up like this?" Logan adds. Everyone certainly wants to know the answer to that.

"Some say we humans once had tails, but our lack of needing a tail had them eliminated over the generations, via evolution. Same thing here. Clearly, we've done *something* to end up looking like this: a nonverbal alien-looking creature. Question is what? What caused mankind to evolve into a species that doesn't need to communicate orally?" Logan asks.

He doesn't wait for anyone to reply. He provides the answer himself. Logan slowly points to the Mindshot on his head and reveals: "It's *all* my fault."

Logan again looks at General Teapard.

The only change in her appearance is that she crosses her arms defiantly. Then she speaks up—and when she does, out of utter deference, the entire crowd goes quiet for her.

"Let's say this is true—that they're human—why then, Dr. Logan, have future humans, these *Homo telethians*, traveled back in time—to here, to this day, to my base?" Teapard asks, trying with minimal success to control her emotions. "What? Is this some kind of millennial family reunion, or did they come back just to show off how we end up looking in the future?"

Logan looks over to Peter and takes a deep breath. This is where it's going to get interesting. He turns back to Teapard. "I haven't gotten the rest of the details myself, ma'am," Logan responds. "Since I'm the only one that can hear him, I'm going to let Peter explain it from here. I'll serve as a court reporter of sorts. Repeating what I hear." Logan turns back to Peter and nods.

Peter begins, and Logan reiterates for the crowd.

"In the coming years, the Mindshot will become a phenomenal success. It will very soon become wireless. It will be used during warfare with great success. Entire regiments, platoons, battalions, et cetera, will communicate with each other directly, while maintaining complete radio silence. There will be no way for an enemy to intercept messages, emails, nothing. Because, after all, *they won't be able to hear what we're thinking.*"

For the first time, General Teapard softens—that got her interest. Even if what he's saying hasn't happened yet, she sees the potential for this now, militarily speaking.

"The Mindshot will eliminate the need to encode communiqués, for instance—secrets can be overtly and freely passed back and forth through the mind. Strategic plans can be openly conveyed. Mission objectives openly discussed. And our enemies won't know how we do it. As far as they're concerned, we will have dropped off the grid and aren't talking to one another. Yet we're still coordinating and mounting complex and lethal offensives at will. As a result, many wars will be won by the American military."

This gets a resounding "*Hooyah*" from the military men and women. Because now they know that in the future, the American military will still be elite, as well as cutting edge.

"Dr. Logan will continue to work, augmenting and upgrading the Mindshot for the American military, until the day he passes away at the age of eighty-six."

Logan can barely get those words out—*eighty-six*. He dies when he's eighty-six—an old man, but still working for Uncle Sam. To erase any doubts about this, they are all shown the proof.

From somewhere on the vessel, a holographic video display is projected out and onto the assemblage—literally—three hundred and sixty degrees around and over them. Logan learns later that in the future, holographic video becomes completely immersive and specific to the vantage point of each individual viewer. Which means, wherever one stands or sits while watching the three-hundred-and-sixty-degree video, *that* would be the angle from which one sees it. If one were to move, however, one would be able to do so *within* the holographic space of the hologram, changing one's vantage point as one moved, without ever affecting the video on display. So right now, from whatever spot he or she stands, everyone watches the same holographic video. Crystal-clear—so clear it appears life-like—and they all see an old man, working in a lab.

Everyone recognizes the old man in a second. There's no denying it; that old man is Dr. Logan many years from now—at eighty-six. Same features, same face, only wrinkled and aged. Logan understands that the future humans are showing him archival footage from *their* past, but *his* future. Logan keeps his eyes on the image of his soon-to-be self and continues repeating what Peter says.

"Dr. Logan's work will then be carried on after his death..." Peter adds. "...by his son."

Logan turns to look at Peter in dismay.

Son? I'll have a son? With who?

He doesn't even have a girlfriend right now. When is his son born? Logan decides he doesn't want to know, and Peter must hear what he's thinking, because he only shows him his son at work—but nothing more. The holographic video switches to that of a young, thirty-five-year-old man, who looks much like Logan.

"The second Dr. Logan won't be satisfied with just continuing to tweak his father's Mindshot for further use only within the military," Peter says. "Dr. *Henry* Logan will have his own ambitions."

Henry. His name is Henry. Why Henry? Why not Norman Junior or Lawrence, after my father? Logan can't believe he's watching his unborn son at some point in the near future.

"Sixty years from now, Dr. Henry Logan will convince the American government to declassify the Mindshot," Peter says. On the holographic video, Henry confers with the joint chiefs of staff inside the Oval Office. A man in a suit sits behind the resolute desk—surely, the future president.

General Teapard shifts her weight, one hip to the other. She's fifty-three, so she won't be around in sixty years and obviously isn't in that video with all the generals, but she tries to see if she recognizes anybody on the video who would surely be a low-ranked officer today, wondering who the idiot is that allowed this piece of technology to be declassified.

"Once declassified, Henry Logan then sells the Mindshot commercially and becomes a multibillionaire."

All eyes turn to Logan. He's still repeating what he's hearing, but this whole time he is struggling to cope with all this information. His son...becomes a billionaire. *His son.*

"Only a few years after that, every human in America will be using the Mindshot," Peter continues. "Then, its use will spread to Europe, Asia, South America—everywhere. The Mindshot becomes a global phenomenon."

Logan repeats all this dutifully, but it's becoming a more and more laborious task. After all, he's not only hearing about the future, he's hearing about the future of his own lineage.

"Soon, Mindshot technology will evolve from a wireless headset, to direct cranial implants," Peter says. "Within a millennia, every human, by law, will have a Mindshot implanted into their heads."

On the video, they see an operation, but no surgeon. A skull is opened and the brain is exposed, but untethered robotic surgical gear somehow *hovers* over the cranium, pivoting with the dexterity of human hands, while it inserts a small chip into the brain. The skull gets sealed back up with fast-firing lasers in seconds. Not even a scar. The patient wakes up right away, totally alert. The robotic gear *floats* away.

The gathered crowd is stunned, but none more so than Logan. His invention—what he created just to make him rich—changes the world. Literally.

"Hard to fathom, I know. Who would make a law that would mandate a Mindshot—a computer microchip—be implanted into our brains, and how is that technology even possible? But keep in mind, even two hundred years ago, the technology that made airplanes, cars, and rocket ships wasn't fathomable. Times change. And laws change."

More stunned silence fills the air. The future seems so foreign to them all now. Otherworldly even.

"In less than three millennia, we will fully evolve into what you see now," Peter continues. "We will one day all be born without vocal cords and only able to communicate with our thoughts. In the future, Ladies and Gentlemen, evolution makes us all mind-readers."

Collective silence as this sinks in.

"We no longer possess the ability to speak orally," Peter says soberly. "That ability evolves out of us. Since all communication is done telepathically, our mouths subsequently become obsolete and evolve away as well."

Logan wonders. *No mouths? That's insane!*

Peter looks to Logan, who responds, "The primary reason our mouths evolved away, Doctor, is *we don't require a mouth to eat anymore.*"

To say this is unsettling is an understatement. Upon hearing this revelation, it gets so quiet one can hear the slight breeze that whiffs past them all. It's so damn quiet now, one can hear the fabric of some people's loose clothing flapping in the wind. And they're all silently wondering the same thing.

In the future, how do we eat then? Logan wonders.

"Sustenance is still needed for humans to survive—even three thousand years from now. We're still human after all." Peter moves forward for more emphasis. "Only, future humans will no longer need *food* itself."

Peter reveals that new technology will make the physical act of *eating* unnecessary. In the future, humans on Earth will subsequently attain all their nourishment *synthetically*—through artificial means. On the video, what appears to be an oversized bobsled dissolves into view. It's enclosed, with glass portals all around it.

Peter identifies this as *a sustenance chamber*.

The video highlights the following:

Sustenance chambers are eight-foot-long, glass-encased capsules that future humans lie in for five minutes daily while bio-engineered probes enter key points of their bodies, and via advanced technology one can't yet fathom, sustenance is literally inserted intravenously into a human being's body. In a mere five minutes, these sustenance chambers provide all the daily servings from each of the five major food groups, as well as every vitamin and mineral a human being needs. Five minutes a day and you are done, ready to go take care of other business.

It was determined that the chambers made human life more efficient by eliminating the need for humans to take time from their busy schedules to eat three meals a day.

Five minutes in a sustenance chamber will allow humans of the future more time to be productive creating art or music or writing or researching new sciences and generally improving their lives. Thus, future humans spend most of their time becoming even more enlightened than they already are.

The obvious result of this was that, over the years, future humans became wholly dependent on the sustenance chambers for their very survival. Going even one day without an infusion from a sustenance chamber was akin to not eating or drinking water for two weeks.

You'd eventually die of starvation.

Soon, humans, who now relied entirely on getting sustenance from a bio-probe in a chambered capsule, who also didn't speak orally, began to evolve further. To hammer this evolution point home, the video now cuts to a morphing sequence, where everyone literally sees *humans of today* evolving over time into the ones *that look like Peter*. This is probably the most unsettling part of the holographic video presentation. Because now, everyone assembled can see it happen right before their eyes.

Peter continues, "Over time, the more we used our mind, the more we learned to do with it."

With that and without warning, Peter levitates, straight upward. Phoenix-like. Everyone gasps. Still not used to the sight of that. Peter then moves out over the heads of the crowd easily, looking down onto them. Then he manages something else.

A moment later, every person gathered begins to levitate too—straight upward—except for Logan. He remains on the ground, continuing to repeat what he hears. Everyone else in suspended animation gasps and squirms, futilely trying to set him or herself down, but it's no use. They're being lifted by the future humans. Peter slowly and delicately serpentines around them, getting up close to most, eye to eye. And while floating among them, he continues to speak through Logan.

"Do not be alarmed," Peter reassures them. "As you can see, over the millennia, we learned to tap into sections of the human mind still unknown to science of today. We eventually learn to move objects—including ourselves—at any speed or to any height within reason we desire. We can do this with just our mind."

Moments later—much to everyone's relief—they are all lowered to the ground and set down gently. Everyone seems stunned except Logan. This all makes sense to him. He understands that once you learn to read minds, it's a gateway to accessing other untapped parts of the brain that provide abilities that today would deem a person superhuman. Logan has learned and confirmed through his own work that the brain works a lot like a radio or a Wi-Fi signal. When we think something, so goes the premise, those thoughts are discharged into the ethers and can be listened to and even accessed.

But taking the concept of mind-waves-in-the-ethers to the next level, the theory of telekinesis has always been based on the notion that the human brain is capable of emitting thoughts so powerful that they can indeed be manifested and applied physically. As in to easily move any object of any size, with just your mind. It'd be an incredible ability to possess. Nobody in the twenty-first century can accomplish this naturally as they can in the fifty-first century, where clearly, these telekinetic abilities are as ordinary as blinking, as proven here just now by Peter.

General Teapard—who did not enjoy being hoisted into the air against her will—has had enough of what she considers a bleak and upsetting and even dystopian picture of the future.

"Jesus Christ! What's the point of hearing all this?" she demands to know. "They still haven't explained why they're here. So enough with the close encounters mumbo jumbo. I want to know why the goddamned hell you're here!"

She's talking directly to Peter now—her no-bullshit gaze locked on him. Peter looks to Teapard with what seems to be a mixture of curiosity and perhaps a bit of annoyance. Logan's not sure which. Peter takes his time to respond, either because he doesn't know how to say this next part or because he's disturbed by what he *has to* say next.

Finally, Peter begins, again through Logan. "I'm afraid that over the last three thousand years, despite all of our amazing advancements, human evolution has burdened us with one tragically unforeseen outcome," Peter says.

Everyone waits with baited breath.

"Because we could no longer speak orally with one another, thanks to the Mindshot and subsequently the sustenance chamber, something as ordinary as dining together, a traditional custom you still enjoy today—and have for ages—faded away over time. Soon, there was no longer a need for *any* traditional social practice. Culturally speaking, these customs also became...obsolete. So eventually, humans in the future were—inadvertently I must add—weaned off the need to even have any *physical* social contact with any other human. Simply put: we detached from our fellow man and humans evolved further still—irrevocably–into a lamentable and permanent new phase in human evolution, I'm afraid."

The truth was sinking in slowly. No physical or social contact led to the unimaginable.

"Through evolution, the ability of future humans to *procreate*," Peter says through Logan, "was eliminated. *Rendering all humans sterile.*"

The air seems to be vacuumed out abruptly, as everyone gasps at the same time. But it gets worse.

"This means my mission team and I are literally among the last humans on Earth. Once we die—and we will die someday—*humans shall be extinct.*"

Oh my God, Logan thinks.

Moments later, Peter continues, "So in order to save the future human race, we have traveled back to this moment in time, to our past, your present, to ask for your help."

Our help? Logan wonders. *How can we help a fully evolved and superior human species?*

"You can help us complete our mission, Doctor," Peter responds.

Mission?

Logan doesn't repeat the next part at fist. He just listens as Peter says, *We're here to find healthy human volunteers of all nationalities, between the ages of eighteen and thirty to take back to the future—we need them to procreate and repopulate the Earth,* Peter clarifies. *We've named this mission, Operation Noah's Ark.*

CHAPTER FOUR

Operation Noah's Ark.

Logan couldn't repeat those three words. He just stared at Peter—stunned.

Are you serious? Is that why you're here? To ask humans of today to save the humans of tomorrow?

The gathered crowd watches a paralyzed Logan put the squint on Peter. The crowd is clearly waiting to hear the next part.

Peter motions to the crowd. *Tell them.*

Reluctantly, Logan turns slowly to the throng and does so. Their reaction is a mixture of excited though hushed whispers and complete confusion. Even fear. Over the next several minutes, Peter elaborates further, revealing that despite all the future advances in technology, despite future humans even having longer life spans as a result (one hundred and fifty years is the average), despite all of mankind's advances, once Peter's generation of humans die off, all of mankind will too.

Logan thinks, *That's our future...extinction.*

Logan yanks off the helmet and seems to exhale in what feels like the first time in minutes—as if he's been holding his breath this whole time. He's had it, can't take anymore. Logan sets down the Mindshot and marches away from Peter.

He scoots past Teapard, through the crowd, and heads back into the main building. Peter and all the other future humans remain still, like a painting. Only their raven-colored eyes watch Logan go.

Teapard shoots Peter one more look and then steps up to him. They're face-to-face now. Teapard doesn't flinch. What's she going to do? Head-butt the future human? No. Instead, she ticks down to the Mindshot helmet and regards it curiously.

Finally, she asks, "If I put this thing on, will I be able to hear you?"

She looks up to Peter, who nods in response.

Teapard considers this and weighs her options. The general knows that whether she likes it or not, this is her new reality, and if she ever wants to know firsthand how Operation Noah's Ark is supposed to work, she'll need to hear it directly from the source.

A moment later, she takes the helmet between both palms and slips it onto her head.

"Fine then. Let's talk."

Logan sits in his lab an hour later, slumped, unsure of what to do now. Unsure of how to even react. He's numb. Distressed. His life has been forever transformed. He sees nothing positive about this.

Can this all be real? he wonders. *Can it really be that mankind's days are numbered? And I'm responsible?*

It's overwhelming. He needs time to process all this.

So the last person he wants to speak to is Teapard, but that's precisely the person who enters his lab and walks briskly up to him with a slight smile on her face.

She carries a leather binder, snug in her arms. "Quit your sulking, Doctor," Teapard orders. "We have a lot to discuss."

Logan groans. He doesn't bother looking up at her. "General, please. I'm not in the mood."

"Like I give a shit what mood you're in," she snarls. "Those clammy bastards had a lot more to say after you sulked away like a child."

Logan looks up at the general and searches her face.

"Of course I put on your helmet," Teapard snaps back. "You think I want to keep hearing all this secondhand? Yeah, your little mind invention worked liked a well-oiled piston."

"An hour ago, that would've made me beam with pride," Logan says. "Now? Now, I wish I'd become a dentist."

"Well, you did invent the Mindshot, Doctor, and humans from the future are here, and they frickin' talk with their minds, thanks to you," Teapard retorts. "Which means, whether we like it or not, we have to deal with the Clammies."

The Clammies. It was common for the military to nickname their adversaries. During Somalia, they were called "Skinnies." During Vietnam, "Charlie" was the bad guy. In World War II, we were fighting the "Japs" and the

43

"Krauts." Now, because future humans are hairless, slick, and oily, they've been christened the "Clammies."

Teapard adds, "I just spoke with the president."

Logan perks up, just as Teapard knew he would. It had been the president, after all, who had personally approved the Mindshot for development. The joint chiefs rejected the Mindshot initially, and the president over-ruled them, even fast-tracking it over other top-secret military projects.

Logan owed the president his entire career.

"The president wants us to cooperate fully with them," Teapard discloses. "He's also calling an emergency session of the UN General Assembly and plans to get the whole damn planet on board. This thing's going global as we speak."

Teapard fills Logan in on what she learned about Operation Noah's Ark.

"There's going to be an involved selection process, starting immediately. We'll put the word out on the news, social media, everywhere, seeking one hundred thousand volunteers—half women, half men. All volunteers are to come here to be evaluated. They'll be thoroughly examined and questioned by the Clammies. If approved, that volunteer will be given a seat on the vessel to the future."

"Then what?" Logan asks.

"What do you mean?"

"I mean, the approved volunteers get a seat on the vessel and then what?"

"Well, shit, Doctor. They travel through time to the future, settle down, pair up, and start making babies—save mankind from extinction. What else is there to know on our end?"

"Details, for one. How long does it take to travel through time? Is it instant or does it take a while. If so, how long is the voyage? How does time travel work? Where will they live in the future? How will they live in the future?" Logan could keep rattling questions, but General Teapard waves him off.

"None of that concerns me," she says, dismissively. "The president has given me orders. Cooperate with the Clammies. Give them what they want and get 'em outta here. Fast. That's it. And that's all I'm going to do."

"Wait. Don't you wonder what will become of the people you'll be sending through time, once they're gone?" Logan asks.

"Not at all."

"Seriously?"

She takes a moment, studying Logan's face, before finally responding. "That's the difference between a scientist and a soldier," Teapard says. "You're paid to ask questions—I'm paid to follow orders. My opinion is a nonissue."

"But you have one? An opinion," Logan probes. "Don't you?"

Teapard glares at Logan. She doesn't like being asked so many questions. Normally, she gives an order, and it's followed. No questions are ever asked. Rather than berate Dr. Logan, Teapard just barrels on.

"The president wants to come down here personally, do the whole PR thing, and get his picture taken with the

Clammies. For security reasons, obviously, we're not letting him come just yet. But this operation is a go. And he wants you to personally assist me with it."

"Me? Why?" Logan asks. "This is military jurisdiction now."

"You're right. Except there are only two helmets and we can't be trading them off whenever somebody needs to say something to them. More than one person has to be able to talk to the Clammies. Which means you gotta make more Mindshots. A lot more. One hundred thousand of 'em."

Logan laughs to himself; he can't help but see the irony. He's being asked to make more of the very thing that will lead to the end of mankind.

"The president even asked me to remind you that without him, you wouldn't be here today," Teapard says in a measured tone. "You owe him, and he's come collecting."

"He can come collecting all he wants. It's pointless. Even if I wanted to make more Mindshots, I couldn't," Logan says. "We haven't properly tested it yet, General, and—"

"Look, you put it on and you heard them. I put it on, and I heard them. Consider it tested. Right now, I need you to make it wireless. We can't be dragging around that damned refrigerator-sized console everywhere we go. So, you're going to make it wireless and then you're *also* going to equip every standard-issue military helmet with one. I want every soldier, sailor, airman, and marine on this base to be able to read Clammy minds."

Logan laughs. "Really? You're serious? That's what you want me to do?" He scoffs. "General, I barely got the prototypes working correctly. Yet now you want me to make a whole bunch? For everybody? In a matter of days? It can't be done. I need time. In fact, I'm years away from being able to—"

Teapard cuts the scientist off midsentence again, this time by slamming down the thick leather binder she's been clutching this whole time onto the table in front of Logan, who stares at it curiously.

"What's this?"

"Open it," she tells him.

Logan exhales loudly. He reaches inside and pulls out a bunch of paperwork—handwritten notes, a thick stack of them, single-spaced and quite copious. There are also thumbnail diagrams sketched throughout the documents. A quick flipping of the pages reveals they are drawings of a helmet, fitted with a complex menagerie of electrodes. More detailed notes are handwritten next to the drawings. Logan seems thunderstruck suddenly by what he reads. He flips through the pages, faster and faster and faster, trying to make sense of what he's reading.

"Do you recognize those documents, Doctor?" Teapard asks.

"No," Logan tells her. "But it's...that's my handwriting." He never wrote in cursive, and he knows the distinct way he writes his M's—with that curving out at end of the letter. His S's—which look like backward Z's—are also unique. No doubt, he wrote these notes. But when?

"I don't remember ever writing these notes, or sketching these diagrams," Logan mutters.

"And well you shouldn't," Teapard tells him. "Those were written by you—*seventeen years from now.*"

Logan freezes and slowly turns to the general.

She nods and smiles. "The Clammies knew you'd tell me it couldn't be done—making more helmets. After all, the technology hasn't been invented yet. By you no less."

Logan looks back down to the documentation in stunned silence.

"So, they brought this along from their archives. Asked me to pass it on to you," Teapard continues. "It's your research from the future to give you a head start today."

Indeed, Logan now recognizes the advancements in his own work. In his own handwriting. Breakthroughs that he will one day make—only he's seeing them now, ahead of time.

"You're all out of excuses, Doctor Logan," Teapard tells him. "In that binder is everything you'll need to let us talk to those Clammy bastards, get them what they need, and get them the hell out of here as soon as we possibly can."

CHAPTER FIVE

Initially, Logan wanted to hole up in his bungalow on the far end of the base and just read his future notes cover-to-cover. There was so much information to absorb. He wanted to consume it all—he'd inhale it if he could—but there wouldn't be any time for that now. General Teapard only needed him to mine the information about making the wireless Mindshot helmets en masse. Later on, she promised, when the Clammies were gone, he'd be able to pour over the notes to his heart's desire. Logan reluctantly agreed with this arrangement.

So with his cheat sheet of sorts in hand, it didn't take long to make the Mindshot helmets wireless.

During the time that it took for Logan to lead a hastily formed team—which included his colleague Dr. Rosenberg and some other cobbled-together military scientists and technicians—to mass-produce Mindshots, the order was upped to one hundred and twenty thousand.

And the word had gone out to the whole world about the arrival of the future humans.

To say this monumental news went viral would be an understatement. Word spread more swiftly than anyone could have imagined, especially when the president declassified the base, telling the world—in a globally televised speech from the Oval Office—exactly where the future humans were waiting for volunteers. All one needed now was a Google Earth app and one would find the base easily.

Initially, Teapard hadn't wanted the president to disclose the base's location and had offered to find another site for the future humans to conduct the interviews—such as Roswell, since that base was the worst-kept secret since Santa Claus—but ultimately, even she had to agree that *this* base—with all of its state-of-the-art fortification and weaponry—was the best-suited venue to control the influx of people that would surely bottleneck into the area.

And what an influx it was.

Logan couldn't believe how quickly people, upon hearing the news, had jumped into their cars, vans, and trucks—hundreds of thousands of them—and driven out here. It was a ridiculously long caravan in the middle of the desert, stretching for miles and miles. During a well-deserved break from manufacturing the Mindshot helmets, he climbed out onto the rooftop of the base's administrative building and joined several other lookee-loos, as they surveyed the trail of cars in the distance, stretching to the horizon, away from the front gate of the base.

New cars, old cars, it didn't matter. People from every walk of life drove out. Within days, the people who rode bicycles would begin to arrive too, followed later by the people who walked.

These volunteers were all compelled to come there for one reason—they all wanted to be selected to save mankind.

But in case any overzealous volunteers or even terrorists tried sneaking in off the beaten path, a battery of fully loaded Apache gunships patrolled the perimeters overhead, around the clock. Then, in the blue sky over the helicopters, the airspace was severely restricted further by a flock of supersonic F-22 Raptors, which buzzed the base endlessly. On the ground below, heavily armed troops, tanks, and a host of fixed gun positions littered the outskirts of the base, all ready to mow down trespassers.

Logan learned later that the future humans allowed the military full use of their armaments again, knowing that:

A. Using them against the future humans was futile, and—

B. If used offensively, the weapons would simply be confiscated again, creating lawlessness amongst the volunteers in the face of an unarmed military.

To avoid either scenario, General Teapard issued a standing order—weapons were only intended to maintain order and security during this selection process, not to mount an attack on the future humans, under any circumstance.

Bottom line: nobody was getting on that base without permission and no soldier was to engage any of the eighteen Clammies.

Within days, the mileage between Santa Fe and the base would turn into one makeshift automobile and RV roadside community after another. Cars were parked and tent cities were erected along the highway to the base as people took up residency on the scorching asphalt—waiting to be allowed onto the base and eventually be vetted by the future humans.

Those closest to the front entrance got a good look at the spacecraft still hovering in the same spot. Smart phones clicked away. The awaiting volunteers took countless photos of the vessel, but even to those miles back from the front entrance, the immense ship was still visible, it was so massive—this only amped up the desire and excitement of the volunteers to get closer.

Then there was the media.

Every reporter from every news network, every blog, and every newspaper in the world wanted access to the future humans. Teapard knew that there was no way this was possible. It'd be the all-too-familiar media circus that usually accompanied anything remotely newsworthy multiplied by a thousand.

"It'd be a royal clusterfuck like no cluster has ever been royally fucked before," she said about the media circus during a meeting with top military and scientific personnel—during which Logan sat right next to her. But this was the news story of all time and it had to be covered, so they couldn't keep the media out even if they wanted to. It was determined in that meeting that the only way to allow the media to cover this unprecedented event and maintain order on the base simultaneously was to select one pool reporter, one pool videographer, and one pool still photographer. That was it. Then, everyone in the world could tap into the video feed, download the same pictures, and get the same information at the same time.

The question now was who would that pool reporter be?

When reporter names started getting tossed around, only the usual suspects were mentioned—the Anderson Coopers, the Brian Williamses, the Bret Baiers—but Logan had a better idea. He smiled when he thought of it, and since he had some leverage in this whole thing, he felt why not use it for this? He hadn't asked for anything special yet, so he raised his hand. Teapard shot him a glance when he did so.

"Jesus, Doctor, this isn't Kindergarten," she grumbled. "You don't have to raise your hand."

Logan sheepishly lowered his hand.

"So?" Teapard asked. "You had something to add?"

"Yes, actually," Logan said. "I do. I have the perfect person in mind for the pool reporter."

Silence. All eyes on him. Everybody waited to hear whom he had in mind, but Logan said nothing.

Suddenly, he was not sure about his choice. Should he mention this reporter?

"Well? Are you going to tell us?" Teapard asked. "Or am I going to have to put on one of your stupid little helmets to hear the name?"

The chosen reporter wasn't going to be there in time for the first evaluation by Peter and the other future humans, which was taking place in the vast and immense Hanger One, situated toward the front of the base. Hanger One was three times the size of a normal hanger and had been built initially to house top-secret military hardware—like cutting-edge aircraft and rockets—but now, it had been retrofitted to the future humans' specifications to allow for the evaluation process to commence.

As Logan marches over to Hangar One with his team in tow, he smiles. He'd been smiling to himself for the last couple of hours, ever since everyone agreed to his suggestion for pool reporter. They didn't even ask why Logan had suggested this particular reporter, which he was glad about. He didn't want to have to explain. Regardless, the pool reporter was more than qualified and since the lead scientist was the one referring this person, nobody gave it a second a thought. Now, Logan is going to prep the first lucky volunteer—*Kyle Howard.*

Kyle is proudly, what one would term, a conspiracy nut and had already been camping out in the New Mexico desert, just on the outskirts of the base, even before the future human events began.

He is one of those who sees a shadow government angle in everything that occurred in the world and feels there is indeed a smoke-filled back room somewhere where shady deals are being made by powerful men puffing cigars. And he also swears that this very base, the one he is now the very first volunteer to be escorted into, had existed all along, despite the numerous official government denials.

Yet, here he is, entering it.

Validation is sweet, so sweet.

He was first the first volunteer in line, thanks to the fact that he was already literally just outside the confines of the base, trying to find it, when he got the tweet about the future humans' arrival and the call for volunteers. He wasted no time. Kyle was in his car so fast, he didn't even pack up his tent in the sand, leaving it there to be blown away by the desert winds. He skidded up to the guard booth fifteen minutes later, number one in line.

In addition to being a conspiracy theorist, he is also an ardent UFO buff. So naturally, the sight of the mother ship was overwhelming. Kyle saw it and sobbed. Uncontrollably. His whole life he'd been ridiculed for what he believed, and here it was—absolute confirmation of his beliefs. He wasn't insane as most had thought—including himself at times. At that moment, he felt a sense of joy that was inexplicable. This was beyond cathartic. This was bliss. Kyle Howard, the scrawny twenty-four-year-old from Janesville, Wisconsin, was going to be the first present-day human to be evaluated by future humans.

Kyle was allowed onto the base only after the stern-looking military men took all his personal information at the front gate—everything from his Social Security number, to bank account info, to family history was recorded onto a secure laptop. Kyle shrugged off divulging all of his private records.

He told them his parents died when he was kid, he didn't have any siblings, and he thought the rest of his family were assholes. He didn't have a girlfriend either—Kyle knew he wasn't exactly boyfriend or husband material. He obsessed over all the things the government was conducting in secret—hence his perpetual singleness. So he wasn't planning to go back to his old life anyhow. The moment he heard the news, he knew he had to go to the future... where a girl *would have to* have sex with him! That was the whole point for the future humans being there after all. They needed people to make babies, and he felt he was as good as anyone.

As he was driven onto the base in the back of that jeep, he couldn't take his eyes off the future humans' vessel towering over the base. As they drove past it, he craned his head all the way around, not wanting to take his eyes off the mesmerizing spacecraft for even a moment. He couldn't wait to board it and see what was inside.

Kyle takes a deep breath and holds it as the jeep pulls up to what appears to be a hangar the size of a New York City high-rise. Kyle exhales that trapped lungful of air as he reads the words stenciled on the side:

"Hangar One."

The two escorting marines order him out of the jeep and tell him to stop just outside a door on the side of the hangar. Kyle can't help but smile at the sight of the hangar's regular-sized, ordinary door, serving as entry into the colossal building. One of the marines places his thumb on a high-tech keypad, situated just to the right of the door, and then he leans his face forward in order to have his retina scanned. The second marine does the same. A moment later, the door opens with a loud clank.

Upon entering, Kyle surveys the vastness of the hangar, wanting to register as much detail as he can. He has no way of knowing if he'll be allowed to stay or if he'll be kicked out at any given moment, so he wants to soak up everything he sees. The open space is clearly divided into a number of subsections by blue-curtained partitions. Kyle tries to see what is on the other side of the partitions, but to no avail. He can't see past that guy in his thirties wearing a white lab coat.

Dr. Logan expected something different from the first volunteer. He thought the first volunteer would be at the very least, you know, showered and shaven—but this guy, Kyle Howard, is totally unkempt, as if he'd been living in a tent. Logan has no way of knowing this is precisely the case.

"My name is Doctor Logan, and I'm going to help you speak with the future humans."

Kyle then realizes who Logan is. "Dude! You're the scientist guy!" he says, pointing at Logan, totally geeking out. "You're the guy that came up with the way to read minds and shit!" Then something occurs to Kyle. "You're not reading my mind right now, are you?" he asks suspiciously.

Logan shakes his head and smiles and then holds up the newly completed wireless Mindshot helmet, fashioned out of a standard soldier's helmet. It looks just like military-issue head gear, except for the menagerie of electrodes packed inside. Clearly, Logan followed his diagrams and notes from the future to a tee. The result? Future technology, applied today.

"No, I can't read your mind without both of us wearing this."

Kyle seems relieved.

"*They*, however, don't need the helmets." Logan then turns toward the partitions. "Follow me."

Logan leads Kyle—who remains flanked by his two marine escorts—down a winding corridor of temporary partitions. As they march along, Kyle is still slow-burning what he was just told by Logan and finally asks, "Wait, *they*? As in the future humans? The *Homo telethians*? *They* can, like, read my mind? Like, right now?"

"Not exactly," Logan explains as they walk and talk. "From what I understand, it works a lot like speaking orally. We have to be within earshot—or within mindshot in this case—for them to hear us."

"Hear us, but with their minds?"

"Yes, with their minds."

"This so crazy." Kyle smiles. But that smile fades fast the moment they round the final corner and end up facing Peter. Kyle is immediately flummoxed at the sight of him—and by just how alien he looks.

This is a human? Kyle wonders.

Logan leads a now trembling Kyle to a chair directly across from Peter. "Have a seat please."

Kyle does so, never taking his eyes off the future human. In turn, Peter doesn't take his eyes off Kyle. Kyle breaks his stare the moment Logan slides the Mindshot helmet onto his head. He recoils instinctively.

"Don't worry." Logan smiles. "This won't hurt. It's like a Bluetooth, but for your head. To read minds."

Kyle nods, and as Logan slips the helmet onto his head, he returns his gaze to the future human. The moment it's on, Kyle hears the words: *Yes, I am.*

Kyle looks around, confused. He doesn't see who said it. Kyle looks from one side of the room to the other until it dawns on him. He turns back to Peter, just as a clipboard floats over and stops eye-level, in front of the future human.

Yes, I am human. Very much so, Peter says in his most soothing voice. *And you are Mr. Kyle Howard, are you not?*

Kyle is frozen, eyes as wide as basketball hoops.

He's talking to me, Kyle thinks. *With his friggin' mind.*

Another voice chimes in: "You get used to it."

Wait, now who said that? Kyle wonders. *That voice sounded familiar.*

Kyle looks over and locks eyes with Dr. Logan, who is now wearing his own Mindshot helmet and grinning, pointing at it.

You do. You get used to it quicker than you'd think actually.

Dr. Logan is right, Kyle, Peter continues. *So just relax and we'll begin the evaluation.*

Kyle tries to saliva up his suddenly parched mouth and then manages a dry smile, responding at full volume, "Yes, I'm Kyle Howard, and I'm here to go to the future with you guys." It just now occurs to Kyle that he was talking out loud. "Wait, was I supposed to, like, just use my mind or whatever?"

It's fine if you speak orally, Peter says warmly. *We'll have to respond telepathically, however, if you don't mind?*

Kyle laughs, giddy. "Wait, wait—no, I want to do this the right way, dude. Let me speak to you...with my *minnnnnnddd*." Kyle then places his fingers to his temples and strains, turning red and veiny in the process. A moment later, Kyle relaxes and grins and then speaks out loud. "Did you hear that?"

Peter looks over to Logan, confused. Logan's brow furrows, trying to make sense of that. He speaks to Kyle, telepathically. *Kyle, did you think anything just now?*

Kyle looks over to Logan and does that same intense thinking face.

Jesus, Logan thinks, *he looks like he's having a painful bowel movement.*

Immediately, Kyle eases up and blurts out, "Hey, I heard that!" He is clearly offended. "And yes, I was sending you thoughts, bro. Just now I was. What? You couldn't hear me?"

Logan looks to Peter, who shakes his head. Neither one can hear Kyle. "Something's wrong. We can't hear what you're thinking," Logan admits while stepping over to Kyle. He removes the volunteer's helmet.

"Give me a moment, please," Logan mutters, totally embarrassed that the Mindshot isn't working properly. "I'm sure I can correct this soon."

Logan tinkers with the helmet, scanning his future notes as he does so. Teapard watches him on closed-circuit mon-

60

itors from her plush private office in the main building next door.

"Moment of truth, Doc," she says, watching the monitor. "Make it work."

Finally, Logan sees what the problem is. He rolls his eyes in mortification, trying to laugh it off. "Sorry. Two of the electrodes inside the helmet are inverted," he announces as he rewires them. "It'd be like connecting a positive to a negative. Honest mistake. But we don't want to do that, do we, Mr. Howard? Then we won't be able to hear your thoughts."

Logan's glad Kyle isn't wearing the helmet right now, so he can continue thinking to himself, privately, what a goober Kyle seems like. Once the electrodes are properly connected, Logan slips the helmet back onto him.

"Okay, let's do a test. Think something," Logan says.

Then, as Kyle strains again, both Logan and Peter hear him this time. *One, two. Tessssttttiiiinnng.*

Logan cringes and cuts Kyle off. He nods with a patient, parental smile. *Thank you. Okay. Got it. We hear you loud and clear. Do we ever.*

Yeah? You hear me? Awesome! Kyle thinks and then turns back to Peter, loudly clapping his hands together. *Then let's do this thang, Future Man!*

Peter looks to Logan, who shrugs, as if saying: "No, I don't know what to make of Kyle either."

Peter then redirects to Kyle. *Well, we certainly appreciate your enthusiasm, Kyle, and your willingness to volunteer,*

Peter says. *But there are a few criteria you'll need to meet first prior to being selected for Operation Noah's Ark.*

Absolutely. Shoot. Ask me anything you want. Kyle's confidence is growing by the second. He leans back, resting the back of his head in his interlocked palms.

Actually, we won't have to ask you anything, Peter says. *This evaluation will transpire rather quickly.*

Peter suddenly glides toward Kyle, who instantly stiffens at the proximity, confidence gone. Peter notices this and gently adds, *You're not going to feel a thing, I assure you.*

Why does everyone keep saying that? Kyle looks to Logan and smiles, just as a futuristic-looking wand, about a foot long, seemingly made of glowing crystal, floats past Peter and settles over Kyle's head, horizontally. A moment later, the wand begins to lower slowly on its own, making its way north to south, all the while pivoting and rotating around Kyle. He is now being scanned. Literally. Anywhere along Kyle's body where the levitating wand physically passes, an oval holographic sectional window opens up above it, like a microscope view, only in thin air, over the corresponding section. This allows everyone to see *inside* Kyle's body in crystal-clear x-ray vision. It's as if he'd been dissected and they're watching every organ beat and pump and pulsate—except not one incision is made. Very surreal technology is being employed. The moment the wand moves on to another part of Kyle's body, the previous sectional window vanishes and a new one is visible further on down, wherever the wand travels. All of Kyle's innards are on display and scanned during this process.

Moments later, the wand shuts off and floats away quickly. Peter says, *This candidate does not meet the requirements for this operation. Thank you for coming in, Kyle. You may go.*

Kyle is stunned. *Wait. What?*

Logan is stunned too. What does that mean? Before he can ask, the pool reporter arrives behind him and walks into the room.

A woman's voice asks, "Am I in the right place?"

Logan turns and comes face-to-face with one of the most stunningly gorgeous women who's never been featured on the cover of a glamour magazine but probably should be.

Logan then smiles at his ex-girlfriend—*Betty Suarez.*

CHAPTER SIX

When the selected pool reporter, Betty Suarez, first sees Logan, she assumes this is some sort of bad joke. She even manages an uncomfortable laugh.

"Norman? What are you doing here..." She doesn't finish her sentence. She can't, not when she sees Peter for the first time.

He's more of a freak than I thought he'd be, she thinks to herself. Later, when Betty realizes that Peter "heard" her think that, she will apologize profusely in utter embarrassment.

Logan and Betty once again meet eyes. She shakes her head soberly and says, "Now I understand why I was selected for pool reporter. Jesus."

Logan realizes he's made a mistake. He should have given her a heads-up—told her he was responsible for her selection, but frankly, he was afraid Betty wouldn't have taken the assignment had she known. He's about to go say hello to Betty and explain this, when Kyle pulls away from

65

the two marines that have just placed their hands on his shoulder to escort him out.

"Get your hands off me!" Kyle blurts out. He then turns back to Peter, pointing his finger, demanding more information. "You! What do you mean I don't meet the requirements for this operation of yours?"

Betty's journalistic instincts spark. She's clearly walked into something juicy here for sure. So she eavesdrops. Except that rather than hear a response, she just watches as both Kyle and Logan, the only other two wearing Mindshot helmets, react simultaneously to something. Clearly, they've just *heard* distressing news.

"What—you're kidding me!" Kyle finally says out loud. "How can that—how can you tell?"

Kyle stands there, the marines having retaken him by either shoulder, waiting for orders to drag him out. Kyle is clearly listening to something disquieting, shaking his head the entire time. "No. That can't be," Kyle mutters.

Despite not knowing what's happening, Betty can tell Logan feels bad for the guy. She's seen that empathetic look before. Many times. Finally, Logan turns back to her and realizes she's in the dark about all this. He approaches and tells Betty what had gone on just prior to her arriving.

"He's infertile. They can tell with their technology," Logan says quietly, motioning to Kyle. "So, he can't go— sort of defeats the whole purpose of their mission."

They watch Kyle, as he deflates and nods his head, accepting all this, however reluctantly. "I can't...Christ," he mutters. "This was my ticket out."

Logan nods, and the marines gently remove the Mindshot helmet from Kyle's head. With that, all communication from Peter to Kyle is severed. He's escorted past Dr. Logan and Betty.

"I'm sorry, Kyle," Logan tells him. "I wish you could've gone."

Before Kyle can be pulled away, Betty reaches out and places her hand on his shoulder. "Hello, Kyle. I'm Betty Suarez, the pool reporter covering Operation Noah's Ark," she says in her most empathetic voice. "I know this is a difficult moment for you, but could you please stick around? I'm sure the world would love to hear what you have to say about your experience with the future humans."

Kyle barely ticks up to her and just shrugs. "Sure. Whatever." He exhales.

Logan nods to the marine escort and tells them, "Take Mr. Howard to the media staging room. Make him comfortable, please. Ms. Suarez will be with him soon."

Once Kyle is gone, Logan turns back to Betty. "You don't waste any time, do you?"

Betty makes sure nobody can hear them, and then in a rage-filled whisper, she unloads on Logan. "Listen, I don't know what you're trying to pull, bringing me in here, but you better not be screwing around with me."

"Settle down. Please. Let me explain—"

"No. How dare you?" Betty is trying to contain her anger. "Maybe you can mess with my head in my personal life, but this...this is my career. This is *mine*. You have no right messing with this."

Logan tries to pull her aside, but she rips free. "Don't touch me!" she barks, a decibel above a whisper.

Logan puts his hands up, apologetically. "I'm sorry. Please. Calm down. Can we talk? Over there? Let me explain."

Betty takes a deep breath. She knows people are starting to look at them. It's in her best interest to calm down too. "Fine. Explain."

As they walk off, neither of them notices that Peter has been watching—and listening—the whole time. Betty follows Logan to a nearby corner where nobody is around—not within earshot anyway. She stands, arms crossed, and waits defiantly for him to say something relevant.

Logan regrets even bringing her into all of this, but he thought she'd appreciate the gesture, that this would be viewed as a peace offering of sorts, considering how things ended between them. He knew he'd broken her heart and desperately wanted to make it up to her. This was the least he could do, considering Betty had been there the day, the exact moment, he conceived the idea for what would eventually become the Mindshot.

"They needed a reporter in here covering this, and I wanted somebody that I could trust," Logan explains to a still-smoldering Betty. "You're the only person I considered."

Betty doesn't seem convinced. Logan knows he doesn't have time to do this—to coddle his ex-girlfriend—yet wants nothing more than to do so. Despite being at fault for their breakup, he knows there's still a lot remaining to work out with Operation Noah's Ark, and people are going to start to wonder any moment now what the problem is between them. Yet, Logan refuses to blow this opportunity to perhaps regain some sort of relationship with Betty, even if it's only a professional one. If that's all she'll be willing to give him, he'll take it. He realizes now he needs her in his life more than ever. Logan knows he made a terrible mistake letting her go. He wishes he'd given up on the Mindshot, sold it to the US military outright, married Betty, and settled down to a much simpler life somewhere in suburbia.

Instead, here they are, tension thick between them, worlds apart, their painful past battering them like an F6 tornado, a menagerie of emotions still entirely unresolved.

"Look, I know you hate me and I don't blame you. Really, I don't," Logan says. "But this is the 'get' of a lifetime for you, Betty. This is history."

Betty looks away—she can't look at him. Emotions are starting to bubble. She fights them. Suppresses them. Pushes them back down. Won't let him see them.

Logan continues, "Yes, I probably should've called or texted or something, warned you. I kind of ambushed you. I get that, and I'm sorry." Logan now thinks he may have to find someone else to be the pool reporter, as Betty hasn't responded yet. He understands. "You don't have to do this."

Logan is about to turn and signal for an aide, when Betty reaches out and places her hand on his shoulder. Platonic as it surely was for her, it's the first time in three years he's felt Betty's touch. "Oh, I'm staying," she says evenly, clearly having composed herself. "There's no way

I'm passing this up." Finally, she smiles. Faintly. Betty has softened—just a bit.

Logan smiles back, relieved. "Good. I'm glad to hear it."

"And I don't hate you, Norman," Betty whispers.

Electricity, right there, right in that moment between them.

"But what you did to me, to us..." Betty's words trail off.

Logan sighs. "Now's not the time. Obviously. But if we can, you know, talk. Later..."

"That'd be good," she responds, sensing that Logan's being sincere in his obvious remorse about this situation. But she refuses to admit that she needs to talk it out with him too.

They remain locked for several moments longer—years of history and friendship and love plays out right there in that silent exchange. Logan expects—*hopes*—this moment will perhaps stretch into something more, but Betty has other plans.

"Right now, I just have to ask *you* one thing." Betty breaks the stare. "When do I interview the future humans?"

CHAPTER SEVEN

The interview would have to wait until Peter felt he'd progressed farther along in his evaluation of prospective candidates. They needed one hundred thousand, and so far, they had zero. There was a lot of work left to do.

Betty's journalistic instincts were to get the story—no matter what. She wanted to know everything she could about Operation Noah's Ark. As a temporary consolation prize, since an interview with Peter wasn't forthcoming anytime soon, Betty was invited by Peter to wear a Mindshot helmet herself and sit in on the evaluation process. She jumped at the chance.

As with Kyle, volunteer candidates were fitted with their own Mindshot helmet and the assessment itself was done fairly quickly. Betty learned that the Floating Wand—as she'd dubbed it—could rapidly diagnose anything and everything about a human's condition. In the future, even common medical examinations were done expediently. It's the main reason *Homo telethians* live so much longer. Advanced science has given future humans insight and access to every ailment ever known, and as a result, remedies and cures were discovered. Within several hundred years from now, all sickness—everything from the common cold, to bipolar behavior, to cancer, to claustrophobia—will be vanquished. Because of advanced science, future humans will eventually access the receptors of the brain that control aging too, thus slowing it down. Betty finds it mildly comforting that future humans have yet to figure out how to eliminate death altogether.

At least they're still mortal, she thinks.

Had they not been, there would probably be no need for an Operation Noah's Ark. Peter and all the future humans would probably just be content with living on forever, always advancing medicine, always prolonging their own lives.

But alas, Betty concludes, *even with all their superior science and technological advancements, immortality is the one human echelon they cannot achieve.*

The evaluations have commenced again, during which time, Betty sits next to her videographer—a nervous-looking Polish national named Aleksy, who was selected at random from a global lottery—to be the pool cameraman. Aleksy wears his own Mindshot helmet, as he rolls digital video onto his HD camera's hard drive. Betty takes copious notes throughout, as a still photographer from India named Mindy—also selected at random for the pool—roams around, snapping photos. It doesn't take long for Peter to find his first affirmed candidate—a twenty-six-year-old male from Cleveland named Josh.

Josh is ideal, according to Peter. No ailments of any kind or mental disorders that he could potentially pass on to future offspring. Most important, he is fertile. Josh had earned a law degree from Ohio State and was working at the Cleveland DA's office when he heard of the *Homo telethian* arrival. As much as he enjoyed prosecuting the city's criminal element and saving the city from hardened criminals, the notion of saving the future of mankind from extinction was far more alluring. He was on a plane and in a rent-a-car before he could think too much more about it.

Volunteers like Josh—who were deemed healthy, fertile, and of sound mind—were immediately dispatched to a secondary process level, where they'd be further evaluated to see if they were truly prepared for the rigors of intergalactic space and time travel. Betty learned that if the future humans felt a candidate wasn't fully prepared to undergo what would be a jolting and life-altering experience, the candidate would be rejected.

"So, just because you pass the physical and mental exam..." Betty sneaks in a question to Peter after one of the evaluations ends in rejection. "...you still have to be what?...*Astronaut ready?*"

Peter turns to her, trying to remain patient. *Not now, Miss Suarez,* he tells her. *We'll conduct a formal interview soon.*

"Yes, just answer the one question, please," Betty presses. "You want to be sure each volunteer is ready to travel to an Earth unfamiliar and foreign to them?"

That is correct. Now if you'll excuse me. Peter moves off to evaluate another volunteer.

73

Many hours later, Betty stands before Aleksy's camera and conducts her reporter's stand-up. "Josh from Cleveland made it past the secondary evaluation, as did a dozen others," Betty reports. "Several commonalities are evident amongst all the selected Voyagers—as the approved volunteers are ultimately being called. The Voyagers are all in prime physical shape, highly intelligent, and well-grounded individuals. It's become clear to me that people who are genetically gifted will be shoo-ins. Unfortunately, this eliminates certain people that the *Homo telethians* deem undesirable—those who have physical ailments, or perceived abnormalities, those who are out of shape, and those who are deemed to be mentally unstable."

Betty leaves out her own concluding opinion, which she felt had no place in an impartial news report. To her, it is clear that the Telethians do not want to taint the future gene pool. Their logic—however callous—is prudent. Why include a Voyager who will water down the future of the human race? Evidently, Telethians want genetic perfection—as close to it as possible anyway. Betty figures the viewers will come to that conclusion on their own. So, she simply reports, unfiltered and without her own bias, documenting the elation of those selected and the despair of those rejected.

Predictably, this strict selection criteria leads to much outrage, as the vast majority of volunteers are discarded—some even before they are allowed onto the base—because they are obese, aged, or exhibit some form of overt mental dysfunction. Some of the rejected candidates are insulted and indignant that they would be deemed unworthy. Others are crushed and break down into tears. These have to be dragged out sobbing, kicking, and screaming.

It's like the auditions on those singing competition TV shows, Betty hears Logan's voice in her head during a break in the evaluations. It's disorienting. She looks around and spots Logan across the room, smiling at her, wearing his own Mindshot helmet. *Remember? Where contestants are stunned when told they can't sing?*

She hadn't taken off her helmet yet, even though Peter wasn't talking to anyone at the moment. Betty had forgotten she was even wearing it still. She smiles, remembering one of their guilty pleasures from when they were still together— watching singing competition shows. Even though those programs were far removed from anything either one of them did for a living, they loved the audition process, seeing contestants achieve their goals. Logan and Betty even cried together when their favorites did well. They never admitted this to anyone. After all, enjoying faddish entertainment is frowned upon by the snobbish elite that exists in both journalism and science. Yet, they loved those shows.

Except these people are being told that they aren't good enough to save mankind. She's still getting used to speaking with her mind. *Stakes are a little higher here.*

A little bit, yeah. Logan laughs. *Hey, you think I can pull you away from all this for a minute to give me a hand with something?*

With what? Betty asks.

A little experiment.

Betty starts to remove her Mindshot helmet, but Logan interrupts.

Actually, I need you to leave it on.

Betty is intrigued and follows Logan outside the hangar, past a line of volunteers waiting to go inside. Logan leads her some distance away and stops, where they stand facing one another.

"What's the experiment?"

You can hear me fine, right? Logan asks with the Mindshot.

Betty nods. *Clearly.*

Okay. Stay there.

Logan now turns and walks several hundred feet away and turns back to her. *How about now? Can you hear me?*

Is this like that commercial? She laughs.

Yeah, sort of.

Logan grins and walks away several more hundred feet. Betty can still hear him, and he continues to widen the distance incrementally. Finally, when they're about three football fields away, Betty can no longer hear Logan and he can no longer hear her. Logan heads back to Betty.

Interesting. Now we know when we're within Mindshot and when we're out, Logan states.

I used to love when you went full dweeb on me.

They smile and then head back inside the hangar, walking back to the evaluation area.

Hey, I know I haven't said it yet, but this has been amazing. Dare I say—historic. So thank you. For bringing me into this, Betty says, still over the Mindshot.

Of course, Logan responds. *I'm glad you're here.*

Their intimate thought transferences are interrupted by a third voice.

Peter's.

He chimes in, *Are you ready for that interview now, Miss Suarez?*

Both Logan and Betty turn and find Peter floating over to the journalist. She does all she can not to seem fazed by this alien-looking human descending before her, like a feather touching ground. Peter looks right into her eyes.

This is the interview, not of a lifetime, but perhaps of all time. Maybe Jesus Christ Himself would be the only other better "get." But now that Betty has "got" Peter, there is the matter of hearing what Peter has to say, considering he only speaks telepathically. It's one thing for them to wear helmets to hear Peter, but how is the viewer supposed to hear him on television if he only speaks via the mind?

Logan already had a solution.

Turns out, he'd been anticipating this moment (and wanting to impress Betty), so he once again went full dweeb at the south end of Hangar One, where the media-center was set up, complete with satellite technology, waiting to beam the interview, live, to the entire world.

Logan devised a system soon after the Mindshot helmets went wireless, wherein he developed proprietary descrambling software that, when patched into an interviewer and subject's Mindshot helmets, processed and routed their thoughts through specially customized fiber optic wiring that was connected into the Mindshot helmets, converting what was previously only a thought into spoken word, transmitting it to external speakers for all to hear. Logan hasn't had a chance to test it, however, and as a result, is a little nervous as he rigs up a virtual bristle pad of tight wiring near the satellite console.

Betty takes her usual spot in the interviewer chair, directly across from Peter, who floats, inches off the ground. Aleksy has set up some lights and is now stationed behind the camera, trying to appear professional, but he is clearly nervous about being around Peter.

Once Logan has finished connecting all his software to the external speakers and hits the spacebar on the Mac desktop, he says, "Ummm, can we get a sound check, Peter?"

Peter looks away from Betty and stares right at Logan. But we hear nothing come from the speakers. Logan returns to the computer and begins checking his setup.

"That's weird; it should be working—" Logan says.

"Oh, it works, Doctor," Peter says over the loudspeakers.

All heads turn to Peter, who deadpans Logan.

"I just wanted to show you, Miss Suarez, and everyone here, that if I don't want to be heard, I won't be," Peter says coolly.

Logan is struck by that. There's a hint of arrogance in Peter's tone, something Logan hasn't heard until now. Even Betty picks up on it.

"Did you not think I had the ability to block your device from hearing me if I chose to do so?" Peter asks.

Logan is perplexed by the question. He stammers, searching for an answer. "Umm, yeah. I suppose. You being an advanced—"

"I will allow for your external sound system to work. Temporarily." Peter cuts Logan off. "The moment this interview is over, so is your ability to hear me over your rudimentary PA system."

Peter not having a mouth makes the fact that everyone can now hear him speak even weirder. Peter swivels slowly–eerily–to Betty and locks in on her.

"Miss Suarez, let's proceed."

Betty steels herself and wipes her mind clean. She knows Peter can hear what she's thinking. Betty then looks up at Aleksy. "Let me know when we're live."

Aleksy seems skittish as he nods and checks his watch, waiting for the designated time to arrive. Mindy—the still photographer—readies her camera as well. An eternity seems to pass before the time comes. At last, Aleksy hits enter on the computer station he's set up next to his camera. His medium-wide shot of Peter is now streamed live all over the world, which is surely watching.

"We are live," Aleksy says quietly and ducks behind his viewfinder—his sanctuary.

Betty faces Peter and notices his whole demeanor seems to shift from antagonistic to pleasant. Like any good politician, he knows when the camera is on.

Betty smiles. *Deep breath. Deep breath. Exhale, mustn't forget to exhale*–She cuts herself off abruptly after remembering Peter can hear her thoughts and composes herself.

After a brief introduction, Betty jumps right into it. "Okay. Let's start with the future—where you're from." Betty's words are measured and calm. "The first thing I'd like to know about is time travel. After all, countless books and movies have been about this very subject, yet here you are—real-life time travelers from the future. How does it work exactly—traveling through time? Obviously, you need that big ship that's parked outside."

"Yes. That vessel is our pride and joy," Peter says, still not moving. "She took us many years to perfect. Traveling through time is rather complicated science, as you would imagine, but we set out to simplify it, so that any one of the eighteen crew members could easily fly it."

"You mentioned the many visits to our time, prior to this one. They were trial runs?"

"That's correct. Admittedly, some of those initial exploratory time-traveling missions ended in the tragic death of many brave pilots," Peter laments. "But we corrected all of our mistakes and perfected the process. We obviously wanted to assure time travel functioned properly and safely, not just for ourselves, but before we could even contemplate asking any of you to volunteer. That vessel is one of a kind as a result—a prototype."

"A prototype? Really? No other time-traveling vessels exist?"

"We only need one."

"I see. So, how does it work—time travel? You get inside the ship and then what?"

"Well, I wouldn't want to get into the detailed algorithms and complex quantum physics that enable time travel, as it would surely bore your audience. Frankly, it bores me," Peter says pleasantly. "But this I will say—all your theories today about how time travel can be achieved are close but missing one key element."

Betty sits forward. "Which would be?"

"Jupiter."

Not what Betty expected to hear. She sits back again, confused. "As in, *the planet* Jupiter?"

"Precisely. Its Great Red Spot to be specific. You know Jupiter's Great Red Spot is an enormous anticyclonic storm—akin to a hurricane on Earth, only the spot is so enormous, three entire Earths can fit inside it. As for those churning red storm clouds in the spot, humans will not understand fully why it hues red until eleven hundred years from now. It had been suggested that certain compounds of phosphorous were responsible for the reddish-brown hue, but we discovered the truth."

Betty leans forward again, expectantly, as does everyone else.

"The Great Red Spot..." Peter pauses, seemingly for effect. "...is *a time portal*."

Dead silence. Did he just say what everyone thinks he said? Betty tries to clarify she heard right.

"A time portal? That's what the spot on Jupiter is? A portal...through time."

"You sound skeptical."

"Sorry. It's just, yeah, this seems so..."

"Fantastical? Yes, I agree." Peter nods. "And I assure you, three thousand years in the future, it still is to some degree. But you're trying to process this and all of our future advancements with your current-day—and subsequently limited, with all due respect—knowledge of the cosmos. Just accept that we have designed and calibrated the spacecraft outside this building to enter the Great Red

Spot, and—how can I explain this—synchronize with lightning inside the maelstrom, which then propels us out of the spot to any point in time that is desired."

Betty glances over to Logan, who seems enthralled and baffled by all of this. She can tell he wishes he could experience it for himself, and she smiles at his still boyish enthusiasm. She turns back to Peter.

"Okay. Let's see if I got this right." Betty looks down at the shorthand she's just scribbled into her notepad. She reads: "You guys discovered Jupiter's Great Red Spot is really a time portal, which means you left Earth in the fifty-first century, flew over to Jupiter, jumped into the spot, and—*boom boom bam*—zipped back out of the spot, and flew back to Earth, only it was now Earth in the twenty-first century. Is that about right?"

"Not exactly. There's the matter of the vessel learning what point in time you wish to travel to first. A very important detail, I'm sure you'd agree," Peter adds. "You see, we've designed our spacecraft in such a manner as to *understand* where we want it to go."

"So the vessel has a computer guidance system that—"

"No. I never mentioned computers."

Betty is puzzled. "Okay. Well then, how does it know where in time to travel?"

"We *tell* the vessel where we want to go."

"You just tell it? Where you want to go?"

"That is correct. For instance, to travel here, we told the vessel our destination: this year, March, the twenty-fifth day. It processes that command and does the rest in conjunction with the vortex within the Great Red Spot."

"Okaaaayyy. So, your ship works like...like Siri on my iPhone?" Betty asks, half joking, half thunderstruck.

Peter nods; he seems to understand her early twenty-first-century reference to the Apple cellular phone. "That's exactly right, Miss Suarez. Just like Siri on your iPhone, only much more complicated."

Betty shakes her head. *Amazing. Truly.*

She knows she can end the interview right there and then and still guarantee herself an Emmy award and a Pulitzer. Only a few minutes in, and she's already learned enough astounding details about the future human race to classify this interview a success, but Betty wants to change the direction of the interview. She never intended this to be a fluff piece about how wonderfully we advance in the future.

She has her own agenda.

"Okay, let's switch gears, shall we?" She smiles. "With all the advancements in health, politics, and technology, why does anybody from the future still have to carry themselves arrogantly?"

Peter visibly stiffens. "Excuse me?"

Logan's brow furrows. Where is she going with this?

"Nobody here has any doubt that you—and all the others with you—can do any number of amazing things with your mind, but is it really necessary to flaunt that ability?"

For the first time, Logan sees Peter show a glimmer of basic humanity in the form of surprise. Clearly, he is taken aback by Betty's question. He doesn't respond.

Sensing momentum, Betty doesn't wait for a reply and follows up. "It just seems to me that ever since you've arrived here, you've flexed your considerable muscles, you've told us what you wanted, and then you didn't give us a chance to debate whether or not any of this was any good *for us*, let alone give us the chance to object to the very premise of your mission."

Betty never once takes her eyes off Peter. She's got him on the ropes; she can tell.

More silence from Peter. Logan can't believe Betty is grilling Peter like this, but he tries to wipe his mind clear. Peter can most certainly hear him, though he doesn't show that he does. Peter remains chillingly locked on Betty, like nobody else is in the room, except her. Peter finally speaks after a very long silence.

"Is there a question in there, Miss Suarez?" For the first time, we detect a shade of annoyance, yet Peter remains calm.

"Well, yes." Betty commits and goes for the jugular. "You have hundreds of thousands of twenty-first-century people out there, lining up, ready to go willingly into the future to restart mankind—to literally save the human race from extinction. Yet, that's the key point, isn't it? You're asking them to go save the human race *because of* mistakes that are *going to be made*, decades and centuries from now—mistakes that haven't yet happened *for us*. So my question is, is that logical, sir? Why go fix our failures in the future when we can just fix our failures in the present and prevent ever getting to the point where we turn out—with all due respect—looking like you."

Holy shit, Logan thinks. *What is she doing?*

Like a spectator in a tennis match, Logan looks over to Peter and awaits his response. For the first time, the future human looks angry. "You're referring to the elementary theory of space-time?" Peter asks calmly. "Wherein, if you travel back through time and interact with the past, you will alter the future. Are you not?"

"That's exactly what I'm referring to. Theoretically, you've already altered the future by interacting with us. So please, tell the viewers of the twenty-first century why you're being here shouldn't simply serve as a cautionary tale."

"A cautionary tale?"

"Yes. Rather than come here to recruit healthy, fertile young humans to bring back with you to repopulate the Earth in the future, why don't you just go around the world, on a sort of lecture circuit, and warn us about where we're headed?" Betty asks. "Wouldn't that resonate today with the way we're disconnecting with our smart phones and not talking to each other in person? Today, we mostly socialize over social networks, or via texting, which seems to me is part of the reason we evolve as we do. Wouldn't it be more effective to simply advise twenty-first-century humans about where we're heading in the future and avoid it, rather than taking a bunch of us to our future to fix *your* mistakes?"

The tension is real thick; everyone can feel it. After several excruciating moments, Peter floats closer to Betty. Aleksy has to zoom out to hold him in frame. The camera shakes a bit as he does so; he's very nervous.

"We're dying off in the future, Miss Suarez. Do you not understand that?" Peter almost growls.

Betty holds her ground. "I do. I really do, but you must also surely understand that your being here has already irrevocably changed your future—our future—has it not?" Betty replies firmly. "How do you know the future you left behind will even still be there when you return?"

"Space-time contamination was a probability we've contended with, which is the reason we've only built and sent one vessel." Peter tries to remain patient. "To minimize contamination."

"So space-time contamination, even minimally done, is acceptable to you?"

"I'm saying it's not an issue, Miss Suarez. That same advanced technology and ability you so flippantly suggest we merely use for our own gain has in fact given us the wherewithal to understand space-time science in ways you twenty-first-century humans can't even begin to fathom. We have discovered layers to space-time staggeringly unimaginable today—truly mesmerizing discoveries that make traveling back in time completely noninvasive—as if it never happened. As a result, Miss Suarez, we are utterly certain, without any doubt whatsoever, that the future we left will absolutely still be there exactly as we left it upon our return."

One senses the indignity in Peter's voice in having to explain this. That doesn't make Betty back down.

"So, let me see if I understand. Forgive me, I am only a twenty-first-century human, after all," Betty replies, not trying to mask her condescension. "You're saying you've discovered how to close off a bunch of space-time loopholes and as a result figured out how to travel back to our time without affecting yours, despite having interacted with your past?"

"That is exactly what I'm saying," Peter snarls. "Hence, our sense of urgency. What you viewed as arrogance on our part is simply a result of the stakes being so high. If this mission fails, then mankind literally has an expiration date. And we will not allow that date to be reached."

Watching the interview from her private office at the north end of the hangar, General Teapard grins. "I like this reporter. She's got balls. Put that Clammy on the ropes. Shows he is human after all."

The rest of the interview is rather pedestrian comparatively, lacking any gotcha moments and takes less than an hour. Betty gleans information about the voyage and about what makes an ideal candidate. Peter felt it was a good idea to get the word out about the latter, so as not to waste any additional time sorting through more unfit candidates. Betty then asks about the living conditions three thousand years in the future. Where and how would twenty-first-century humans live in the fifty-first century? Peter explains that to avoid culture shock, housing and neighborhoods, exactly as they'd find in this century, have been erected in the future. The plan, however, is to gradually integrate and assimilate the Voyagers into fifty-first-century life.

Betty has one last question. "Can I see the inside of that magnificent vessel parked outside?" Betty asks. "Since you're only bringing back one hundred thousand humans, there will be a lot of people—about seven billion or so—that won't otherwise get a chance to peek inside."

Again, Peter remains still, but something in his eyes seems to suggest a smile. "Of course, Miss Suarez. Once the selection process is complete, I intend to take the Voyagers on a tour of the vessel prior to the departure. You may accompany the tour at that time."

"Thank you very much for your time, Peter," Betty adds a smile of her own.

But Peter does not respond; instead, his attention has suddenly moved over to Aleksy the cameraman.

Betty nods to Aleksy. "Are we still live, Aleksy?"

Aleksy's eyes are trained on Peter, consumed no longer by fear, but by what seems to be...hatred.

Betty is perplexed by this. "Aleksy? Take us off the air."

Aleksy's breathing only quickens. He's not blinking—his eyes are watering, getting bloodshot, and are fixed on Peter.

Peter stares back, having just heard what Aleksy was thinking and, more important, what he is *planning to do* next. He heard it mere moments before Aleksy actually did it. Peter heard two words, being repeated.

Kill it...Kill it...Kill it...

Then, all who wear a Mindshot helmet hear it now as well.

Kill it...Kill it...Kill it...

Aleksy gets as far as opening his jacket–it had been zipped shut this whole time. But when he pulls down on the zipper, whips the jacket open, and reveals the bomb belt strapped to his chest, he is milliseconds from detonating the remote in his hand, which he had kept hidden this whole time.

But Peter had heard Aleksy coming.

So before Aleksy can get any further than butterflying his jacket open, he is abruptly levitated into the air—launched quickly straight upward and hurtled savagely into an overhead skylight. He shatters right through it. Violently. Glass shards spray, clawing train tracks of bloody scratches along Aleksy's body. He continues out, skyward, rockets into the clouds, away into the desert.

On the ground below, onlookers crane upward, having seen a man cannon shot out of the main hangar and flung far out over the desert where he suddenly explodes.

A fireball of flesh and blood rains down in the distance.

Back inside, Peter has not even flinched. His eyes sway back to Betty, who sits there in abject horror. Neither she nor Logan can comprehend what just happened.

"It seems your cameraman had objections to Operation Noah's Ark," Peter says coolly and then adds, "Duly noted."

At that moment, Logan's computer explodes in a small puff of smoke and sparks. His prototype for hearing future humans via external speakers is destroyed.

Peter floats past Betty, glares at her, and keeps going. Moments later, he's gone.

It's quiet for several seconds. Finally, Betty has to laugh in sheer disbelief. She turns to Logan and says, "Guess I need a new cameraman."

CHAPTER EIGHT

Now Betty understands the reason for Aleksy's nervousness.

It wasn't because Peter intimidated him. Turns out, Aleksy wasn't even the real pool cameraman that was selected at random. Polish authorities found that guy dead inside Aleksy's Krakow apartment a few days later, his press credentials missing. During the crime scene investigation that followed, NCIS found Aleksy's single-spaced manifesto tucked inside a side pouch of his backpack, where they learned he had been a Doomsday extremist who felt the very presence of the *Homo telethians* signaled end times. Aleksy—and the recently formed fringe group of like-minded believers he belonged to—considered it a Holy Crusade to eliminate the future humans, noble intentions be damned.

Like the volunteers, Aleksy was also determined to save mankind, only he felt mankind of today needed saving from mankind of tomorrow. So he strapped on the belt to his midsection, loaded with C4, and waited for the opportune moment to detonate. Opportune being the end of the interview, when they were live with the whole world as an audience.

Most startling was Aleksy's obvious ability to keep his mind clear of his dark intentions until moments before he acted on them.

Immediately after the incident with Aleksy, Peter and the other future humans took on an almost businesslike approach to the selection process. Gone were the pleasantries and niceties. Aleksy's incident seems to have turned off future humans to present-day humans, creating deep feelings of suspicion.

Who else, they surely wonder, is able to keep their minds clear of hostile aims?

Peter seems to be conferring in private with the other future humans quietly and more frequently.

This makes Logan nervous. He'd seen what they were capable of doing and worries about what they'll do if provoked again. So considering how terrifyingly close they'd all come to dying already and perhaps even feeling thankful that Peter had intervened to save them all, Logan feels it necessary to let Betty know she had treated Peter disrespectfully during the interview. Not being a meek wallflower, Betty digs in.

"Oh, please! That wasn't some *Access Hollywood* vanity piece," an indignant Betty shoots back when Logan confronts her in the privacy of his office. "I'm a journalist—a real one—and I *will* ask the tough questions."

"I get that, I do, but that wasn't just some corrupt politician you were interviewing," Logan counters. "We don't know what they're capable of doing."

"So, this is about fear?" Betty asks, pointedly. "About you being afraid of what they'll do if they get their feelings hurt by a few tough questions?"

"You didn't see how they came in here, Betty!" Logan fires back. "What they were able to do. Nothing could stop them. Nothing! So yes, I was afraid, dammit! Afraid that he'd do *something to you*."

Whoa. That last part slipped out fast. Logan wishes he hadn't said it. Betty wasn't expecting that either.

"Afraid of what he'd do...to me?" she pries after several moments of silence.

Logan is embarrassed. He hadn't realized that was what he was upset about until those words were blurted out. Now he understands his anger. He wishes they were both wearing Mindshot helmets, so he wouldn't have to say anything else, so she'd know what was on his mind. That was why he built the Mindshot after all. Then he reconsiders, glad actually that she *can't* read his mind, because then she'd be able to see how he *truly* feels about her. Even after all this time apart, she'd see how terribly he feels about abandoning her. She'd see that he still realizes he made a huge mistake in letting her go. But he doesn't want her to know that. Not just yet. Not until he can confirm he has a shot at winning her back.

This is his second chance with Betty, and he has no intentions of blowing it.

"I suppose that *is* what I was afraid of. I don't know. Yeah," he says, trying his best to be coy. "Look, I brought you here because I feel you're the best reporter I've ever seen, but I also brought you here because..." He trails off, unable to finish the sentence.

Betty leans forward, a faint smile on her face.

Logan curses to himself. *What's wrong with me? Why can't I keep the running spigot that is my mouth, closed?* he wonders.

Betty asks, "What? You also brought me here because of what?" There is a hint of devilishness in her eyes.

Logan smiles at her now. *What's happening? Is that flirting?* He's not sure, so he treads lightly.

"Look, we just have to be careful around them," Logan says. "That's all."

"That's *all?*"

"Yes, Betty, that's all."

She searches his face—reads his eyes. She's known him long enough to know that there's something else behind his cryptic words, and she suspects knowing what it is. Although she'd never admit it, part of her was indeed thrilled earlier to see Logan again, even after so much time apart. Her feelings for him had never abated, which frustrated her. It was all she could do, when she first saw him again, not to go over and hug and kiss him. Luckily, anger was the *very next* emotion that overcame her and that suppressed her feelings of ardor—anger toward Logan because he'd meddled with her career.

That said, she knew that there was something else going on with Logan, something hidden under a quilt of suppressed feelings. Most likely—and she can only guess—this is his way of making up for how things ended between them. But now, the moment after he revealed he was afraid for her well-being, she has a sneaking suspicion that the man she is still madly in love with, feels the same and is taking steps to rekindle and renew their romance.

"Fine. That's all then," Betty finally says.

They remain locked for several more moments. It seems they're each about to say something else, when there's a knock at the door. Logan sighs and opens it.

He finds a lance corporal standing there. He says, "Sorry to interrupt, Doctor, but Kyle Howard wants to know when his interview is happening?"

"Who's Kyle Howard?"

Betty jumps in. "Oh my God. I forgot about him," she says. "Poor guy. He's the first volunteer, Norman. Remember? The one that got rejected."

"Oh right. Shit. He's *still* here?" Logan asks.

"Yes, sir. We were told to have him wait in the media room, but he's getting antsy and keeps asking when he can leave."

Logan and Betty enter the media room, but it's nothing more right now than the spot that Betty leaves her stuff— just a bunch of empty tables and chairs. Seated at one of them is Kyle. He throws his arms up in exasperation when he sees them enter.

"Finally! It's about time!" Kyle exclaims. "I was starting to feel like a *prisoner* in here."

"I am so sorry, Mr. Howard," Betty apologizes. "I got sidetracked, and well, I'm here now. May I still interview you?"

Kyle seems torn. Clearly, he's frustrated that he's just been sitting around such a long time, exasperated because he knows he's not going to be part of Operation Noah's Ark. Maybe it's because Betty's beauty can be very persuasive, but he relents and agrees.

Then something occurs to Betty. "Except that, damn it, my cameraman was...I don't have a cameraman," Betty remembers. "It's fine. Doesn't matter. I ran my own camera in college. I'll lock it off on a tripod, and we'll be good to go."

"You know, I operate camera. Done so my entire life. Not too many people want to camp out in the desert with me, waiting to videotape UFOs. So I had to learn how to do it myself."

"Good! Wonderful. Then you can help me set it up," she says, turning on the charm.

Logan shakes his head slightly, with a smile.

She's good. Kid has no idea he's fallen victim to Suave Suarez, he thinks.

Then, Colonel Canoga appears, walking into the room briskly. He looks grim.

"There's been a development," Canoga tells Logan.

"Yes?" Logan asks.

"The future humans have just completed their selection process," Colonel Canoga reports. "They have their hundred thousand Voyagers."

It's as if the air has been sucked out of the room.

"That's impossible," Logan says, reeling. "How can they be done so fast?"

"I'm not sure, sir," the colonel responds. "But they're about to give the Voyagers a tour of the ship."

In the time it takes to walk briskly from the media room to the lower gantry of the future human vessel still hovering in the same spot, Canoga debriefs Logan and Betty about what just transpired.

"A short while ago, a dozen Clammies went airborne. Floated out of the base."

"To do what?"

"Well, at first we weren't sure. After the attempted assassination, we initially feared hostile retaliation. Later, we learned they were doing fly-overs."

"Fly-overs?"

"They're clearly concerned we don't have our shit together. The fake cameraman got past security and got real close to going jihad on them, so now they're concerned about copycats. They want to expedite the selection process—get it over with fast. I don't blame them. Thing is, they decided to assess the volunteers in line, right where they waited."

Canoga holds up a digital tablet and taps on a paused security video. Once it begins to play, it shows twelve future humans emerging from the gantry below their vessel, fully levitating. They zip off at high velocity, out and over the base, then out and over the miles and miles of volunteers still waiting in line.

Colonel Canoga chimes in. "We've called these guys diagnostic scouts. They're picking viable candidates *right out of line now.*"

Logan continues to watch the tablet and indeed sees exactly that happen. At any given moment, a scout will stop in front of a volunteer who seems young and healthy, bypassing all the ones who look old and sick. Immediately, the scout releases the diagnosis wand and scans the dazzled and confused volunteer. *At that point*, if he or she passes muster, said volunteer is literally levitated into the air and whisked back toward the base. No conversation is had. No warning is given. If selected, they're just taken. As the other volunteers soon realize what's happening, they cheer happily each time one is plucked out of the crowd.

From obscurity to savior of mankind.

A wider angle on the video reveals dozens upon dozens of airborne volunteers, befuddled but dazzled—floating through the air like a squadron of air force bombers—all making a beeline directly into the base, over its high fence, and into the immense hangar.

It wasn't long until Peter deemed the selection process complete. He then patched into all the Mindshots and radios on the base and made the announcement to all military personnel that they were done, that they'd found all their Voyagers for Operation Noah's Ark—one hundred thousand qualified volunteers, half women, half men, who embodied a person from every corner of twenty-first-century Earth. According to Peter, every nationality from today was duly represented because, in addition to health, the scouts thoroughly scoured the many miles of volunteers to guarantee diversity.

The future humans were satisfied the collective salvation of mankind was assured with this group.

Canoga admits that what's most aggravating however is that the future humans aren't bothering to tell the throng of *rejected* people still outside the base, still hoping for a chance to be selected, that the process is now over.

"They're leaving the bearing of bad news to us. Can you believe that, sir?" Canoga asks, shaking his head in dismay. "There's going to be a riot when we tell them, and I really don't blame them."

The future humans are now making final preparations to depart the following morning. This is why a tour of the vessel was imminent for the selected Voyagers. A few notables, like Logan, have been invited to attend as well.

For her part, Betty isn't about to let Peter forget that he'd personally promised her a tour of the ship. She has it on tape, so even though she isn't on the VIP list, she seeks to get on board anyway, intending to report back to the world.

Logan certainly isn't about to dissuade her from collecting on Peter's promise, but this last-second development keeps Betty in a bind—she has no cameraman still. Since there is no time to wait for a new pool cameraman to arrive, she needs to figure something out right away. She doesn't even have a still photographer anymore, because Mindy quit earlier. Despite Betty explaining why Peter had killed Aleksy, Mindy still feared she'd be next. She was terrified the future humans had a vendetta against the media. The fact that Mindy also felt Betty was purposely antagonizing Peter during the interview didn't help either. So Betty has no way of documenting any of this and finally asks Kyle if he can really run a video camera, since he'd claimed he knew how.

The UFO nut swears repeatedly he can and is giddy as a schoolboy when Betty agrees. Shaking nervously with excitement, he hastily gathers up the camera equipment. The fact that he knows exactly what gear to bring and what gear to leave behind comforts Betty. Still, as he follows Betty out—practically skipping—she has to lay into him a bit.

"Okay, you gotta dial down the dork. Remember, the world is counting on you to see what the inside of that ship looks like," Betty says, as they walk toward the ship. "Worry about focus and good framing and sound—don't just geek out at all the cool sciency shit you're gonna see. Got it?" Betty glares at him.

Kyle nods right away. He understands; this moment is serious.

"Yes. Right. I got it. I'm totally cool. Totally," Kyle says, still unable to erase the ear-to-ear smile from his face. "I will operate the crap out of this camera. You'll see."

Betty is already regretting this, worried she's made a huge mistake. There's not much she can do about it now. Worst-case scenario, she'll take the camera from the UFO geek and operate it herself.

As the group rounds the corner and comes upon the splendor that is the spaceship, Logan, Betty, and Kyle see all the selected Voyagers gathered together for the first time—one hundred thousand of them. All young. Nobody over thirty.

These are the *Voyagers* who will save mankind from extinction.

CHAPTER NINE

The volunteers stand in two orderly lines—men in one row, women in the other. Each gender seems to be sizing up the other, a lot of them perhaps even already locking in on potential mates.

Logan and Betty each notice this and exchange grimaces.

"Something salacious about this whole thing, isn't there?" Teapard asks as she steps up, clearly arriving for the tour of the craft herself.

"C'mon, General. That's a little cynical, isn't it?" Logan cracks, barely concealing his half-cocked, snarky smirk. "They're going to repopulate the Earth after all. They should at least be allowed to find a partner they're attracted to."

"Do I detect a tad of sarcasm there, Doctor?"

"Just a tad."

Teapard steps closer to Logan, serious now. "Well, on the bright side, this whole thing may be over soon."

That's when Teapard notices Betty and Kyle standing behind Logan. "I don't recall seeing your name on the tour manifest, Miss Suarez," Teapard says. Her eyes narrow, as she directs her gaze to Kyle. "And certainly not a rejected volunteer."

Before Betty can respond, Peter floats over, gliding to a stop in front of them all. They put on their Mindshot helmets—which they've been carrying under their arms. Once the helmets are on, they turn to Peter.

The general is correct, Peter says evenly. *You were not invited.*

"Why not?" Betty asks sharply, not trying to hide her indignation. "Because I didn't toss you softballs during our interview?"

That is precisely why, Peter responds coolly.

Betty's defiance fades. She was expecting him to deny it, to be diplomatic.

But then I reconsidered, Peter goes on, his voice a tad condescending. *I simply forgot that in this century, freedom of the press is still crucial in keeping the powers-that-be in line. I simply wasn't accustomed to that type of questioning.*

This intrigues Betty. "Wait, that sounds like you're saying there's no press in the future."

Peter holds his inert eyes on Betty for a moment or two before responding. *In the future, freedom of the press is a nonissue.*

"So, yes then? That means no press?"

What I am saying is everyone plays by the same rules. Everything is equal and just. There is no need to have a hostile press to keep us honest. We already are.

"You're not answering the question—"

Miss Suarez, I've already given you an interview. Peter cuts her off. *Would you like to come aboard or not?*

Betty feels there is something about the future Peter's not telling her. She's sat across from many savvy politicos and knows when somebody is ducking a question—and Peter is ducking.

"Of course I want to go aboard." Betty notices that Peter has turned his gaze to Kyle behind her. "I needed a cameraman, and Kyle is an accomplished cameraman—self-proclaimed—and he'll be shooting the tour."

Peter considers this for a few moments and then says, *Very well.* He moves closer to Kyle. *I'm glad, Mr. Howard, that you at least get the opportunity to go aboard.*

"Yeah, thanks!" Kyle blurts out. "I'm super pumped, dude."

"Did you just dude a superior intellect?" Betty whispers.

Their attention is then redirected skyward. Floating en masse from above are a hundred thousand Mindshot helmets. The floating-helmets swarm like bees and swoop downward. Logan last saw these helmets in the mill, just after they'd been manufactured in bulk. But now, they're all up in the blue sky, coming down at them. He glances over to Peter and the other future humans and knows instantly that *they* are bringing the helmets over, telekinetically.

Moments later, each helmet descends onto the head of each Voyager in line. It's like a simultaneous multiperson coronation, only with Mindshot helmets. Before any of them can object, each of the one hundred thousand Voyagers is now wearing their very own Mindshot.

General Teapard leans into Logan.

"I'll say one thing about the Clammies," she whispers. "They're efficient."

Kyle has been rolling video this whole time, with Betty looking over his shoulder, watching him work. He's in focus, well framed, and tilted down with the descending helmets smoothly. She's relieved. Now she can focus on reporting what she sees.

Peter rises straight up into the air, Phoenix-like, about fifteen feet or so—high enough so everyone gathered can see him. Because they all have Mindshots on, they can all hear him too.

Welcome, Voyagers. The future awaits you, Peter says. *And all of mankind thanks you.*

Except for those selected in the initial stages, this is the first time the Voyagers have experienced a Mindshot. They cheer enthusiastically, as if they were at a rock concert.

Once they settle down, Peter continues, *In a moment, you will all walk up this ramp..."* A ramp lowers underneath the gantry. *...and come aboard to take a tour of the vessel that will transport you to the fifty-first century, where you will save mankind from extinction.*

Again, everyone cheers.

For some reason, each time they do so, Logan is disturbed. It's just now dawning on him that none of these people have a clue about what awaits them. Yet, they're cheering wildly, as if the home team has just scored a touchdown. It's bizarre, almost cult-like. He now notices Betty staring at him, and then he hears her voice in his head.

Remember, we can hear what you're thinking, she reminds him, tapping her helmet.

Logan realizes she's right and immediately clears his mind and focuses on the future humans and the Voyagers. He doesn't want to think about anything else lest he be caught judging this operation.

Peter continues, *We will depart in the morning, following a farewell ceremony that your fellow twenty-firsters have planned for you.*

This brings on another thunderous ovation.

For now, Ladies and Gentlemen, if you will please, Peter motions to the vessel. *Let's take a tour.*

The Voyagers begin to walk up the footbridge into the mother ship.

Logan, Betty, Kyle, General Teapard, and all the other non-Voyagers have to wait for all one hundred thousand actual Voyagers to board first, before a future human finally waves them on.

The first impression one gets is that the ship is surprisingly sparse. It's certainly not what you'd expect from erudite geniuses like the future humans. The interior of the craft looks vacant, even plain. There are no blinking lights or buttons and shiny knobs of any kind. There is no high-tech gadgetry or machinery. In fact, there isn't even a single piece of avionics or equipment of any kind visible anywhere.

"Where's the hardware?" Teapard asks nobody in particular.

They're standing in a vast, open, cavernous space, about the size of a football stadium. This immense chamber vaults up several stories. What's even more peculiar is that there aren't any ninety-degree angles anywhere. The walls and ceilings are all rounded and grooved by what appear to be vertical capillaries running up and down the length of the walls, like pin stripes, giving the appearance that they're inside the mouth of humpback whale, rather than in an advanced space vehicle from the future.

The only accouterments they see are one hundred thousand plush chairs off to the side, way in the distance of this expansive volume. Clearly, that is where the Voyagers will sit for the journey forward through time. The chairs are divided into pairs, with each chair facing another. Logan figures that's so a man can sit in one and a woman in the other, ostensibly so they can begin the process of getting to know each other right from the get-go.

The group of visitors hears Peter's soothing voice. *You're wondering how we operate the vessel?* he asks.

They all turn and find Peter gliding down to them.

"As a matter of fact, yes," Teapard says. "I don't see any navigation equipment, an ignition, or even a yoke. Nothing. How do you drive this thing?"

The problem is, General, you're looking at this ship with twenty-first-century eyes. Try looking at it with fifty-first-century eyes.

Everyone sizes up the surroundings. It's silent for a while as their imaginations run wild. Teapard is the first to speak.

"Are you saying that in three thousand years, we do away with...*technology?*" Teapard asks in disbelief.

Not quite. But that is our intention, Peter says. *We've done away with most of it. The goal is to do away with* all *of it.*

Logan starts to understand. "Because in three thousand years, most everything will be powered by the mind. Literally."

That's correct, Doctor. Thanks to you and the Mindshot, the road to this inevitability was paved. Once you unlocked the know-how that made it feasible for us to speak with our minds, endless possibilities opened up. Over the course of many centuries, we started to rely less and less on mechanical contrivances and more and more on our own brains to power the world.

Logan pieces it together and says, "Which means the need for actual physical gadgetries is minimized, if not eliminated. This is why there isn't any hardware in here. They power this entire interdimensional spacecraft *with just their minds.*"

Betty steps forward. "Whoa! You're saying you flew this ship through time and space with *your thoughts?*" she asks now, her journalistic curiosity working on overdrive.

That is precisely what I am saying, Peter says, with a hint of pride. *If you'll direct your attention to that the area directly to my right, you'll see what is for all intents and purposes, our cockpit.*

They turn and see an alcove, a nook seemingly carved into the wall as if by a human-sized ice cream scooper, where a panel of some sort is visible. The panel has no buttons, knobs, or lights on it either. Instead, it appears organic—like the rest of the ship—as if it's made up of a half a dozen protruding veins.

Those are essentially levers. We operate them telepathically in order to power and fly the vessel. Peter tells them. *Simply put, those levers function in the main as our steering wheel and gas pedal.*

"Just to be clear, which you then operate entirely with your mind?" Teapard inquires.

With only our minds, yes. Peter nods.

Silence, as that percolates.

Yet this is but a mere spacecraft, certainly not the heights of our capabilities. This vehicle is the proverbial tip of the proverbial iceberg, Peter declares proudly. *In the future,* all *is done with the mind. Physical labor is nonexistent. Hammers, screwdrivers, and saws exist only in museums, as relics in our twenty-first-century exhibits. In the future, everything is built, manufactured, and operated with the mind.*

"Telekinetically?" Logan asks.

Indeed. It's really not that complicated once you know how to properly access that part of your brain. We learned how to physically accomplish everything we needed with just our minds.

Everyone gathered is mesmerized, as Peter continues, *We concluded, a long time ago—or a long time* from now *in your case—that our reliance on technology was unacceptable. The computer in our head, after all, is* endlessly *more powerful. More so, certainly, than any computer we could ever build and program. So as we continued to advance in our thought-trans-*

ference abilities, computer technology was eventually abolished altogether. There was no need for them anymore. We do everything with the mind now. So during space travel, for instance, we can chart a course, navigate, and power this special vessel to arrive safely at our destination. Along the way, never having to worry about a computer malfunctioning or crashing. Our brains are always on, always providing the power we need, thus making technology obsolete.

"That is, so long as you keep the brain properly nourished?" Teapard asks, pointedly.

All heads turn to her.

"That's why you people still need those sustenance chambers, right?"

Peter seems impressed she remembers that.

Our sustenance is one of only a few areas of future life where we still rely on computer technology. Unfortunately so, Peter reports. *We've compressed the time it takes to receive sustenance while inside the chamber; however, as much as we've tried, we have not been able to eliminate the need to feed our bodies—and our brains. So yes, we still need nourishment to survive.*

"Hence the sustenance chamber?" Teapard says.

Hence the sustenance chamber. As Peter says this, he motions to a different section of the vast ship where two eight-foot capsules, leaning at forty-five-degree angles, are. They all recognize them instantly from the holographic video presentation from earlier.

We needed to bring two of them on the trip, Peter says with a hint of disdain.

He then floats off to attend to several Voyagers, waiting with questions of their own.

Teapard shakes her head, while staring at the sustenance chambers for a bit. She then realizes Logan is watching her, and she grins.

"I'll take eating a cheeseburger and fries any day over having a cheeseburger and fries injected into me," she muses.

Logan chuckles. "I'm with you on that."

As they all exit the craft, the one hundred thousand enthused Voyagers are told to keep their Mindshot helmets on as they're led back inside Hangar One, where a very large co-ed dormitory has been set up for tonight. They're told to find a cot and rest up. In the morning, they will reboard the vessel and fly off to the future.

With the tour having ended, the lance corporal races up, a bit sweaty. "General, ma'am! We've been trying to reach you!" he says quickly.

Then, they all hear it.

Chopchopchopchopchopchop.

A Sikorsky VH-3D helicopter coming in toward the base. Fast. General Teapard recognizes its markings right away.

"Is that Marine One?" Teapard asks.

"Yes, Ma'am. That's what I needed to tell you." The lance corporal pauses to take a deep breath. "The president of the United States is about to land."

CHAPTER TEN

Because of security concerns, President Carlos Beltran didn't want anyone to know he was coming. Not even Teapard. This breach of protocol didn't surprise Logan. President Beltran had always done things his own way. But this—arriving unannounced onto a base that is for all intents and purposes being occupied by a foreign invader—this is new, even for a media-savvy president like Beltran.

"He must really want to get his picture taken with the Clammies," Teapard remarks, sotto voce.

Logan overhears and raises his eyebrow at her. So she walks it back.

"And for the record, I fully support his choice in doing so," Teapard adds.

Logan smiles at her, as Marine One touches down about a hundred yards away. He knows she's fighting the urge to curse the president out, but the general knows Beltran as well as Logan does and understands there is no way he'd let an opportunity like this pass him by. Security issues be damned.

President Beltran looks sharp in his navy-blue Georges de Paris suit as he steps jauntily out of the twin-engine, all weather helicopter. He salutes the marine stationed at the foot of the stairs sharply as he passes and then smiles broadly when he sees Teapard walking up, hand extended, ready to greet him. His smile has a calming quality. This was, and is, Beltran's greatest asset—his ability to charm.

"General, it's a pleasure to see you again," President Beltran says, shaking her hand and not letting go. His hand sits atop hers, instantly asserting his power.

"I wish I could say the same, sir," Teapard says, also with a smile, unfazed by his obvious power play. "With all due respect, the base isn't as secure as I'd like it to be."

Beltran pulls his hand away and looks away as if surveying the base. He then walks away, making Teapard follow—another shallow power move. Teapard rolls her eyes, which the president doesn't notice.

"Nonsense, General. I'm sure you have this base sufficiently locked down."

Beltran studies the future humans' vessel. Even though it's off in the distance, its overpowering presence staggers the commander in chief. He even seems to gasp a bit.

"Oh my God. The pictures don't do it justice."

He admires it in wonderment. The greeting party around the president stands back, allowing him this moment to absorb the ship for the first time. Logan and Betty are among them, waiting for their moment to address him.

President Beltran takes a few steps toward the ship, more and more captivated by the sight of it. Gone is the flashy smile; gone are the charm offensive and the petty power plays. He's now just another twenty-first-century human being trying to make sense of what he's looking at. Finally, he realizes all eyes are on him, and he snaps out of it. As with any president, Beltran has become acutely aware that everyone always watches him, trying to decipher what he's thinking. So as with any president, he works very hard not to reveal much. He whips back around, faces the greeting party, flashes his perfect dental work again, and points at the vessel behind him.

"C'mon, General. Why don't you build me one of those things, huh?" the president jests.

Everyone laughs. Beltran then spots Logan.

"Well, if it isn't the man himself!" President Beltran exclaims. "Doctor Logan! You want to thank me now or later for having the foresight to green-light the Mindshot?" The president takes Logan's handshake and pulls it into man-hug. One arm around the back, while keeping palms pressed. "How are you?" Beltran asks.

"Good. Thank you. How about you, Mr. President?" Logan asks once he's released from the bro-embrace.

"Eh, as well as a president who's been visited by humans from three thousand years in the future can be," Beltran quips, to more laughs.

Logan gestures toward Betty. "Mr. President, I'm not sure if you remember Betty—"

"Do I remember Betty Suarez?" The president lights up. He is always a notch or two more charming with the

113

ladies, especially the attractive ones. "Of course. I thought you two broke up?"

"We did," Betty admits, with a sheepish smile and a firm handshake. "I'm here on business."

Beltran never loses his amiable smile. "All right then. That makes sense. You're a wonderful reporter—a fair one. How are you?"

"I'm fine, thank you, sir," she replies, fighting the impulse to like him. Betty knows the president uses this charm tactic to disarm reporters so when they interview him later, they'll give him the softball questions.

"Outstanding. Glad to hear it," the president says.

He looks around and sees several other people in the greeting party waiting their turn to say hello. Rather than go glad-hand each of them, President Beltran stands back and makes an announcement.

"If you all don't mind, the pleasantries will have to wait," he says for all to hear. "I need to speak to General Teapard. Alone."

The general perks up. The president leans in and whispers to her. "Someplace we can't be heard?" he asks, motioning with his eyes toward the future humans' vessel.

Logan's housing unit on the base is rudimentary—bachelor funky—but is somehow still cozy and lived in. He's decorated his bungalow with the few furnishings he brought over from his old apartment in San Francisco. The centerpiece is a plush leather couch that overlooks a flat-screen TV.

His tastes haven't evolved much since I saw him last, Betty observes as she steps through the front door. Logan enters behind her.

"Sorry about the mess," Logan says, with a grin, locking the door behind him. "Wasn't expecting my ex to pay me a visit today."

"It's actually comforting—oddly—seeing your mess again," she says, plopping down onto the couch. "It reminds me of..." Betty sinks into the deep cushions a bit and finishes the sentence warily. "...us."

Logan stands there, just getting an eyeful of Betty. Smiling. He feels something between them right then and there. She's staring back at him. There's something amorous happening, for sure. It's overwhelming. Which is why Betty changes the subject.

"So, what do you suppose the president wanted to talk to the general about in secret?" she asks, feigning interest in a magazine on Logan's coffee table, as she flips through it.

"You know, he is the leader of the free world and she oversees his military," Logan jibes. "Could be anything."

Logan sits down next to Betty—really close.

She stiffens immediately at the proximity but keeps her back to him, still pretending to show interest in the magazine. He doesn't see how her eyes have opened wide as panic sets in. She starts to reconsider her decision to come to his apartment. Betty thought she could do this and not feel anything—or at the very least suppress her feelings. She was wrong about both.

Logan peeks over her shoulder. He smirks. "Weird," he says.

"What?"

"I didn't know you were interested in *Scientific American*."

"Umm, yeah. Totally love it." She flips a few more pages, stops on an article, and reads the headline, with feigned interest. "'Astral Physics in Quantum Tunneling.' I mean, wow. That is fascinating-*ly* boring. Do you *really* read this stuff?"

Logan gently pries the magazine from her fingertips and sets it down. "Why do you seem so nervous?" he asks, smiling slightly.

"Me? Nervous? Do I seem nervous?" she responds, unsure of what to do with her hands without the magazine in them.

"A little bit. Why?"

"Well, first of all, I'm not nervous," Betty says without much conviction. "But let's suppose I was nervous. Just supposing."

"Of course. Totally hypothetical."

"Exactly. Hypothetically, I'd maybe...maybe be nervous because, I'd possibly be, maybe have, still, have some unresolved issues," Betty stammers. "With my ex."

There! She said it. But she's not done.

"So the question should be," she continues. "Why aren't *you* nervous too?"

"Do I not seem nervous?"

"Wait...are you? Nervous?"

Logan nods. "And for the exact same reasons you are."

"Well, hell, you don't seem nervous," Betty says, suddenly more nervous than before.

How is that possible? she wonders.

"I work for the United States military developing top-secret, state-of-the-art weaponry," Logan reminds her. "I've learned to not show when I'm nervous."

They stare at each other for a bit, not saying a word. Now what?

"I'm sorry," Logan blurts it out, not wanting to mask how he feels anymore. So he's going to tell her, right this moment, how he feels. That's it; no longer can he hold it in.

"I should've never let you go, Betty. I should've kept you by my side. I should've stayed by yours. I can't believe that I ever felt my career was more important than you were. Than us. It wasn't. And it isn't. You were the most important thing in my life. Betty, I still love you with all my heart."

He said all that very fast. He'd rehearsed that speech in his head hundreds of times, wishing to one day get the chance to tell her, and here she was, looking at him with doe eyes. He wasn't about to miss the opportunity.

Tears well up in Betty's eyes. She tries to stop them, but they just flow out. There are only a few at first, but the longer she looks at Logan—the man she's never for an instant gotten over—the more her tears gush.

Logan reaches out and wipes them away gently. The moment his hand touches her face, she closes her eyes. In rapture. She lets his touch linger—fingertips to her skin. She kisses his knuckles tenderly, not opening her eyes. Logan's hand remains on her face, caressing it softly, rubbing away the still streaming tears with his fingers. She kisses his fingertips, keeping her eyes shut. Betty can't bring herself to open them.

Is this a dream? she wonders. She hopes not.

Then she feels his lips on hers. Lips still soft—just as she remembers them—velvety as they press against hers. With her mouth open slightly, she kisses back. Same way. And then she pulls away. Just for a moment. Eyes open now, they bring their foreheads together, just as they used to do. This is real. This is happening.

They move in again, connect–kiss–touch each other. They've longed for this moment so long. They both weep and finally embrace.

"I never stopped loving you," Logan whispers in her ear.

"Me neither," Betty says, after a gasp.

With that, they melt into each other. Nuzzle. Remembering what it felt like—loving again what it feels like. And then they kiss again. This time, they don't—they can't—won't stop.

Passion now. Triggered. Hungry. Pent-up sexuality unleashed. First Betty's blouse is opened. Then the bra comes off. His pants follow. They can't wait.

It's not long before they're making love.

When it's over, they lie there holding each other. Their bodies are still warm and slick with perspiration. Their chests heave against one another. They don't speak. They can't.

Finally, they pull away. Not too far though—only inches apart. Face-to-face now, they laugh—delirious, content, satisfied, and very much in love.

"Well…" Betty finally says, composing herself as best she could. "…that was…unexpected."

"Are you feeling all right?" Logan asks.

"Am I feeling all right?" Betty smirks, lightening the mood. "That's not what you really want to ask me."

Logan clears his throat. "Huh?"

"C'mon. You wanna know if you still got it. The chops…" Betty continues. "…the *sex* chops."

Logan laughs, embarrassed. She's nailed him. Still, he pretends to be indignant.

"That's outrageous, young lady," he says doing some obviously fake acting. "But since you've brought it up—"

"It was amazing." Betty purrs. "Just as I remembered it."

They embrace once again and begin kissing anew, but it's interrupted by a door-rattling knock.

They both tense up, prone one atop the other, wondering who's knocking. They're unsure about what to do.

There's more knocking—louder now. Then they hear General Teapard. "Doctor, it's General Teapard," she says, knocking again.

Oh crap!

Now Logan and Betty bolt upright, scrambling out of bed, naked, and start getting dressed as quick as they can. He tosses over her panties. She flings over his pants. They can't dress fast enough.

Can this get any worse?

"I'm here with the president, Doctor. Please, open the door." She knocks louder.

Logan and Betty freeze. *It just got worse.*

They finish dressing—pat down their hair, tuck in shirts and blouses, trying to make themselves presentable. Logan heads for the door and looks back at Betty. She nods.

A beat later, he opens the door.

General Teapard and President Beltran look past Logan and see Betty. Seeing how inelegant she looks, they put two and two together.

"Well, this is certainly awkward," the general says.

"We should've called first, yes?" President Beltran chides.

Behind the president and general, there is the flotilla of troops who escorted them. And they're also all seeing Logan and Betty standing there, together, postcoital.

CHAPTER ELEVEN

The president and general sit on Logan's couch in silence, ill at ease about having caught Logan and Betty together.

The lead scientist had been caught hooking up with the pool reporter on the eve of a monumentally historical moment in time by the president of the United States and a bunch of military personnel. It made for a gauche situation.

Finally, Logan clears his throat and attempts to regain some semblance of decorum. "You both know I would've been happy to come see you at your office," he says, delicately.

He still doesn't know why they've shown up like this, unannounced.

"Actually, it was my idea to come here," President Beltran says.

Logan and Betty exchange puzzled looks. "Why is that, sir?"

The president nods to General Teapard, clearly referring to some recent conversation in that look, giving her permission to respond.

She then turns to Logan and leans in. "Why did you call your invention the Mindshot?" Teapard asks.

Logan is puzzled by the question. "Well...the name was based on the concept that the ability to read minds would function much like the ability to hear conversations. You'd have to be within mindshot so somebody can hear—" Logan cuts himself off. He suddenly understands why they're here. "...what you're thinking."

Teapard nods. "Your housing unit is clear on the other side of this base, as far away from that future human vessel as we can get."

"Which means our minds probably can't be read at this distance," Logan concludes. "Which means, there's something you have to tell me, something you don't want *them* to hear."

"Are we?" President Beltran asks. "Are we out of mindshot here?"

"I can't say for sure, Mr. President," Logan admits. "But I've conducted some elementary experiments, and it seems that the farther we get from the future humans, the more questions they end up asking about what we're doing. That suggests they can't hear us from a certain distance. But again, it's just a theory."

"That's what we've concluded as well." Teapard nods.

"Which means what I'm about to tell you, in all likelihood, isn't being heard by them," the president says. "And even if it is, it doesn't matter. They're going to hear it soon anyway."

Once again, Logan and Betty glance at one another. The president and the general appear dire. Something huge is definitely happening. Logan takes a deep breath. He knows it somehow involves him. Otherwise, they wouldn't be sitting in his living room.

"Yes, sir?" Logan says quietly.

The president stands and begins to pace. He looks to General Teapard, and she nods. Whatever it is, it has her full support. He then faces Logan and Betty and smiles pensively.

"The other day, my daughter climbed and stood on top of the monkey bars in the playground we have in back of the White House," the president recalls with a parental smile. "She's not supposed to climb and stand up there, mind you, but she'd been watching gymnastics on the Olympics and decided she wanted to test her balance. She was using the top of the monkey bars like they were a balance beam, you know? Now, had she fallen off, she would have indeed gotten hurt, no doubt about it, but not seriously, bruises at most. We have it all padded on the ground. So, part of me said, 'Let her fall. Let her get hurt. She'll learn not to climb up there anymore.' But another part of me said, 'No, *don't let her fall*. That's your job. To protect her. Stop the fall from happening, and then explain why you're stopping it.' I chose to stop it and got her down. She was so mad at me—she looks just like her mom when she's angry with me. Anyway, she stormed off in a huff and wouldn't talk to me for a while, but I prevented that fall from happening. My job as president, Dr. Logan, is to sometimes be dad to this country."

Logan and Betty are intrigued. Where is he going with this? A moment later, they learn where.

"*I'm withdrawing the United States' support for Operation Noah's Ark*," he says. "Effective immediately."

Ton of bricks. The proverbial kind. That's what hits Logan and Betty. They're stunned.

"Prior to arriving here, I signed an executive order, instructing that all American citizens be pulled out of here and returned to their homes," President Beltran continues. "Furthermore, I have spoken with every world leader—literally all of them, one after the other—and it's unanimous. Turns out, not one of my fellow leaders feels comfortable either, sending their citizens off with these...people. I've been authorized to pull their citizenry as well. There won't be a mission to the future."

Logan and Betty try to process this. Fast as they can. Thoughts racing. Questions lingering. This is historic. Especially at the eleventh hour. Clearly, the president has been considering this for a while, perhaps from the onset of their arrival. Logan has never seen President Beltran so grave. Gone is the jovial charmer. In his place is somebody who is carrying the weight of what is certainly a monumental responsibility.

"Your interview, Betty, with that...*human* raised a lot of good questions." Beltran nods to Betty. "It's what prompted this whole change."

Betty beams.

The president continues, "Turns out every world leader felt the same—this whole notion of sending our people into the future to correct mistakes humans *will make* hundreds, if not thousands, of years from now seems...wrong."

Teapard seems to sigh with relief.

"You were right to ask that, Betty. How can we, in good conscience, send our citizens on a journey with the understanding we will never again know of their well-being," Beltran continues. "The moment they leave, we won't know what becomes of them. We won't know if they succeed or fail. We won't know how they're being treated. We won't know a thing. Even if the future humans assure us up and down, backward and forward, that these people will be well treated and looked after, we won't know for certain. Yet, here we are on the eve of sending these people into a great unknown."

"Just doing the devil's advocate thing here," Betty chimes in, "but nobody is forcing these people to go. They're volunteering of their own free will."

"That's true, but how many of them would've opted not to volunteer had I and every other world leader strongly urged them not to?" Beltran responds.

"I believe volunteers would've still shown up. Regardless. This is far too irresistible," Logan adds. "There would be people who felt they hadn't anything to lose and all to gain. Those kind of people would have absolutely still shown up, regardless of what you or any world leader advised."

"Sure, I agree. A lot of volunteers would've still insisted on partaking, no matter what, but that's where I have to step in—as their leader—and lead. They voted me into office to lead, not to look at poll numbers and act in my own self-interest."

Logan has never seen Beltran this solemn. *He's* definitely *had some sort of come-to-Jesus*, Logan concludes.

"So that's what I'm doing. Leading," Beltran says somberly. "As president, I've concluded that I can't allow a single American to go on this goddamned voyage. Period."

These are emotions Logan's never seen pour out from this president.

"Look, the future humans have shown us what we become—what we evolve into, my God, what we end up looking like—unless we alter where we're headed. Make changes. Starting today. Right now. If we do that, we won't ever get to the point that humans need to travel back in some desperate Hail Mary move to gather up healthy people to procreate and carry on the race. No, if we change course as humans, going forward, starting right this instant, mankind can and will go on."

Damn it. Betty wishes she had her camera. *Why did I leave it in the media room?* Here she is without a way of documenting a moment where history is happening in Norman Logan's living room. She considers fishing her iPhone from her purse to video all this, but her journalistic juices are flowing.

"If you do this, no matter how well you explain it, some will call you the president who refused to save mankind. That's how you'll be remembered. That will be your legacy," Betty says gingerly. "You're okay with that, sir?"

"Absolutely," Beltran responds without hesitation. "Because I believe it's the *right thing to do.* Just like I did with my daughter when she stood on top of the monkey bars."

"Don't let 'em fall?" Betty asks.

"Don't let 'em fall." The president nods.

Teapard turns to Logan and leans toward him inquisitively. "Now that that's settled, there's one more thing I've been wondering about, Doctor." She searches Logan's face. "When Kyle Howard first put on the Mindshot, the Clammies couldn't hear his thoughts."

"That's right. Must you remind me? I inadvertently—" Logan cuts himself off the moment he realizes *why* she's brought this up. "...I had the bio-electrodes inverted, blocking thought transference rather than sending it."

"Doctor, you may have already figured out how to once again keep our thoughts private," Teapard says with a smile.

CHAPTER TWELVE

It didn't take long for Logan to flip over all four of their Mindshot helmets and rewire them, just as he'd first done—albeit unintentionally—with Kyle. They all slip the helmets on and stand in silence, looking at one another. After a while, General Teapard speaks up.

"Unless you've all managed to clear your minds," the general says, "I can't hear what any of you are thinking."

"I was thinking about washing my dishes. They've been sitting in the sink for days," Logan says. "Anybody hear me think that?"

Everyone shakes his or her head.

"Me? It was the weather," Betty adds. "I regretted not having brought a sweater. Anybody hear me think that?"

Again, more head shakes.

"I was thinking about the nuclear launch codes, what they were," the president says.

He laughs when everyone gasps in shock.

"I'm kidding! I was thinking about my dog. Anybody?"

Everyone smiles and shakes his or her head.

"Okay, that settles it. These Mindshots are reversed," General Teapard says, with a hint of relief, knowing she has regained some form of tactical advantage. No matter how minute. "Good job, Doctor Logan."

"There's just one problem," Betty warns. All heads turn to her. "We'll be able to hear their thoughts, but they won't be able to hear ours now?"

"That's correct," Teapard says.

"Am I the only one thinking of this? If they can't hear our thoughts, we're going to have to speak with them orally," Betty tells them.

"Yeah. That's kind of the intention," Beltran adds, with a confused laugh.

"Right, but that also means, *they* will know immediately that we're somehow *blocking our thoughts*."

"Your point being?" Beltran crosses his arms.

"Her point, Mr. President, is that if they know we're blocking our thoughts, then they'll know we're up to something and so perhaps we shouldn't all go talk to them at once," Logan suggests. "We wouldn't want them to think we're being cagey."

Teapard retorts with a taste of disdain, "With all due respect, kids, why don't you leave the strategic implications of doing this to me." She heads toward the door.

President Beltran chimes in, "I think they're right, General. Maybe it should just be me. Approaching them—breaking this news. And also Doctor Logan, he should be with me since they trust him. Perhaps the presence of military force will give the wrong impression."

"Or the right one, Mr. President. The impression of strength. I don't think—" Teapard starts up.

Beltran cuts her off with a hand wave.

"I'm sorry. No. The more I think about this, the more I want to keep this meeting friendly. After all, it's going to be a huge disappointment for them, and I don't want them thinking we're being aggressive."

Teapard can hardly contain her frustration.

"My mind is made up, General," Beltran continues. "You'll stand down and wait in your quarters. I don't want military anywhere in sight. For peace to work, my talk with them has to be free of anything that may be deemed aggressive."

Teapard's frustration does not escape Beltran.

"Look, I have my Secret Service detail, Anne. Believe me, I'll be fine." Beltran smiles. "I will go in with Dr. Logan. Alone."

"And the media too!" Betty interjects. "Sorry, sir, as the pool reporter, I must insist on documenting this moment."

"Fine. The media too. Having a record of this will be historic," Beltran says.

Teapard shoots Logan and Betty daggers with her eyes. "Yes, sir," she growls.

"It's not their fault, General," Beltran says. "This way just makes for good diplomacy."

"Understood, sir." Teapard nods, begrudgingly.

"Where are the Voyagers right now?" the president asks.

"They're in a holding area, getting settled into their dormitory, sir," General Teapard replies.

"Good," President Beltran says. "I'll want to talk to them afterward. Break the news to all of them personally."

Peter descends past the gantry, floating down, accompanied by a few of the other future humans just in time to see the jeep carrying the president approach. A barrage of military personnel, protection vehicles, and security detail escorts the jeep, as usual.

Peter notices that Doctor Logan, General Teapard, and Betty Suarez accompany the president. They are all wearing Mindshot helmets, yet interestingly, he can't hear any of their thoughts.

As the jeep comes to a stop, Kyle Howard races up to them, already turning on his video camera. "I got your message. Sounds like something big's about to go down."

"There is. Roll on everything."

President Beltran and General Teapard exchange looks one last time, before they spin on their heels in opposite directions. He heads toward the vessel with a few Secret Service agents in tow. Teapard heads toward the main building where Colonel Canoga steps up to greet his commander.

"Colonel, have everyone fall back away from the vessel," she orders. "The president is going rogue."

"General?" Colonel Canoga asks, confused.

"He's got his Secret Service detail with him and has ordered the rest of us to fall back. So fall back."

The colonel nods and immediately radios the order. Soon after, the entire military presence around the ship rolls backward or flies off, as ordered. Once that happens, the general marches past the colonel.

"As for you, me, and the all the other troops out here, we're withdrawing to the bunker right now," General Teapard says as she walks past him.

The colonel radios more orders, as he tosses one last look toward the president, who is curiously headed right up the gantry of the vessel. Unsure of what to make of this, Colonel Canoga falls in quickly with the general, stride for stride.

"Have Doctor Rosenberg join us down there too," the general orders as they enter the main building and disappear behind a slow-closing door.

Meanwhile, like a descending paper airplane, Peter glissades down to the president, who is flanked by his security detail, consisting of two dark-suited Secret Service agents. The fact this has become an obviously impromptu meet-and-greet, sans any military presence, does not escape Peter.

He also notices that the whole area around the vessel has been vacated. There are some Apache helicopters circling overhead, but aside from Beltran, his two agents, Logan, Betty, and Kyle, General Teapard has gotten rid of *everybody*.

Mr. President, it's a pleasure to meet you, Peter says soothingly. *My name is Peter.*

This is the first time Beltran sees Peter and is the first time he hears him over the Mindshot helmet. Even the leader of the free world has the same reaction everyone else did: disorientation.

But Beltran quickly pulls himself together and says aloud, "It's a pleasure to meet you too!"

Silence now. What next? Clearly, Beltran is nervous. He does his best to hide it.

"I speak for the entire twenty-first century when I say that your being here, this day, is a monumentally historic moment—probably one of the biggest moments in history, if not the biggest. Your mission to save mankind is one that any human, no matter what century they're from, can understand and want to fully support."

As Beltran continues to wax poetic for Peter, and for Kyle's videotaping camera, Logan looks at Peter and can tell he is confused—another common human emotion on rare display. Peter turns his head slowly like a wind-up doll and fixes his eyes on Logan. Very creepy.

What's happening, Doctor? Peter asks, a trace of annoyance in his measured voice.

Logan looks around curiously to see if anyone else hears Peter. *Nobody else can hear me. Just you,* Peter reports. *Respond, please. Why I can't hear your thoughts? Or Betty's or the president's? To where did the general pull all the soldiers back? Why is the president giving me this lengthy speech? Respond, Dr. Logan.*

Logan gulps, shrugs, and smiles sheepishly. He shakes his head and points to his ear, then points to President Beltran, as if to say, *Just listen, this will all make sense in a moment.*

Peter's eyes narrow. He seems irritated now and holds a contemptuous look on Logan for a few moments longer, until in disgust, he refocuses back on the president, who is just now finishing his unscripted speech.

"—which is what brings me here, right now," the president says.

Beltran takes a deep breath, places his fingers in the steeple position and reveals his change of heart—how there is complete unanimity among the entire world's leadership about this, exception of none, and that he is authorized to speak for all of them.

Then, he breaks the news, none of the one hundred thousand Voyagers will be allowed on the journey.

Beltran's bedside manner is exceptional—it's like a tender and heartfelt breakup. There is nothing arrogant or aggressive in his voice. Peter remains motionless. Occasionally, he glances at Logan and then Betty, but otherwise, he remains focused on what Beltran is saying.

After wrapping up what became a fifteen-minute dissertation as to why the twenty-first century is pulling out of Noah's Ark, the president stands back and smiles.

Everyone waits to hear the future humans' response.

Thank you, Mr. President, Peter says with a smooth, even tone. *I deduce that this is a final decision, with no possibility of reconsideration?*

"That's correct. I'm sorry," Beltran empathizes. He genuinely feels bad for them. They've worked so diligently, perfecting time travel, building this magnificent vessel to do so, and are now going to leave empty-handed.

Peter looks back to his fifty-first century cohorts, and in that single moment, in that single look, a good amount is determined between them about what to do next. Logan is sure they're speaking telepathically, but evidently, they can block their thoughts as well.

Finally, Peter turns back to the president.

We understand why you've come to this conclusion, Peter finally says. *We certainly do.*

Beltran seems to be relieved, proud of his diplomatic prowess.

Perhaps I can still use this to win reelection this fall, he thinks, knowing nobody can hear his thoughts right now.

But to Logan, something's not right. Something deep down in his gut tells him something terrible is about to happen.

To his horror, he was right.

*However, we **reject** your desire not to participate,* Peter says coolly.

Beltran stiffens. Did he just hear him right? They're *rejecting* him? Betty practically double takes. Kyle fights the urge to lower the video camera and look on with only his eyes.

But Logan just mutters to himself, "Oh no. Oh no. Oh no." He fears where this is going.

Surprised, Mr. President? You shouldn't be, Peter continues. *Did you really think we'd accept this? That we'd say, 'Thank you for your time,' and simply pack up and leave?*

Peter is floating closer and closer to President Beltran, menacingly. So close that the two Secret Service agents are forced to draw their weapons.

Peter keeps approaching regardless.

I now understand why you pulled back your entire military infrastructure, Peter says without inflection. *You wanted the appearance of peaceful negotiations. Not a wise move. You were left defenseless.*

Beltran looks over to his Secret Service agents.

*Really? You think **they** can protect you from me?* Peter snarls.

Hearing that, the agents bolt to extract the president. The moment they do so, their semi-autos are ripped clean out of their hands. Levitating, the guns whip around—one hundred and eighty degrees—the barrels now facing the agents. Up close. Point-blank. Then each gun discharges twice. Muzzle flash obliterates their faces; they blast the Secret Service agents backward with armor-piercing bullets shredding apart their skulls.

Grisly carnage and instant death.

But Peter never even flinches, except that he keeps moving closer to the president.

*Did you really think we'd allow you to **change your mind**?* Peter asks, now face-to-face with Beltran, who manages to hold his ground, yet is clearly shaken by what's just happened.

No. We will not, Peter says, eerily calm. *Operation Noah's Ark **will** continue.*

Logan's instinct is to protect Betty. Yet, she's got her eyes on the future humans, terrified. So he starts to move toward her, instincts desperate to pull her away to safety.

Here's what's going to happen now, Peter continues. *First, this conversation never happened.*

Kyle has been videotaping this whole time, trying to keep his spastic hands from trembling, when suddenly the camera begins to get warm. Very warm. And then hot.

Piping. To the point that, Kyle can't hold onto to it anymore. He hot potatoes it to the floor, where it combusts suddenly, engulfed fully in flame.

Secondly, you and Dr. Logan and Kyle Howard are under arrest, Peter says.

It happens fast.

The moment Logan reaches out to Betty, inches from clasping her hand—he, the president, and Kyle are levitated upward, hoisted abruptly into the air, straight up unceremoniously—just like Aleksy.

Then they are jettisoned—still airborne—away from the vessel as if shot out of a cannon.

The only person not whisked away into the air is Betty. She remains planted, alone, stunned and horrified.

Peter turns his ice cold gaze onto her.

CHAPTER THIRTEEN

Airborne.

They're moving not out into the desert but rather toward the main building on the base. Moving so very fast. G-forces push on Logan so fiercely that he thinks he may pass out up here, midair. But despite the nauseating inertia, Logan notices something *below them*.

He sees that every several hundred yards or so, a different hovering future human is stationed underneath them, seemingly watching them fly past, overhead. At least four of them in a row spaced out evenly for some reason. And when they arrive at their destination, the military penal brig, they find yet another future human stationed, also watching them wing past briskly.

Logan, President Beltran, and Kyle are now swept inside the building. Throttling down a long hallway, they pass two more future humans, who watch them land inside of a large cell, where a heavy steel door slams shut behind them. They are set down somewhat gently but still tumble, end over end, onto the concrete floor. They try to catch their breath, gather themselves, and get their bearings.

Even as he composes himself, Logan realizes why there was a future human spread out every few hundred yards. That's how they were able to whisk them in here so easily—a levitation relay system of sorts. Peter sent them up, flying to one future human, who then sent them to another, who sent them to another, until they reached their destination.

The president is the first to get to his feet and stumble toward the door. He tries it, but it's locked. So he looks out the small, vertical, rectangular window on the cell door, seeing if he can make anything out, and comes face-to-face with the two future humans on the other side of the glass, startling him.

They're looking in on them. Glaring.

President Beltran backs away, frustrated. He turns to the others, still trying to collect themselves after the jolt of being brought here.

"Well, it seems like we've just become their prisoners."

The Apache pilots overhead witnessed the whole thing.

The instant Logan, Kyle, and especially President Beltran are swept into midair, the military response is immediate.

"They've taken the president! Agents down!"

Teapard's voice crackles in on overlapping radios, urgently. "Engage! Engage!"

The United States military does just that.

Starting with the Apaches, they unleash the full might of their implements of war upon the future humans.

And a hellish firestorm descends from above.

Betty instinctively dives to the ground, arms over her head, as the Apache gunships pivot in, weapons hot, strafing the future human vessel. No sooner does that happen, than Peter simply raises his hand at the incoming choppers, where they and their streaking ordinance stop midair and freeze. Then the gunships buckle, like beer cans in a drunkard's palm. The choppers are crushed and implode in fiery bursts that rain down as twisted balls of steel and flame.

A moment later, just as the F-22 Raptors dive in, weapons blazing, a slew of future humans emerge from within the vessel, with their hands up—but not in surrender.

This is how they wage war.

Inside the jail cell, everyone listens to the muffled sounds of war raging outside, filtering in through the walls. This creates some glimmer of hope, however fleeting. Perhaps the future humans will be done in by American shock and awe. President Beltran glances out the window of the cell and looks to the future human guards.

They no longer look at him. Instead, both are turned away and have their arms extended upward, hands up in the direction of the battle.

Inside the dormitory in Hangar One, the one hundred thousand Voyagers hear it—explosions, screaming, whistling missiles. Moments earlier, the mood had been festive. Now all are silent, fear-struck, as they listen to bedlam outside. They're not sure what's happening, and none dare investigate. Some of them even cover their ears.

Since he was the first to be selected, Josh from Cleveland has become a self-appointed leader of the group and addresses them all.

"Let's stay calm until we know what's happening out there. Okay? Just stay calm."

It is hard to do so when the marines stationed in the dorm, looking over them, had long ago scrambled from their posts after hearing the blasts, racing out to join in whatever melee was transpiring outside.

After a few moments—as if somebody pounded the mute button—there's silence.

Whatever was happening outside is over.

Betty still has her hands swathing her head and is still lying prone on the dirt, when she hears the mayhem abruptly stop. During the clamor of the battle, she considered crawling to safety.

*But where is **safe?*** she wondered. So she stayed where she was until it was over.

She slowly looks up, not sure what she'll see. And what she did astounded her.

Utter destruction had befallen in every direction.

Every military vehicle commissioned at the base, from tanks to choppers and fighter jets, lay on the ground in smoldering heaps. Some severed in pieces, but the majority had simply been disabled and flung down onto the sand, where they no longer presented a threat.

The rest of the air support...is in full retreat.

Betty can't believe she's seeing this. Apaches and F-22s, fleeing into the far reaches of the desert, withdrawing from the fight. Betty would learn later that General Teapard painfully ordered the retreat when defeat was imminent.

What had happened was immediately obvious to Betty. Within a matter of minutes, the future humans had once again, with relative ease, prevailed over the US military.

This time, tragically, perhaps to send a message, soldiers had been killed. Betty averts her eyes when she sees the blood-drenched bodies of Americans—strewn where they fell.

The slaughter is too devastating to bear.

She then turns her attention to Peter and the battalion of prevailing future humans behind him. They all lower their hands at once.

It is over.

Peter moves toward Betty now. She wants to scream, to run, but she stays put and braces herself. She doesn't know why she's still here. Alone. With them. *With him.*

I am curious, Miss Suarez, Peter finally says, when he is only mere feet away from her. *How is it that you can still hear my thoughts, but I can no longer hear yours?*

Betty knows the answer but won't respond. Instead, she asks questions of her own—always the journalist, especially in times of crisis.

"Do you realize you've just declared war on us?" she asks out loud, knowing Peter won't hear her thoughts.

This makes Peter pause with what seems like amusement.

Have I?

"Yes! And I don't know what you've done with the president, but you've just killed…no, you've just murdered—"

I know full well what I did, Miss Suarez! Peter barks. *I have arrested the president because he reneged on our arrangement. And yes, we killed many soldiers and marines, because **they opened fire on us,** despite our repeated warnings not to do so. Do you believe we derive some sort of sick pleasure in killing? That we are barbaric?*

Betty does not respond.

So now I ask you—if war has been declared, then who did so first?

"Spare me your trite outrage and moral equivalency, all right? Just shut up!" Betty doesn't know if she will live or die. She may as well go down swinging haymakers. "We have every right, no matter the timing, to reconsider! Especially something life-altering like Noah's Frickin' Ark. You had no right to slaughter all these people. None!"

Peter moves closer to her, so close she can now smell his repugnant body odor—like a spoiling fish pulled out of a gym locker.

I have a confession to make, Peter says. *You get on my nerves.*

Betty's Mindshot helmet is pried off her head with a taut yank, where it then floats to Peter and is flipped over, bottom up. Peter inspects the wiring of the electrodes on the inside of the helmet and immediately sees what's been done to it. He tosses Betty a look as the wires begin to move on their own and get rewired back to normal.

During this time, Betty tries to clear her mind—tries to think about the weather, sports, anything—knowing that Peter can now hear her thoughts again. She's doing all she can not to send out any vulnerable thoughts, but she's furious and terrified—furious because the future humans have just escalated matters with overt hostility and terrified that she stands in the midst of the total defeat of the US military and also because she doesn't know what's happened to Logan or the president. She is terrified about what will happen to her but tries her best not to think any of these things.

Moments later, the helmet floats back over Betty and settles onto her head, where she can now hear Peter again.

Much better, Peter tells her.

"So answer me this," Betty demands, "why am I still here? Why wasn't I whisked away with the others?"

Because you are not under arrest.

"I'm not?"

No. I'm going to take you back to the fifty-first century. Peter's tone makes it seem like he's smiling. *Congratulations, you are now part of Operation Noah's Ark.*

Betty takes a step back. "Yeah right! You can torture me all you want, pal, but it won't happen. I will not participate!" she says angrily, barely able to contain tears of rage. "I won't procreate for you or any other asshole in the fifty-first century!"

One of the by-products of having an advanced mind is that it heightens certain senses. Much like a dog that smells fear. We can perceive certain...conditions, Peter says calmly.

Peter then inches forward for emphasis to reveal:

*You're **already** pregnant.*

Betty gasps. She goes ashen, tries to comprehend what he's just said. But she can't process this. Not this.

"But...I...but..."

You copulated a short time ago, did you not? I can hear you thinking about it. Peter interjects. *So, you're wondering how can you **already** be pregnant?*

With that, the familiar diagnostics wand floats over to Betty and levels off at her midsection. That's when the holographic sectional window opens over her womb—revealing an egg inside her ovaries, spinning, pulsating. *Alive.*

***That**, Miss Suarez, is the fertilized egg in your ovary. Your offspring has already been conceived. And your son will be born three thousand years in the future.*

Betty begins to weep.

Kyle peeks out the window.

The two future human guards have lowered their arms and resumed watching the cell door. He turns back to the president and Logan.

"They're unarmed. That's gotta help us, right?" asks Kyle.

"Don't be fooled," Logan informs him. "Their minds provide them all the weaponry they need. They can gun us down right now and never use a pistol."

Logan looks to the president somberly.

"Which is what I suspect just happened outside."

Logan wonders where Betty is and gets scared. He wishes he'd been able to bring her with him. He feels utterly helpless.

Beltran looks out the window and deflates. He doesn't like being in this position. He's the president of the United States—the greatest super power the world has ever known—yet, here he is, powerless.

"Where the hell is Teapard?" Beltran asks.

"She's either wisely in hiding...or dead," Logan says. "We're no match for them, Mr. President."

Kyle starts to get angry. "So you're saying we can't fight back? We can't disarm them? That's what you're telling us?"

"I'm afraid so." Logan nods with a sober expression.

"That can't be right. Every bad guy has a hidden weakness, an Achilles' heel. We just have to find it and exploit it!"

"Let me guess—you read a lot of comic books?" Logan asks.

"What's that got to do with anything?" Kyle snaps back.

Logan shakes his head, exasperated. "Kyle, knock it off, okay? This isn't a comic book."

In disgust, Kyle stomps off to the far side of the cell and slumps against the wall, putting his head down into his knees.

Once he's gone, Logan turns to the president.

"Except...he may be right." Logan smiles slightly as he points to the Mindshot helmet he's still wearing.

Logan whispers, "They didn't confiscate our helmets—our *reversed* helmets—when we were tossed in here. Which means: they can't read our minds right now. Obviously, this was human error. Even if it was a fifty-first-century human error, it was an error nonetheless.

The question now is how do we exploit that? 'Cause it's all we got."

Beltran smiles and whispers back, "Well, it's something."

Betty is transported via levitation into the vessel, which is empty, still waiting to be filled by the hundred thousand voyagers. Betty doesn't seem to notice this as she floats into the volume. Sullen and shell-shocked, Betty doesn't resist as she is lowered onto one of the comfortable seats intended for the voyagers. She doesn't fight it when a set of straps secures her, via telekinesis, firmly to the chair, snug across her shoulders.

Betty's life has been irrevocably changed forever. She's pregnant. She's been taken captive. She's going to travel into the future.

Oh my God.

She hopes to stave off insanity by shutting her eyes—so tight she sees twinkling spots.

Then come the memories, flooding like milk into a glass. She mostly remembers the past she's shared with Logan. She remembers how their intersecting lives led to this day. She remembers that she was instrumental in Logan's success. This is a tragic irony she cannot help but lament. She wonders if this is that moment you hear about—where your life replays before you die. Maybe she's already dead? Is that what's happened? But no...she knows she's very much alive, and she knows this is happening. She keeps her eyes closed and allows her life with Logan to replay on the back of her eyelids.

It comforts her to recall the farce that was their first—and only—high school date at the mall in San Jose. It makes her smile.

Then she fast-forwards to after graduation. Logan and Betty didn't see each other again for years—until that wonderful night, their chance reunion in a San Francisco bar.

They were twenty-eight. High school and college was behind them. Logan was still finishing his doctorate. Seeing Betty again that crisp evening brought back all sorts of nostalgic feelings for Logan, he told Betty later. The attraction was still there for both—and not just the physical kind.

Both being Rembrandt-painting beautiful provided each access to a steady sea of other attractive people. Over the years, they'd had their pick of the gorgeous. Yet, nobody had ever truly sparked to either. Aesthetics weren't everything clearly. They longed for something else. So now, that very instant, something was different between them. Perhaps it was maturity, or perhaps it was the years apart, but they had chemistry like never before. After warmly hugging each other tightly, both very happy to see the other, they began the process of catching up on the other's life.

She was single, having broken up with a boyfriend several months back. Logan was also single. He'd dated here and there but had avoided anything serious for fear it'd interfere with his Mindshot work. Yet, the moment he set eyes on Betty again, that fear of commitment had vanished. Right then and there, in that dimly lit Pacific Heights bar, on that cool San Francisco night, Logan and

Betty were just a man and a woman, who happened to know each other when they were a boy and a girl and had now met up again.

They talked, caught up, and laughed—mostly about that horrible first date they had in high school. Logan explained that he'd literally gotten his idea for what became the Mindshot while on that date and had become so obsessed about it, that he forgot he was even on a date.

For her part, Betty was blown away that she was there at the moment of inception for what had become Logan's passion—his life's work.

Logan then gushed at how impressed he was at the type of reporter Betty had become over the years. Of course, like most people in the Bay Area, Logan had been watching Betty report the news on the local Fox affiliate. She was still stunning, maybe more so today than in high school, Logan admitted. But Betty could also conduct a thoughtful, probing interview. She was the complete package. He admitted that he'd been watching her reports online and was struck by how unbiased she was. Journalism, by most accounts, had all but died thanks to an influx of partisan politics in almost every newsroom, but Betty had managed to hold onto a wildly independent temperament and biting curiosity. Her reports weren't burdened with one-sided agendas waiting to be doled out to the masses. Betty was journalistic integrity in a pinstriped pantsuit.

Norman Logan and Betty Suarez officially started to date that night. Making up for lost time, they became virtually inseparable. When she was covering an international summit in Geneva, Logan flew out to meet her and keep her company. He was the only one who knew she threw up prior to each interview with a head of state. Despite how cool and collected she was on camera, he knew that Betty was a wreck on the inside and was always immensely proud, and impressed, at how well she carried herself.

It worked the other way around too. Before running into Betty again, Logan was obsessed with his Mindshot. He was certain he was about to hit the mother lode with it. After years of trial and error, he'd finally revolutionized and made possible the ability to speak only with your mind. This was the invention of the ages. He figured all he had to do was shop the Mindshot around and listen to offers. He felt, finally, after all he'd sacrificed in his personal life—marriage and children—while earning his doctorate in neuroscience and obsessively designing and building his Mindshot all these years, he was at last ready to put his creation out on the open market and reap the rewards. He'd hoped to emulate Mark Zuckerberg, Bill Gates, and Steve Jobs and accomplish what they did—conceive and make the ultimate product that everyone would want and then make billions off it.

But it didn't go as planned.

There was a lot of interest in the Mindshot, just not the type he'd anticipated. The Mindshot was dismissed, out of hand, as a nefarious device that would invade people's private thoughts, and that was when he wasn't being called a charlatan for trying to pass off a phony paranormal scam as real science. The accusations of false science turned him into a joke among the scientific elites. Telepathy was widely regarded as occult mumbo jumbo—certainly not real science. All this while advocacy groups assailed Dr. Logan as having breached the last frontier of human privacy: their inner thoughts.

No matter how eloquently and soundly he defended the Mindshot during countless presentations, seminars, and private meetings with just about all the Fortune 500 companies—nobody wanted any part of it. Even when demonstration after demonstration proved it worked, nobody wanted to buy it. The notion that Dr. Logan (or anyone) was literally hearing their internal thoughts when they were wearing a Mindshot disturbed most. And because of this, nobody saw the marketability of the Mindshot. They all claimed that as remarkable an invention as it was, it'd never pass legal muster and any company selling it would surely be crippled by an onslaught of lawsuits from privacy advocates.

It was still rejected, even when Logan tried to push the Mindshot as a device that could potentially help the paralyzed move their arms and legs by triggering injured parts of the brain. As appealing as that sounded, the thought-transference component was still present. The Mindshot could still read your mind, and that premise alone was a PR risk no company was willing to take.

Logan had what he felt was an amazing invention that nobody dared purchase.

As Logan flew around the world trying to sell to international conglomerates, Betty was there to console him during his countless rejections. It was her idea to feature Logan's work during one of her news reports.

She put together a slick *20/20*-type feature on the Mindshot, which instantly got him more free publicity than he could've imagined.

At first, he didn't want her to produce the package, as he felt he'd be abusing their relationship if she did so. But it was her idea, she reminded him and insisted on doing it. This single TV report was seen across the globe, especially when it went viral online. And it was because of this television report that Logan got offers from the third-world despots to buy the Mindshot.

Predictably, the rogue nations and mobsters made lucrative offers for the Mindshot, but Dr. Logan wasn't about to sell his invention, or soul for that matter, to any of these degenerates either. He knew that if the Mindshot fell into the wrong hands, it'd surely be used for illicit mind control. Naturally, Logan declined all those offers, and these murderous people didn't take too kindly to being rejected. Death threats soon followed. It was a terrifying time, as Dr. Logan's life was suddenly in mortal danger. If he wouldn't sell the Mindshot technology outright, nothing was stopping a despot from killing Logan and simply taking it for himself.

After he began to get the death threats from these tyrants and warlords, an indignant Betty put together yet another TV report that revealed the threats—where she named names and provided emails as well as voicemails chronicling the death threats. The report ended with a dire warning: *Should Dr. Logan be killed and the Mindshot stolen, the repercussions would be tremendous and reshape the world, as we know it. After all, America's enemies would have the ability to eavesdrop on what we were thinking.*

Within hours of the second report's initial broadcast, the US Government had swooped in and offered Logan the irresistible job he holds currently developing the Mindshot for Uncle Sam. Logan accepted immediately. It wasn't what he expected to happen, but he was now safe from warlords and gangsters, not to mention he was genuinely intrigued by how the United States wanted to implement the Mindshot.

Betty accomplished what she had intended for her man. She gave him what he desired most, yet that moment he took that job as a military scientist marked the end of their relationship. As grateful as Logan was finally to be doing what he loved and to have the full weight of the US military backing him, thanks to Betty, he became obsessively consumed with the Mindshot. Logan was not about to let this once-in-a-lifetime opportunity go to waste.

This meant he started to sacrifice his personal life with her. Gone were the international trips to support Betty on her interviews with heads of state. Gone were the date nights, because so much was now expected of Logan. Gone was everything in their relationship they held dear. Before long, they couldn't even schedule a monthly dinner.

Betty, at first, tried to be understanding and not pressure Logan. She tried to give him space to work. But soon—much to her heartbreak—it was all gone. She hardly saw him, and if that wasn't bad enough, Logan was one day abruptly transferred to a top-secret base, where he was now sequestered, forbidden from even telling her where he was. But worst of all, until the final stages of his work on the Mindshot was complete, he wasn't allowed have any contact with her or anyone outside the base.

He assured her he still loved her, but that he needed to do this. That was what he told her. This was, after all, the moment he'd been waiting for his entire life. Only, he had no idea how long this process was going to take. They might be apart a few months, he told her, maybe a few years.

It should've been their proudest moment, but she remembers it as her most painful heartache. The price Logan had to pay for finally realizing his dream was to fully break off his relationship with Betty.

She gave him the best years of her life.

He gave her a broken heart.

After he drove away from the roadside diner where they split up on an overcast Saturday morning, Betty broke down into tears and didn't see Logan again until three years later, when she walked onto the military base she hadn't known even existed.

Betty opens her eyes. She has to so the stream of tears can flow more easily.

As Peter and the other future humans glide into the dormitory in Hangar One where the Voyagers still await, Peter is pleased to find that they are nervous and rattled but still calm and orderly. They had been prepared to take all hundred thousand voyagers forcibly if need be, which would've complicated matters when they returned to their time. Surely, had these Voyagers been brought back by coercion, they'd most certainly not adhere to the requirements awaiting them. Not willingly, anyway. After a scan of all their thoughts, none seemed to be in panic mode, and since none of the future humans are picking up any notions suggesting sedition, Peter is relieved he doesn't have to use strength on the Voyagers—at least for now.

They have all kept their Mindshot helmets on, just as they were instructed to do. Peter is pleased and feels he selected wisely among all the volunteers. This group will undoubtedly submit to their authority when the time comes.

Ladies and Gentlemen, Peter says, as he floats up and rises above them. *Surely, you've heard the commotion outside and are wondering what's happened.*

The Voyagers look inquisitive. So Peter does what he needs to do to maintain order.

He lies.

A group of disgruntled volunteer outcasts decided to take up arms against us in an attempt to force their way onto Operation Noah's Ark, Peter tells them. *I'm happy to report, they were beaten back.*

The gullible Voyagers seem pleased, as they all nod in relief.

Unfortunately, these rebel outcasts managed to kill several American military personnel, Peter goes on lying.

The Voyagers gasp upon hearing this. Most get visibly upset.

We hope there won't be any more violence, Peter adds. *But because that possibility still exists, we've decided to move up our departure. **We leave immediately.***

CHAPTER FOURTEEN

"I was going to lose my reelection bid. *This* was supposed to have changed that."

This whispered admission from President Beltran during a quiet moment in the cell strikes Logan as odd.

"Wait...How did you know you were going to lose reelection?" The moment Logan asks, he realizes the answer:

Peter revealed it.

President Carlos Beltran's approval ratings were abysmal, even though he'd won election four years ago in a landslide. He was the product of the American dream, born in Dallas, the eldest son of Mexican immigrants, Beltran worked his way through college, majoring in political science. He became, by all accounts, an expert on United States history. Carlos Beltran the political junkie and American history geek soon became Carlos Beltran the city councilman, then mayor, then governor, and finally, president. He'd breezed into office and was loved by the majority of Americans, with approval ratings in the stratosphere. Beltran was untouchable...until he directed a botched raid on the wanted terrorist, Abu Sahid, who was holed up inside a Syrian safe house. Many Navy SEALs were killed during the ill-fated incursion, and the sought-after terrorist they were after ultimately escaped.

As the reddish-yellow dust settled, all fingers of blame pointed directly at Beltran, who ordered the raid despite having faulty intelligence and being warned not to conduct it—even by General Teapard herself. The deaths of Americans, especially those of the beloved Navy SEALs, was more than the American public could take. The incumbent was doomed to lose his reelection bid this fall. No way he would win. But nobody can know for sure what the future holds, right?

Until now.

Beltran goes on to admit that after his initial shock and disbelief that people from the future had arrived, he was soon intrigued and wanted to know one thing and one thing only. The president wanted to know about the election outcome this November.

Who wins it?

"Can you blame me?" Beltran shrugs, keeping his voice down so Kyle won't hear. "What politician wouldn't want to know the future?"

Beltran admits that, at first, Peter didn't want to reveal what the future held for him, but then Beltran ordered Teapard to tell Peter that no president in history would allow his citizenry to volunteer for something like Operation Noah's Ark—*unless he had something to gain personally.* Reluctantly, Peter divulged that the incumbent president would lose his reelection.

That was *Beltran's* future.

"Only now...*I saw a way of changing all of that*," he admits. "This event, this monumental event, this mission from and to the future, could perhaps save my presidential legacy. All I had to do was cooperate and go down in history as the president who saved mankind from extinction. That's one hell of a campaign slogan, ain't it?"

Beltran doesn't seem prideful of his actions; rather, he seems contrite, which perhaps explains this confessional of sorts.

"This was very seductive. Especially for me, who now knew, with absolute confirmation, that I would lose reelection."

Logan got the sense that Beltran was disgusted with and ashamed of himself. This was one reason he liked Beltran—he was guy's guy. He was great over a beer and quick with a joke. Logan also liked the president, naturally, because he'd championed the Mindshot when nobody else would. Despite all this, Logan had always suspected Beltran was a political opportunist and didn't really have the country's best interests at heart—just his own. Logan hoped this wasn't true; deep down, he felt it was but never admitted this to anybody. He always felt that the president wanted the Mindshot for his own nefarious reasons— after he once joked that he'd like to have a Mindshot all to himself to read the minds of his enemies.

It was a joke, but the moral implications didn't escape Logan.

What if, Logan wondered, *the president—or any president for that matter—decided to abuse the Mindshot under the guise of national defense?*

Not much can stop an immoral executive order. Logan decided to ignore the comment back then, hoping it was indeed a joke.

Beltran moves away from Logan, reflecting. He peers out the window absently—and that's when he catches a glimpse, a quick glimpse of a fully equipped recon marine. The marine peeks around the far corner, right behind the two future human guards. The marine, who was decked out in battle-ready tactical gear, was only there for a split second, and then moved back out of sight, but the marine was there! Beltran is *sure* he saw him.

But he concludes, even more importantly, that the future humans did not see the marine.

Beltran whips around, eyes open wide and moves to Logan.

He whispers, "Stay calm. Act normal. But I think there's a rescue attempt underway."

Logan stiffens and takes a deep breath.

"Answer me this," the president again whispers. "If we have marines out there, about to breach, why don't the Clammies hear their thoughts?"

Logan thinks about this and then a moment later, knows the answer. He points to his helmet.

"That's what I thought too." Beltran nods. "Which is why this has to stay between us. If we tell Kyle over there, who isn't wearing a reversed helmet, those Clammy guards will be tipped off, right?"

"That's exactly what will happen, sir," Logan whispers back.

Beltran nods and moves nonchalantly back to the window on the door and peeks out again, checking on the guards. The future humans still have not moved. It's obvious they haven't been alerted yet to the marines Beltran believes are around the corner—waiting to strike.

President Beltran walks casually back to Logan, trying not to let on that anything is happening.

But Kyle notices the president's strange behavior. He cocks his head, trying to figure out what's going on. Kyle sees the president is whispering something to Dr. Logan, but he can't hear what.

Unaware that Kyle is watching them, the president does indeed whisper to Logan, "They're going to need our help. Otherwise, the Clammies are going to have too much time to react."

"Are you sure you saw a marine out there?" Logan asks.

Beltran narrows his eyes with indignation and is about to respond, when Kyle heads over to them, curiously.

"Hey, what's going on? You two are all whispery-whispery over here."

Beltran winks to Logan. "I'm positive," Beltran says, smiling.

Logan knows the president didn't become president because he was timid. Here they are, in a life-or-death situation, and the president is engaged and calm, collected, even excited about the possibility they may be about to take the fight to the future humans.

The president turns to Kyle, and before he can say anything else, Beltran whispers, "Go with me, kid."

With that, Beltran grabs a puzzled Kyle by the lapels and whips him around, a hundred and eighty degrees, slamming him against the door so hard, it rattles.

The president of the United States then proceeds to yell at Kyle, full throat. "Do something! Make your move, damn it!" the president shouts. "*I'm giving you the green light! Go!*"

Logan realizes the commander in chief is not talking to Kyle, but rather giving a veiled, yet direct order to the marines he believes are hidden around the corner.

Logan looks out the window, wondering if they're actually there, or if the president was hallucinating—a victim of wishful thinking.

Both future humans move toward the window of the cell to peek inside and see what all the racket was about, just as Beltran had hoped they'd do.

Thankfully, the president is right about what he saw. It was all the distraction the marines needed. The future human guards never saw the kill-team rounding the corner behind them. They were stealth defined—library quiet. Three recon marines emerge, in cover formation, M4A1 carbines eye level.

And once all three have clear sights, *they open up.*

Headshots rip apart the future humans' skulls like dry eggshells, and their brains splatter onto the window of the cell. Beltran recoils as bloody chunks ooze down the glass. The marine fire team methodically finishes the job. Center-mass rounds shred the future humans' hearts, as they are hurled back, recoiling, hitting the cell door with a resounding thud. They leave a vertical streak of blood in their wake, as they both slip down the length of the door, onto the linoleum.

The one hundred thousand Voyagers are being lined up for their march toward the vessel, when Peter jolts upright. He just felt something and immediately glances over to the other future humans. They felt it too. They can no longer hear two of their comrades.

Something has happened to them.

It's as if they were abruptly silenced. And if that's so, Peter and company can't continue readying the Voyagers for departure. They have to go investigate.

This changes everything, and Peter turns to the throng.

Ladies and Gentlemen. Change of plans... Peter speaks pleasantly, hiding the angst he's suddenly feeling. *There's going to be a short delay in our exodus. Just conducting some last-minute security sweeps. Nothing to be concerned about. We'll be on our way shortly. Thank you for your patience.*

Peter orders a few of his comrades to stay and watch over the Voyagers. The rest are to follow him downstairs.

More marines pour into the hall from around the corner and converge on the scene, all blazing M4A1s—all being pointed down at the fallen future humans, in case they aren't dead.

But they are. Bloody heaps the both of them.

A moment later, Teapard appears carrying her own M4 carbine. She nods to a marine next to her, who immediately sets an explosive-frag against the door of the cell.

The marine looks into the window lathered in blood and brain, makes eye contact with a jubilant President Beltran, and barks, "Sir, get back, please! Fire in the hole!"

Beltran turns to the others and waves them to the far side of the cell.

"The marines are going to blow the door. Back away right now!" he orders Logan and Kyle.

They both comply. Seconds later, the direct explosion causes the door to buckle and dislodge from its hinges.

The marines gain entry methodically, coming forth through the cloud of smoke, clearing the room, and taking protective flanking positions around the president.

"The president is secure, ma'am!" one marine shouts out as General Teapard enters the cell.

"Glad to hear it." She smiles at the president.

The president salutes the general, grateful and proud. "Well done, General Teapard. I can't thank you and your men enough." They shake hands firmly.

Kyle is shell-shocked. "You used me as a decoy?" he blurts out to Beltran. "So they wouldn't notice the guys with the guns behind them?"

"That's right, son," President Beltran says in his best politician's voice. "You've done your country a great service. Thank you."

Beltran walks away from Kyle, who slow burns before he realizes the truth. Then he beams. "I'm a frickin' hero."

Logan leans in to Teapard. "Do you know anything about Betty? If she's all right?"

Teapard shakes her head. "No. I'm sorry. We've been down below this whole time."

Logan sighs and moves over to look down on the dead future humans. He can't believe it. Two of them were *killed*.

"When they can't read your mind and know you're coming, they're just as mortal as any other human. Regardless of century," says Teapard, as she crouches to take a closer look at the dead bodies herself.

The president joins them. "Very impressive, General. Your team moved in so fast that they never got a chance to sound an alarm."

"They don't need alarms, sir," Logan jumps in. "They don't use technology. Just their minds, remember? Which means Peter will know, if he doesn't already, that these two are dead."

The president gets it right away and says, "And when these two don't respond, they'll come here looking to figure out why."

General Teapard stands and grins. "I'm counting on that."

Both the president and Logan turn to her.

"What?" Logan asks. "General, where's the sense of urgency? The only advantage we have over them is the element of surprise, and the only way we can maintain surprise is when you're wearing the reversed Mindshot helmets, but if they do know where we are, we're done for. Right now, they know where we are and are probably sending everyone. Here. Now."

"Tactically, I doubt they'd send everyone," Teapard corrects him. "I'm sure they'll leave a few behind to guard the vessel and some to look after the Voyagers."

"Why do you care if they leave some behind to guard the vessel?" Logan is perplexed. "*They are on their way here!*"

President Beltran and General Teapard exchange calm looks. Beltran now understands fully exactly what Teapard is up to and yet again, seems impressed.

"The general is planning an attack on the vessel." The president nods. "Which is why she needs more of them here and less of them there."

Teapard smiles and pats Logan on the back. "All thanks to you, Dr. Logan, we do indeed have the element of surprise back on our side."

She then gets serious, waves over her marines, and gives them the exit signal, which consists of a rotating finger in the air.

"Now, let's boogie, Mr. President. Dr. Logan is right. The Clammies are on their way here."

This base is bottom-loaded with numerous, highly classified subterranean levels that are known to just a few select people—like General Teapard. Dr. Logan always suspected these secret lower floors existed but didn't know where they were or even how to access them. Yet, here he was, part of a large group that included a heavily armed squadron of marines, descending deep into the bowels of the base, circling down a labyrinth of staircases, passing through countless security redundancies—like retinal scans and palm interfaces along the way.

"These lower floors provide the most secure areas we can bring you to, Mr. President," Teapard tells him. "It's where I holed up during your...*talk* with the Clammies."

Beltran says nothing—he knows he was wrong to attempt that without the military and should've listened to his general.

Logan pipes up. "I hate to be the bearer of bad news, General, but the future humans punched pie holes into every floor. They made it down to my level with no problems."

"That's true, Dr. Logan, but only because they knew where you worked and made a beeline right for you. They'll have to scour this whole base to find us down here, and hopefully by then, Operation Goliath will have been successful."

"Operation Goliath?" Logan asks.

"It's already underway. We can monitor it in here."

A final steel door opens vertically before them, like an elevator, and reveals a laboratory filled with several dozen marines, standing in line, as Dr. Rosenberg tinkers with their Mindshot helmets. He glances up and sees Dr. Logan.

"Logan, you son of a bitch!" Rosenberg shouts out with a huge grin. He's also wearing a Mindshot helmet. "Leave it to you to figure out how to get us out of this mess!"

Rosenberg hands a marine back his helmet; he immediately puts it on. "There you go, Marine," Rosenberg tells him. "Your thoughts are once again private."

It's now evident that Rosenberg has been the one mass-reversing the helmets.

"Operation Goliath," Teapard says, getting Logan's attention. "We're going to go David on these Goliath sons of bitches."

CHAPTER FIFTEEN

Logan found it somewhat amusing that Teapard was responding to the future human operation with one of her own.

Operation Goliath was already well underway, as Logan settles down next to the president in the makeshift command bunker, several stories below the base. The space isn't that large, about the size of an average office, and is made up of thick, cinder-block walls, with simple furniture, yet is equipped fully with the latest in advanced communication gear. Enough to operate securely, but it isn't exactly the lap of luxury.

"Talk to me, General." Beltran cracks his neck and rotates his head in a circle.

"There isn't a lot of time for details, sir, so I'll stick to the headlines, if you don't mind. Head-to-head, we're no match for the Clammies. We all know that. It's evident they don't need guns or ammo or equipment of any kind. Their minds are so advanced, they've figured out how to use them to fire off what I can only describe as cannonballs of energy. Right from their clammy hands. These energy cannons can blow holes in walls or floors—and surely even soldiers. If that weren't enough, they can disarm us and simply float our weapons away."

"Jesus, sounds like we can't beat them." President Beltran shakes his head. "What's your plan?"

"We need to equalize our enemy," Teapard says. "If they can't hear our thoughts, they can't know we're coming."

"Don't tell me you're hoping to sneak up on them, one by one, and put a sniper bullet in each of their heads?" Beltran asks with a chuckle.

"We considered that actually, but I came up with a better solution."

"Which is?" he asks.

"Weaken them," Teapard replies.

"How the hell are you going to weaken them?" he asks.

Logan snaps his fingers. "By destroying the only piece of technology they still depend on—the sustenance chambers!"

She's nods. "That's correct, Doctor. If we can get to the two sustenance chambers on board their vessel and take the chambers out—"

"They'll be weakened by lack of sustenance." Logan smiles.

Teapard smiles slightly. "Thus, evening the playing field."

"So basically, you want to starve them?" Beltran asks.

"That's exactly what I want to do, Mr. President. If they can't eat, they get weak. If they get weak, they can't fight. If they can't fight, we can kill them, or they die on their own of starvation. Either way, we win."

"What if they use their mind powers before that to simply take the helmets off our heads and destroy them?" Beltran asks.

"Sure. They can do that, *but they'd have to find us first*. With our helmets all reversed, they can't hear where we are. So that task has been made slightly more difficult for them, giving us all the opportunity we need at beating these bastards."

Beltran brightens. "Sounds simple then. Let's do it."

Teapard frowns. "I wish it *were* that simple," she says.

Beltran laughs, clearly optimistic all of the sudden. "You mean launching a counteroffensive against an evolved group of human beings won't be simple? Shocking."

"Yes, sir. We still need to gain access to their vessel. Which is why, as you pointed out, I'm trying to get as many Clammies away from the ship as possible. If my men are spotted, by even one Clammy, we don't stand a chance. They need to remain covert for this to work."

"Understood." Beltran nods. "How far along is this operation?"

Teapard smiles. "A strike team, all equipped with reversed helmets, is already on sight. I just got word moments ago that the Clammies have scrambled away from the vessel, probably off to check on the two dead ones upstairs. We got their attention now. Recon did a head count of the sixteen remaining Clammies—they left only one sentry behind to guard the ship."

"Just one? They're underestimating us, aren't they?" Beltran muses. "They don't think we have the balls to attack their ship."

"That's what I was counting on, sir." Teapard nods.

Beltran studies Teapard for a few moments, smiling and nodding. "You've been planning for this since they arrived, haven't you?" he asks.

"I'd like to say I have, sir," Teapard admits. "But since I knew they could read my mind, I decided not to even *think* about a counteroffensive. Had I done so, they would've surely picked up on it. So instead, I took a position of curiosity. I wanted to learn all about them, as much as I could absorb—the sustenance chambers in particular. The moment I saw those chambers, I knew they'd be key. It was all I could do not to make war plans right there and then. Which for somebody like me is torturous."

Everyone chuckles.

"Mr. President, the moment you arrived, I moved on this plan. I had Dr. Rosenberg deliberately repeat Dr. Logan's fortuitous error. Voila, private thoughts for all again. Then the moment you decided to speak to the Clammies alone, I gave the plan the go-ahead. Came together very fast after that."

Beltran isn't sure if General Teapard is knocking his choice to speak to the future humans alone. He tries to read her face for a hint of condescension but finds nothing to give away her true feelings.

"Well, excellent as always, General." Beltran says.

Peter left three comrades to look after the Voyagers in Hangar One and a sentry to look over the vessel outside. He and the remaining eleven make their way down to the brig. Forming a squadron. Tactical formation. Ready for a battle. They hadn't anticipated having to take this precaution. They thought the twenty-first-century humans posed no credible strategic threat.

Up until this very moment, the only emotion Peter had felt in earnest was *irritation*—irritation that the twenty-first-century humans were so primitive, yet also frustratingly headstrong in their beliefs. This isn't what he is used too. In the fifty-first century, there is no opposing viewpoint, no conflict, no war, not even a minor disagreement—ever, about anything. All humans in the fifty-first century are like-minded, and as a result, they are completely peaceful and docile. Yet, here in the twenty-first century, not only is there strife and dissension and animus, but it seems like humans of this era thrive on it. Humans today feel debate results in better conclusions. Fifty-first-century humans know better than that. It's not the better result that's reached, but rather the compromised one. Peter knows true righteous living is never actually achieved when one has to compromise values with someone who is so obviously wrong in theirs. How long can this kind of contentious life go on for humans? Not too much longer, Peter bears in mind with relief. Thankfully, a few hundred years from now, a true era of peace will be ushered in.

Which is why Peter takes great pride in his family legacy, knowing that a Logan has been there at the center of every recent pivotal and historical moment leading to peace.

As they move down the winding hallways, Peter begins to consider his family history, replete with triumphant Logans. Beginning with Norman Logan inventing the Mindshot, followed by his son Henry, who made the Mindshot available to the world. Then, generations later, in the twenty-second century, the Nobel Peace Prize will be awarded to *Dr. Anthony Logan*, (Norman Logan's six-times great-grandson) who stepped out of the shadows of his prominent and wealthy family, after having worked and written many dissertations in the area of global governance. His globalist papers were considered the Magna Carta of a concerted movement to equalize the entire world for every single human on Earth. Anthony Logan maintained that humans at their core, no matter where they're from, all want for the same thing and have more in common than perhaps we care to admit.

Subsequently, Anthony used the Logan family status, pedigree, and wealth to lead a worldwide crusade, mandating global laws be passed determining that no one human ever be greater than another. Which meant, in accordance with the scripture of Anthony Logan, no *one nation* could ever be greater than another.

So powerful and far-reaching did Anthony Logan's global campaign for equality become, that wars would be fought to erase the concept of national sovereignty. The rationale behind these wars was that without borders, the desire to ever again wage war over a piece of land or jurisdiction would end. By design, the stated goal of these final wars was to intentionally eliminate and vanquish borders.

Just a few decades later, what was called the Great Final War was fought between a consortium of Globalists and a coalition of individual nations, led by the United States. Brutal was the war, yet eventually the vast numbers of Globalists overwhelmed the coalition into ultimately surrendering.

At long last, Anthony Logan's vision of abolishing national borders was achieved. Countries were disestablished, and the varied potpourri of different nations, with their own identity and specific laws and traditions and values, *vanish entirely*, thus forever eliminating separate allegiances to heterogeneous republics, states, and commonwealths.

All of them are wiped out.

In their place arose the peaceful global allegiance of all humans, seeing one another as equal.

However, now that all humans were without country, Anthony Logan convinced the masses that collectively they still *needed to be* governed and determined they should be subjugated by one supreme, but *benign*, global government. And soon, the populace agreed.

Thus, *the Global World Order* was born—the GWO for short.

All laws passed by the GWO applied to every single person on Earth. Equally. Unconditionally. Nobody was above anybody else. We had all become equal.

A supreme panel of fifteen elected persons, called the Supreme Council of the GWO, was put together. Its members hailed from every corner of the Earth, and it was made up of people of different skin colors, who sat side by side in an ornate and echoing hall that dwarfed the United Nations, where they looked out at the general assembly and enacted equality laws.

And ruled.

Because Dr. Anthony Logan led the global revolution that brought about the very formation of the GWO, he became one of the *refounding fathers*, one of the first to sit at the GWO Supreme Council. These fifteen influential men and women that made up the governance of the GWO were charged with making the wise and complex decisions for the planet entire. The GWO's mandate was to be wise, compassionate, and most of all, fair. In turn, every citizen went along with their decisions willingly.

The GWO's authority over terra firma was absolute.

The formation of the GWO is inevitable, Peter acknowledges, considering the path these twenty-first-century humans are on. After all, how can anyone live productively let alone peacefully amidst so much discord and divisiveness? This is why Peter is glad he is from the fifty-first century, where as a sitting member of the current Global World Order, he proudly relishes making decisions that the people need and want him and the GWO to make *for them*.

But just as the refounding fathers, led by Anthony Logan, had to take up arms and eliminate rebellion in their time, Peter has to persevere today with this twenty-first century rebellion and prevail. They've come too far to let the unenlightened rise again. This mission is *his* defining historical moment–the mantle has been passed to Peter, and he has no intention of failing. Peter sees this mission and the hardships it's suffered as his historic challenge to overcome. Books will soon be written about this day, glorifying his achievements. One day, the future Logans, starting with the one in Betty's womb, will look back on Peter's achievements with pride.

Even though he's been taught that personal aspirations should never be coveted over the needs of the collective, Peter can't help but imagine his own glorious individual triumph, and be pleased.

Then he shakes away these blasphemous thoughts, angry for even having them and reminds himself why they're here, why they've traveled back in time, what is at stake, and this grounds him once again. He wishes there had been a way they could have healed their inability to procreate and not needed to undertake this mission, but even with all their advances, evolution proved to be insurmountable. They certainly explored every scientific avenue, but all roads eventually, and ultimately, pointed to traveling back in time to this era, the era just before the Mindshot went public, just before the evolution began.

But now, in the face of mounting challenges, Peter is feeling a whole new emotion. It's an emotion he's only felt three times prior in his life: when they learned humans were now sterile, when the mission to the past was first conceived, and when the saboteurs began impeding the mission.

The saboteurs...

Peter shudders at the thought of them and the countless setbacks they caused. But he doesn't want to think about them right now. He'll deal with them upon returning to his time.

For now, he must focus on and cope with this rarely felt emotion—*concern.*

As they round the corner, Peter doesn't know what to expect, which he doesn't like.

Uncertainty is staggeringly unbecoming, he thinks.

Usually, by now, he'd be hearing the thoughts of anyone within several hundred yards. But he hears nothing. Why is that? Could it be that they have reversed all the Mindshot helmets, giving them the ability to hide their thoughts? Peter's compatriots hear this notion and seem troubled by this possibility. Could it be that Peter was misguided in trusting future data to Norman, one of his own family members? For the sake of efficiency, it was Peter's idea to pass along the binder filled with future notes. Despite protests from the other fourteen GWO members, Peter insisted he could trust Norman Logan.

Could it be Peter was wrong? About his own family?

Now the entire twelve-man squad feels concern. That concern is only exacerbated when they come upon the two fallen future humans, dead, their brain matter sprayed onto the walls and on the wide-open cell door. They begin to scan the immediate area, listening for any thoughts, listening for any clue that would give away where the twenty-first-century humans are hiding.

But they hear nothing.

Even though each of the future humans is having a visceral reaction to seeing their dead comrades sprawled in an indignant bloody cluster, they remain calm. This has now become a full-scale military mission. Still, death—certainly not in this gruesome, violent manner—is not something they're accustomed to seeing. There hasn't been a war in any of their lifetimes. The final war was fought centuries before their births. They knew there was a potentiality that twenty-first century humans would resist complying with Operation Noah's Ark and that war could be necessitated, but nobody in the GWO ever counted on war and death being brought to them by an inferior human race no less. It'd be like Neanderthals defeating Cro-Magnons. Yet, here they are, facing that exact scenario.

Everything has changed.

Peter and the other future humans decide it best to replenish their energy and strength, readying themselves for anything else these twenty-first-century humans can possibly inflict. So they all agree it is prudent to head back to the vessel immediately and nourish up in the sustenance chamber. After doing so, they will load the Voyagers onto the vessel. No more delays. Peter knows they have to leave as soon as possible, or history will not be good to him.

Colonel Canoga can't believe how close he and his strike team are to the vessel. From their vantage point, Canoga and his squad of elite special forces—hidden behind supply crates stacked just outside the main building—are but a scant one hundred yards away from the sentry guarding the front entrance of the vessel.

They'd arrived undetected.

Canoga moves immediately to the next phase: quietly dispatch the sentry. Canoga nods to his sniper, who then inches forward into a standing supported position with his SR25 sniper rifle, silently resting his elbows on a low crate. He turns to the unsuspecting future human sentry, places the palm of his nonfiring hand at arm's length against the crate, and locks it straight, letting his left leg buckle until the sniper places his body weight against his nonfiring hand. He forms a V with his nonfiring hand and then places the fore-end of the weapon into it. The sniper nods to Canoga. The colonel keys his secure radio.

"This is CC-1. We're at Tango Zulu," Colonel Canoga whispers. "Permission to engage."

Teapard's voice comes back. "Granted. Fire at will."

The colonel taps the sniper on the helmet, nodding and signaling the go-ahead.

The sniper then dutifully lowers his firing eye three-and-half inches from the scope and begins taking control of his breathing. In the circular scope, he centers up the sentry, who shows no signs of being aware he's about to die. The sniper takes a slightly deeper breath, exhales, pauses, and then fires.

The future human's head ruptures on impact, reeling him backward with a taut snap. He lands with a thud. Shattered skull and brain matter is peppered across the sand.

Moments later, the ten-man kill team emerges from hiding. Two of them clear the body while the rest of the squad moves onward, weapons blazing, toward the ship's gantry.

CHAPTER SIXTEEN

Betty sits, still strapped into the chair that the future humans left her in, when she hears footsteps coming up the gangway.

At first, she assumes it is the Voyagers, finally being brought back aboard. But instead, materializing from the washed-out daylight pouring into the vessel, she sees American Special Forces troops—many of them—and they're breaching the ship!

Am I imagining this? She blinks, not sure, until she hears one of them speak.

"We have a friendly," Colonel Canoga reports. "It's the reporter."

Down in the bunker, Logan perks up when he hears this. *Betty is alive!* He's relieved and terrified for her.

Get her out, he thinks. *Just get her out!*

As the other Special Forces clear the ship, making sure there aren't any more future humans lingering about,

Canoga makes his way to her, flipping open his Carson knife, and her binds are cut away.

"Are you injured, miss?" Colonel Canoga asks.

"No. I'm fine," she replies, still disoriented. "What's happening?"

"We have to get you out of here right now," Canoga informs her brusquely.

Betty looks past him and sees another handful of soldiers moving in, directly onto the sustenance chambers, weapons raised.

"This way, miss," Canoga tells her as he firmly takes Betty by the arm and tugs her toward the exit.

But Betty continues to watch what is happening over at the sustenance chambers. Two of the commandos remove two sandwich-sized items that were strapped to their front vests. She knows what those are immediately.

"C-4? You're going to blow up the ship?" she asks, always the reporter.

Colonel Canoga keeps dragging her to the exit. "Not exactly," he responds.

Canoga knew Teapard had considered doing just that, blowing up the entire vessel once the guard was taken out. But there would be no time to set the amount of explosives needed to do so and air support would be too far away, hiding deep in the desert on standby; she feared Peter and the remaining future humans would "hear" them coming and prevent an airstrike. The best plan, Teapard determined, was to have commandos, led by Colonel Canoga, destroy the sustenance chambers.

"Just keep moving, miss," he orders her.

Even as they rush to the exit, Betty is still craning her head back at what she now knows is a Special Forces demolition team. They attach several C-4 bricks to each of the two sustenance chambers. As Betty reaches the exit, they punch a few numbers on a small keypad sitting atop the C-4, which activates the timer to detonate the charge.

Sixty seconds. Then boom.

The demo team immediately moves away from the rigged sustenance chambers, bearing quickly toward the exit, where Betty awaits.

She's about to turn and exit, but Colonel Canoga shoves her back inside the ship, shielding her with his outstretched arm. He looks past her to the rest of the team, waving for their attention. When he has it, he places the stock of his carbine against his shoulder, with the muzzle pointing in the direction of the enemy.

"Bogies. Incoming!" Canoga whispers loudly for the others to hear. Betty glances out the exit and sees Peter and all the other future humans outside.

Floating right toward them.

When Peter sees the dead sentry at the foot of the vessel, his worst fears are confirmed. The twenty-first-century humans are on the offensive.

They've regained the element of surprise. Neanderthals versus Cro-Magnons, Peter reminds himself.

The future humans all turn in unison toward their vessel, ready for battle. They can't see or hear the twenty-first-century humans, but they know they're there.

"I repeat, I have Clammies incoming. We're boxed in. We can't get off the ship. We need backup," Colonel Canoga whispers into his com.

The other commandos move up behind Betty, pull her back—gently but firmly, setting her behind them, as much out of harm's way as possible.

"Get down, miss. Now! Stay down," one of them orders her.

Betty immediately drops onto her knees and elbows, keeping her head as low as possible.

"We gotta pick off as many of these Clammies as we can and then make a break for it," Colonel Canoga orders. "We have thirty-five seconds to do it before those C-4 charges go off."

Indeed, the ticking timers on the C-4 explosives count down: *35...34...33...*

Canoga keys his radio, "Sniper detail, headshots only. Remember: wounded, they can still use their minds. We need head shots." Then he orders: "Fire on my target! Attack! Attack!"

The sniper, still concealed behind the crates, takes the first shot.

Just as they were about to enter the ship, Peter heard the report of the weapon. It rang out a whole second after he was blood-sprayed by the ruptured head of the comrade directly to his left. Peter had never seen anyone from his time killed like that—in grisly fashion. They all turn in the direction of the shot but see no one. The sniper has already moved.

That's when the hailstorm of gunfire descends like raindrops of hot nails—but not from the sniper position. To their dismay, the relentless salvo of ordinance originates *from inside their own vessel.*

In no time, two more future humans are mowed down, perforated with hundreds of bloody holes before Peter and the others even have a chance to retaliate. Present-day humans have inflicted heavy damage—three more dead *Homo telethians*—but this also means they've revealed their positions.

So Peter and the other future humans raise both arms, palms facing the ship and strike back.

Inside the ship, the commandos are still midattack when suddenly, they are simultaneously jolted backward harshly, as if sucker-punched by an invisible coldcock they didn't see thrown. Before they hit the ground, they come to an abrupt halt, levitating to a stop only inches from the surface, *and they float there.* Then, the unseen power of the future human mind snatches their weapons away from them.

And just that fast, they've all been disarmed.

Moments later, all ten commandos, as well as Colonel Canoga and Betty are levitated quickly toward the exit and brought outside of the vessel, still alive, but not able to squirm, unable to move. They are suddenly powerless, trapped in a midair mind-vice.

Once they're hovering outside, Canoga, all the commandos, including the elusive sniper, and Betty, are put on display, up high, suspended in midair for the future humans to regard. Peter and the surviving future humans look them over, obvious animosity and even intense hatred in their coal-black eyes.

Before anything else happens, Canoga speaks. He knows what's about to happen. "We've been captured, base," Canoga says into his voice-activated mic. "Ordinance set to go in three, two, one…"

Two huge explosions emanate from inside the vessel. The concussion rattles the ship, making it convulse and shudder from within. Black smoke plumes outward.

"Food supply-E. Kablooey," Canoga reports bravely, never taking his eyes off Peter. "I repeat, Food supply-E. Kablooey."

A new emotion overcomes Peter: *wrath*. Peter glares at the floating commandos, and Canoga accepts his fate.

"It's been an honor serving with all of you," Canoga says, defiance and genuine pride his voice. "Especially with you, General."

Peter instantly lashes out—with his mind—exerting pressure, crushing their helmets—helmets that Canoga and the other commandos *still wear*. The horrid sound of flesh and bone collapsing onto itself beneath the heft of their Kevlar helmets sickens Betty who turns away, just as the heads of the elite troops implode. She weeps now, uncontrollably.

This butchery is overwhelming.

A moment later, Canoga and the rest of dead fire team is released from their levitated perch and dropped limp to the dirt. But Betty is left up there, levitating above the fallen. She won't look down, crying still. She then senses someone right in front of her. A familiar rank smell comes over her. She opens her eyes and gasps. Peter has floated up to her—his ebony eyes bloodshot with rage. She's not sure if he's crying, but it doesn't matter. He looks terrifying.

Your being pregnant is keeping you alive. She can still hear him through her Mindshot. *But do not tempt me again.*

With that, Peter and the others glide into the vessel to survey the damage.

Down in the bunker below, Teapard is hunched over, listening to the radio transmission, where she's been monitoring the offensive. She stares at the monitor that no longer transmits Canoga's voice, distraught by what she's just heard.

Behind her, President Beltran stands, stoic.

Logan stands off to the side, simply trying to stay out of the way.

"The E stood for enemy," Teapard responds, never taking her eyes off the monitor, fighting back tears. No time for that. "The kablooey is self-explanatory."

Beltran grins. "So, they did it? They blew up the sustenance chambers?" he asks.

"Yes, sir," Teapard replies, clearly trying to keep her emotions in check. "Perhaps you didn't catch it, but my men, including Colonel Canoga—a great soldier—paid the ultimate price in doing so. They're all dead, sir."

The president's grin fades.

Nobody in the room wants to say anything now. Logan doesn't know if that includes Betty. He assumes so, and he begins to cry quietly, moving away to the back of the room.

Teapard doesn't want to show her emotions. There will be time to weep for the fallen later. For now, she needs to analyze the operation, play it back in her head, and determine what was done poorly. Men died. How? What did she miss? She acknowledges this combat theater is unprecedented in the history of warfare, but Teapard is unaccustomed to losing so many soldiers in one operation.

After all, her rise to general is a storied one in the annals of US military history.

During the first Gulf War, then Sergeant Teapard refused to accept the rules pertaining to female soldiers, which prevented them from any frontline active-duty. In fact, rumor was she'd been made sergeant faster than most because she'd repeatedly ask to be assigned to infantry and the top brass hoped in giving her rank, she would be persuaded to abandon this notion that she'd ever fight in actual combat. It just wasn't good for morale, they feared, a female soldier out on the front lines of the battlefield.

But the promotions only emboldened Teapard. She took pride in being a professional soldier and didn't want to be treated any differently than any man serving. Finally, early in the first Gulf War, she was assigned a squadron of ten troops to watch over a weapons cache inside a nondescript warehouse in eastern Kuwait. It wasn't forward action as she'd hoped, but she also recognized it was the best she was going to get for now.

As luck would have it (good fortune in Teapard's view), her first night on watch, a platoon of Iraqi Republican Guard attacked the warehouse, looking to take back the cache. With no air support to be had, Teapard and her squad were on their own.

An intense firefight ensued, where Teapard showed considerable poise under duress. She skillfully coordinated a counteroffensive. Going head-to-head with a larger armed enemy was suicide. She tapped into her favorite period in US history—the Revolutionary War—and adapted a technique that worked well for militiamen: sneak attacks. Strike fast. Strike lethally. Move away. Never engage head-on. Pick off the enemy in small numbers. Change positions. Hit them again. Repeat as needed. Which is precisely what she did that night in Kuwait.

It worked so well that within an hour, she and her outnumbered squad had killed half the Iraqi Republican Guard. The other half scattered into the desert night, in retreat. Not one American was killed or injured. By all accounts, it was Sergeant Teapard's steady battlefield leadership that produced this victory.

From there, she was quickly promoted and was already a decorated colonel when she led another brilliant raid years later against the KLA in Kosovo, wiping out their terrorist leadership hidden in the damp forests of Macedonia. Once again, Teapard showed she was a mastermind on the field of battle.

The word *genius* was used often, too often she felt, to describe her uncanny instincts in combat. Soon, she became brigadier general, finally moving up all the way to five-star general, in record time, where she was then given the extraordinary duty of protecting the US Government's most high-level, top-secret base, hidden in the New Mexican desert, which she is now charged with the extraordinary task of defending from superior beings.

And for the first time in her illustrious career, she's facing defeat.

Beltran breaks the silence.

He asks tenderly, "Okay. Now we wait, right? They can't last long without sustenance."

Teapard exhales now and turns. "Yes, sir. Hopefully, that'll further even things out. But we need to move to the next phase of this operation. Now. I get the feeling, after this, the Clammies are gonna be hell-bent on vengeance."

Both sustenance chambers had been destroyed—total losses, the pair of them.

Because the implications were immediate, Peter understands at this moment *why* they blew up the sustenance chambers, and he admires the brilliance of their strategy.

The future humans would be starving within twenty-four hours.

This meant they had to gather the Voyagers up and depart immediately, without further delay. They were now in full crisis mode. A few even suggest cutting their losses and leaving right away, but Peter overrules them all.

History will not show him a failure.

Besides, the duo of explosions has also caused considerable residual damage to the vessel itself. The twin blasts ruptured a sizeable hole in the ship's hull, just beyond the sustenance chambers. Thankfully, the future humans are relieved that, other than the sustenance chambers, they carry no other technology susceptible to destruction, being that everything else on board is powered with their minds.

However, without the necessary sustenance, their minds, as well as their bodies, will soon begin to shut down.

They need to repair the hull immediately, and it will certainly require the exertion of valuable mind strength to do so. Also, the repairs are going to take some time to complete. Even with their powerful minds providing the necessary machinations, the repairs have to happen in real time.

So Peter immediately assigns one future human the task of repairing the hull, while leaving two others with him, on guard. The other nine and Peter are charged with another mission: round up the Voyagers, secure them all on board, find the remaining humans on the base, and kill them.

Kill every single one of them.

Since she'd already been restrapped back into the same chair, Betty overhears the plan.

"No! You don't have to kill anyone else!" she blurts out. "Take the Voyagers. Take me even. But please...no more killing. Just leave, please!"

Peter doesn't respond. After a few agonizing moments of deafening silence, wherein he just stares at her, he moves out the exit with what is now a kill-team of future humans. But before he goes, Peter tosses one last contemptuous look to Betty.

Once they've gone, she helplessly turns her attention to the future human tasked with repairing the vessel—she calls him the Repairman—and watches as he floats up, about six feet in the air, where he holds out his arms while facing the hole in the damaged hull. Instantly, the organic-like material before him—which makes up the ship's super-structure—begins to contort and twist. It's clear that he is patching it up *with his mind*.

But then something odd happens...

The Repairman stops abruptly and drops suddenly, straight down and unabated, only stopping his free fall mere moments before slamming onto the surface. He seems to be collecting himself, summoning strength.

One of the future humans guarding the ship goes over to check on the Repairman.

Are you all right? the guard asks.

I think so, the Repairman responds. *Just got light-headed.*

And that's when they realize Betty is listening to this whole conversation. A moment later, Betty's Mindshot helmet floats off her head and levitates away. She can no longer hear them, but it doesn't matter. She knows what's happening.

They're starting to weaken.

CHAPTER SEVENTEEN

Ever since Logan was rescued from the cell, he'd been relegated to observer—something the workaholic was unaccustomed to being.

However, fearing Betty was dead, Logan felt the slow drip of insanity consuming him. He needed to get his mind off all this. He needed to preoccupy himself with something else—anything else—but all he kept doing was retracing the steps in his life that led to this very moment, trying to make sense of how he ended up here.

How could he not have seen the negative ramifications to the Mindshot? Were the naysayers correct? Did his blind ambition impair reason? After all, Logan recalls, even as a child, he had wanted to be an unqualified success someday. In fact, Logan couldn't ever recall not having lofty aspirations.

He'd always coveted success.

As an only child, he wasn't raised in a terribly successful home in Folsom, California. His parents were working class and modest. His father worked at an eyeglass factory, topping out as a shift manager before he retired, and his mother was a homemaker. His was a loving home, yes, but hardly one replete with examples of great success. Despite that, or perhaps *because of that*, he wanted more.

Because being successful consumed Logan as a child, he was labeled odd. When others his age were busy playing video games or football or sneaking looks at porn stolen from their fathers, he was reading the biographies of successful people. These were the days before the Internet. Back then, he had to go to the library and check out every book about a successful person. He wanted to know how people attained success, when they did so, and what they did to reach it. He was intrigued by how many of them reached success before age thirty and remembers feeling like an underachiever that it took him until thirty-three—his age now. But his age didn't make success any less sweet or less rewarding. He cherished his newfound success more because he'd had to wait for it longer. He'd been waiting for success since his senior year of high school when the idea for the Mindshot was first born.

He was a science geek even back then, and that was fraught with all the usual teen angst that being a geek of any sort brings. The ace up his sleeve was that he was always a remarkably handsome guy. His classmates didn't know what to make of this geek—who relished things like the periodic table of elements and algorithms in quantum science—yet had movie-star good looks.

Logan, however, resented the constant emphasis on his looks. He dismissed his appearance as nothing more than fortuitous genetics. He aspired to be a great scientist for NASA one day, work on rocket ships and the like. Nobody in the real world was going to hire him just because he was easy to look at—Logan knew that. Still, he was able to play his genetic hand when it mattered—like when he asked out Betty Suarez.

Betty was the girl every guy wanted—maybe even some teachers too. She was one of those girls who appeared fully formed by the time she was fourteen. Betty was so staggeringly beautiful, she intimidated every male around her. As a result, she never got asked out by anyone her own age. There were the degenerate older men, mostly college guys and some creepy thirty and forty-year-olds, whom she naturally rejected, but boys in her generation? They never asked her out. She was so pretty, they insisted, that she was out of everyone's league.

Betty was also a member of the high school wrestling team—not the girl's wrestling team, but *the boys' team*, where she lettered. Betty had been so tough, beating any girl she wrestled, that the coaches eventually moved her over to compete against the heaviest boys in school. Betty took them all down too. Her scissor hold was fearsome. If Betty got an opponent between her thighs, it was sure defeat for him.

Naturally, there were some boys—the crass jock-wrestlers who underestimated Betty—who figured they'd manage a cheap thrill, getting to place their head between this gorgeous girl's legs, but when they got on the mat with her, and she swung and twisted her legs around them, slamming them to the mat like tattered rag dolls, and held them there helpless, an inch from snapping their neck, most of them were reduced to tears.

Betty never got a rematch, and because of that, she gave up wrestling. Being a novelty was no fun.

Because of all this, Logan found Betty fascinating. He couldn't understand why teenage minds went to mush around her, rendering them unable to speak to her coherently. Betty's skills in wrestling notwithstanding, she was just another girl and Logan wondered why nobody approached Betty, let alone asked her out. He scoffed at his fellow teens who were intimidated by her and insisted that could never happen to him.

Logan had never bothered asking Betty out initially because he was too busy, particularly obsessing about his future success. He was busy reading books and trying to come up with that one great idea that would propel him into the stratosphere of success he so coveted. But eventually, Logan's seventeen-year-old hormones got the better of him. He finally asked Betty out, and she accepted that date quicker than he thought she would.

The date itself was an unqualified disaster.

As soon as it began, Logan's bravado and charm were gone. Much to his chagrin, he ended up behaving exactly like every other teenager before him. She was beautiful, flawless, a talker, well-read, and oh, she could also kick his ass if she wanted. Suddenly, Logan didn't know how to speak to her. He babbled. He couldn't believe it; his mind had also gone to mush in her presence. For her part, Betty tried to spark conversation, help Logan along, but it was no use. He was just another bumbling idiot, at a loss around her.

All Logan wanted to do was speak to this beautiful girl—after all, he fancied himself quite a brilliant mind, and yet...he could not.

That was when Logan thought to himself, *If she could only read my mind, look into my brain, communicate with me telepathically, then she'd totally swoon at my intellect.*

This was it! His eureka moment. His ticket to success.

What if he could come up with a way that people could speak with just their minds? Shy people, especially really smart shy people, wouldn't ever again worry about clamming up under pressure. Their minds, replete with a high IQ, their most important attribute, would do the talking *for them*.

It was perfect!

Logan spent the rest of the date ignoring Betty and jotting ideas down on a napkin from Nathan's Hotdogs. He was writing fast. Stream of conscience. Adrenaline flowing.

Betty was perplexed and tried to see what he was writing. Logan became very protective, covering the napkin with his hands. When Betty persisted, trying to see what he was writing, Logan got up and moved to another table. He was so busy writing he didn't notice that she left.

Logan stands, stretches, and flits around, trying to clear his restless mind, still looking for something to do.

The president and Teapard are busy mounting a counteroffensive. Dr. Rosenberg is still in the makeshift lab, reversing all the Mindshot helmets.

When Logan offered to help, Rosenberg dismissed him, "I got this. You go take it easy, Logan."

It was obvious to Logan that Rosenberg saw this reversing of the helmet for the marines as his shining moment in history, his contribution to the cause. Far be it from Logan to interfere.

This means everyone is busy—except Logan. This leaves him little to do, so he resorts to what he loves to do—experiment.

Luckily, in order to reverse the Mindshot, Rosenberg had the leather binder filled with all of Logan's future notes brought down to the bunker.

So Logan reads over his future notes, feasting on all the nuggets of new information from the future that he finds enticing, in particular the data on *telekinesis*.

To become a telekinetic, he reads, *it was necessary to tap into the pituitary body and the pineal gland, establishing a connection with the cerebrospinal nervous system.*

The explicit instructions on how to do this are there, in his own handwriting from Logan in the future to Logan in the present. A step-by-step, how-to guide to make himself telekinetic.

Why not try it? he thinks.

His scientific curiosity gets the better of him. Besides, it will also take his mind off Betty and be good for him to go back to experimenting anyway. So, he follows his future notes and overhauls and rewires and rebuilds his own Mindshot helmet considerably. Then he puts the helmet back on.

Which is when it happens. Dr. Logan brings a ceramic coffee mug over to himself—*with his mind.*

Minutes before it occurred, he had been sitting at a beat-up folding table, tired, having just moments prior, poured himself a cup of coffee. But he'd set his mug down on another table over at the far end of the room. Wearing his newly refashioned Mindshot helmet, Logan looked up at his coffee and sighed. He didn't want to get up and get it and wished it would simply just *come to him.*

And then it did. Well, it started too anyway.

By the time Logan had noticed what was happening, the ceramic coffee mug was floating over to him, midway between where Logan left it and where he sat.

At first, Logan can't process what he is seeing.

Is that...is that my...coffee mug? Levitating. Moving toward me?

And then he reacts with a gasp, sitting bolt upright, thereby releasing the mug from suspended animation. It drops and shatters on the linoleum. Hot coffee spills everywhere.

All heads whip around, turning to Logan, as he immediately takes off his helmet in shock, staring at the wiring inside.

Have I just wired this helmet to give me...telekinetic powers?

"You all right over there, Logan?" Rosenberg asks obliviously from across the room, still reversing Mindshot helmets for the troops.

Logan slowly looks from his Mindshot helmet to the shattered ceramic pieces dipped in spilled coffee on the floor and responds without even looking over at Rosenberg.

"I'm fine. Just fine," Logan mutters.

A moment later, once everyone has gone back to their business, Logan turns back to the jagged pieces of mug littering the floor before him. His instinct is to gather them, clean up the mess, but then he pauses.

He has an idea.

Logan surveys the room, makes sure nobody is looking, and then slips the helmet back on. He takes a deep breath, exhales, and locks in on the broken shards. The pieces begin to quiver—slowly at first, then faster, as if the fragments are gathering momentum.

Finally, they rise *and float.*

Logan keeps his focus on the dozen or so pieces of broken mug, dripping with coffee, and looks over to a nearby garbage pail about six feet away. A moment later, the debris glides over to that pail, where Logan releases them. The debris drop down into the trash—exactly where he wanted them to go.

Logan lets out a shriek of joy.

A few people look over for a moment but just as quickly resume their business. Logan is beside himself. This is both astounding and outstanding. He takes off the helmet again and enthusiastically studies the new wiring and arrangement of the electrodes. He glances at his future notes and back to the helmet and then laughs one more time.

He now has another thought, *Can I levitate **people**?*

Logan stands, faces Rosenberg and the other scientists, busy scurrying about the lab. He takes a deep breath, shuts his eyes, and raises his arms outward.

Logan keeps his eyes closed and then imagines *lifting the people.*

He is not sure how long he was doing this, how long he was deep in focused concentration, when he finally hears Rosenberg's voice.

"Umm, Dr. Logan?"

Logan opens his eyes and gasps, unable believe what he sees happening.

Rosenberg and the other scientists are levitating five feet *over* their workstations. They're all oddly calm about this, yet visibly frightened.

"Yeah, um, I think you should tell the general and president that you can do *this* now," Rosenberg says, still trying to remain calm.

Logan nods. *This* changes everything.

CHAPTER EIGHTEEN

After the death of Colonel Canoga and his team, Teapard had wanted to retreat, to lay low and wait out the future humans until they starved and weakened, then launch a new definitive offensive. But Beltran was concerned about the Voyagers still holed up in the dormitory—people he was charged with protecting and saving—so he ordered that each Voyager be saved immediately and brought down here to the relative safety of the lower floors.

Teapard doesn't like the orders, but she follows them dutifully and dispatches a two-man scout team consisting only of a patrol leader and a rifleman, keeping the unit purposely compact and elusive in order to conduct covert reconnaissance missions to determine where the Clammies were at any given time, so she could identify the right moment to move in and rescue the Voyagers. Many men and women willfully volunteered for this very dangerous task—even after the horrific deaths of Canoga's team, which Teapard is profoundly moved by. But she only needs two.

The job is perilous, yet simple: find Clammy positions, report back, *but nothing more*—no engagement. She knows if the recon team is discovered…it will be their sure death.

So Teapard is tense as she monitors the team's progress.

The hallway that the patrol leader and his rifleman are canvassing seems empty and quiet when they enter it. They hadn't seen any sign of the Clammies in a while.

Which is why, when the recon team rounds a corner, they are startled to suddenly come upon Peter and two other future humans—just hovering there, waiting, at the far end of the hallway. The element of surprise for the recon team is gone.

So the following happens fast.

First, the rifleman's helmet implodes as if trapped in a fast-closing vice. His death is quick, yet gruesome.

The future humans never flinched once.

The dead rifleman collapses forward, and the patrol leader expects to be next, braces for it…but instead, his Mindshot helmet lifts off his head and is hurled violently against the wall, where it shatters as if made of brittle balsa wood.

Now the future humans move toward him. Menacingly. *What are they doing?*

The terrified and helmetless patrol leader isn't sure. He wonders what they're up to, until it dawns on him and he finally realizes what they're doing. The patrol leader's eyes bulge.

He reaches for his radio and speaks as fast as he can, "Command, they're reading my mind. They know everythi—"

He's dead before he can finish the sentence.

Peter telekinetically eggshell-crushes the patrol leader's skull, casts the body aside, discarding it, and then turns coldly to his strike team.

Now we know where they are.

In the control room, Teapard waits and listens for the patrol leader to complete his sentence. He never does. Her jaw tightens and her shoulders slump as she attempts to maintain her wits.

"Recon's been compromised," Teapard steadily reports to Beltran, who paces nervously, looking over her shoulder. "We're in the goddamned shit-soup now. We have to abort."

"What? You have a team just outside Hangar One, don't you?" Beltran asks.

"I do, but after what we just heard—"

"How many Clammies are guarding the Voyagers?"

Teapard turns back to the console and barks into the command circuit headset, "Company V, can you confirm? You are at the area of operation, and only report having a twenty on one watcher?"

"Yes, ma'am. Affirmative," a voice quietly reports back in whisper. "I repeat, we have only one watcher on patrol."

"Great! One sentry. Take him out!" Beltran spews. "Save those people!"

Teapard shakes her head and tries not to lose her temper with the commander in chief. "They left one guy minding the store. Doesn't that strike you as odd? Where are the others?"

"Maybe they're busy looking for us," the president tells her. "The situation may not be perfect militarily, General, but rescuing those innocent people right now may be the only chance we have to do so." Beltran pulls rank. "Do it. Now. Save them. That's an order."

Despite it going counter to her every instinct, she keys the command module.

"Company, turn to. Zone and sweep," Teapard orders. "Take out the watcher. Rescue the people."

"Roger that," the stoic squad leader responds from his hiding spot around a corner, just outside the front entrance of the dormitory in Hangar One, where the one hundred thousand Voyagers are corralled.

The squad leader turns to his three-man fire team and holds up two fingers, signaling that target is within two hundred meters of range. He extends his arm in front of his body, hip high, palm down, and moves it horizontally several times.

This is the signal to commence fire.

They raise their weapons, lining up their sights on the lone sentry looking over the unsuspecting Voyagers. A moment later, they open up, pulling triggers, but the bullets that spew from their M-4 carbines, *never hit their target*. In fact, they don't even travel very far.

Instead, the moment they're fired, the airborne slugs come to a sudden and abrupt dead stop, midflight.

And remain there, frozen in midair—like a snap shot.

The kill team ceases fire. That can only mean one thing. It's now that they sense their presence. The squad leader and his team turn and, to their horror, find Peter and three other future humans but scant feet away—floating—glaring down at them.

The squad leader speaks calmly into his radio, "You were right, ma'am. They didn't leave just one. It was an ambush."

That's when the frozen bullets move again—only this time reversing course 180 degrees. Projectiles redirect, and fire right back whence they came. The diverted rounds plow right into the Special Forces team at the speed of a typewriter flurry, wiping out all four instantly.

"Company V, come in. What's your status?" Teapard asks, an urgency in her voice not heard before. There is no response. She fears the worst. Agony. Again—more dead troopers on her watch.

She glares at Beltran, who doesn't know what to say.

"My instincts are never wrong! Sir! Ever!" Teapard snarls. "Because I didn't listen to *my* instincts, four more of *my* men are now dead."

Before Beltran can respond, they all feel the forceful concussive blast coming from above.

The building rattles and shakes down to its foundation. Items on tables spill onto the floor. All heads look upward. Sudden dread consumes them all. A few moments later, it happens again. This earsplitting boom bellows even more thunderously than before, shuddering the edifice more ferociously. Again, it comes from above, but it feels closer.

Teapard looks back at the president, who's eyes are fixed upward. *Now he's scared*, she thinks.

Then, they all see it on the LED security monitor. A security camera frames five floating future humans, emitting the now-familiar shock wave of energy from their downward-facing palms. Like an archer flinging flaming arrows, they rip open a twelve-foot-wide hole in the floor below them. The building once again quivers brutally, this time accompanied by the sounds of concrete, steel, and infrastructure cracking above them.

Closer, they're getting closer.

On the monitor, the five future humans descend into their newly opened hole, working their way downward.

"They know where we are," Teapard says through gritted teeth, eyes locked on the monitor. "And they're coming right for us."

She whips around to the president.

"We have to evacuate to the fall-back position."

The president doesn't move. He sounds frustrated when he says, "Run? Is that the best plan from my best general?"

"Yes!" Teapard can't believe they're even discussing this.

At that moment, another booming explosion reverberates from above. Dry plaster rains down on everyone. Dust clouds billow.

They're getting closer.

This is when Dr. Logan, breathing hard, comes racing into the room. He skids to a stop, wearing his rewired

Mindshot helmet. He would have come sooner, but Rosenberg demanded an explanation as to how Logan pulled off telekinesis. Once he'd shown Rosenberg the reconfigured helmet, Logan bolted out to tell Teapard and Beltran.

"I need to talk to you—" he shouts, trying to catch his breath, but he isn't heard because Beltran and Teapard are locked in a terrible argument.

"But, the Voyagers!" he calls out. "They'll be taken!"

"They volunteered! They knew there were risks!"

"Mr. President! General!" Logan tries futilely again to get their attention.

The president won't concede. "We can't just abandon them!"

"Jesus, look at that monitor! That's real time! That's happening as we speak!" Teapard is shouting now. "They're coming down here right now! They're blowing holes in the floor with cannonballs that they shoot from their slimy little hands! *They* can do that. *We* can't."

Logan tries again. "Please, I have to talk to you!"

Teapard ignores him. "So, head-to-head with them, Mr. President, it's no frickin' contest. We're dead. The end. We *must* retreat!"

Another fulminating blast sends down a cascade of sparks and dislodges wiring and jagged pieces of ceiling.

Logan ignores it and tries again to get their attention. "Hello!"

"You're my responsibility now, Mr. President. So are you coming or am I dragging you out of here?"

The president and the general suddenly levitate—straight up—and hover. They squirm, but it's no use. An unseen force is making them float six feet off the ground. In horror, they look over, expecting to find a future human standing there. Instead, they see Logan, his arms extended outward, palms up, a sly smile on his face.

Before anyone can react, five future humans arrive, plowing in from above, dropping like five anvils of death.

CHAPTER NINETEEN

To Peter's annoyance, all one hundred thousand Voyagers witnessed what the future humans did to the commando team, and they're aghast.

This means Peter's plan to keep them all calm is on the verge of collapsing. Heightened communal murmuring begins, as the Voyagers talk among themselves, trying to make sense of what they saw—some voicing outrage at having seen American soldiers get gunned down by their own bullets no less. There's no mistaking it. They died at the hands, or the minds in this case, of future humans.

But Peter knows he didn't have another choice. He must maintain order and put down this insurrection, which is why he already dispatched his five best men to the lower floors—he sent them down there to kill the humans in hiding. So right now, all he has to worry about is not further alarming the Voyagers. He needs them to remain calm and submissive so they'll go along peacefully, without a need for him to burn any more precious mind strength. He needs the Voyagers to exit the dormitory willingly, get on the ship, travel through time, and live their lives in the future the way he and the rest of the GWO wishes. The Voyagers mustn't suspect anything is amiss. The challenge that Peter needs to overcome as quickly as possible, however, is how to spin this so the Voyagers believe what they saw isn't what they saw. It doesn't help, though, that Peter and the others have all been physically deteriorating a bit each time they've exerted their minds to conduct a bodily undertaking. So, even though he has already weakened considerably, Peter gathers the strength needed to face the assembly.

Ladies and Gentlemen, please, Peter says into their Mindshot helmets, as he floats up over them, so as to be seen by all. *I regret to inform you that an insurrection is underway. But not to worry, we're doing all we can to stop it and protect all of you.*

Looks are exchanged among the Voyagers. They know something is wrong and are wondering if this account of an insurrection is true. Peter can hear doubts in their thoughts, even if nobody is vocalizing them. He continues his charm offensive, hoping they buy it.

*A rogue element of the United States military has defied explicit orders and is now engaged in a coup d'état, trying to subvert this whole operation. Thankfully, we've received the go-ahead directly from the American president himself, to put down this rebellion ourselves, using our **full might**, which unfortunately, most of you just witnessed us carry out.*

Peter can hear the thoughts of some accepting this premise. He's frustrated, though, that there are many still, too many, whose doubt has only amplified.

One of them speaks up. Peter recognizes him immediately as Josh from Cleveland—the first Voyager selected.

"How do we know that's true?" Josh calls out. "Why are you the only one telling us these things? I mean, we haven't seen anybody else—other than you people—for the last few hours. Where is everyone else? Why aren't we hearing this from the president himself?"

Well, there's his security to consider in the face of a revolt, Peter offers.

"Okay. Fine. Then let's have that general—what's her name—Teapard. Have her come talk to us," Josh responds. "Or the doctor dude. Either one. Look, a lot of us Voyagers think something shady is going on, something *you're* not telling us, and we need to hear what's what from somebody other than you."

Peter isn't surprised that Josh is starting to persuade most into nodding in agreement. The Voyagers were selected for, among other things, their intellect, and inherent doubt is a characteristic of the highly intelligent. Peter acknowledges to himself that this is one of the reasons every single person in the future is equally intelligent, everyone having the exact same IQ. If each person is exactly as smart as the next, then nobody will ever attempt to outwit another, as it'd be impossible.

But any more of this doubt among the Voyagers and Peter could have a legitimate uprising on his hands. Meanwhile, Josh stands among the throng, turns in every direction, trying to make eye contact with as many people as possible.

"I say we stay put, stay right here, until we can verify this whole story of theirs!" Josh proclaims, pointing his finger at the future humans.

The Voyagers are getting more animated and more dubious now, as several of them speak at once, over one another. Peter looks over to his comrades and nods.

Meanwhile, the emboldened Josh continues his rant.

"So, Mister Future Human Man, we're not going anywhere until you tell us what—"

The energy blast that shoots from Peter's palm encases Josh like sunshine and then *vaporizes him* like a dandelion in the wind. Nothing is left except microscopic human particles, backlit by incoming sunlight, wafting away like tiny shrapnel, sprinkling onto those closest to him.

A collective horrified gasp ensues followed by terrified silence. They all turn back gingerly to Peter and the other future humans. Aside from a smatter of whimpers, hushed stillness befalls.

Anybody else having doubts? Peter asks, coolly.

As the five future human assassins land, after descending violently into the subterranean level, Logan sets the president and general down, and they immediately mad-scramble away, down winding corridors in retreat, as far and as fast as they can. Moments prior to following them out, Logan looks back at those five future humans and notices something peculiar about them.

They seem exhausted, gassed. They seem to be trying to summon breath like a runner does after a sprint. Logan regards this for one final moment and then races off.

He quickly catches up with General Teapard, who is further down the maze-like corridor, urging everyone out of the area—including Kyle—through an open door with a set of stairs that lead further downward, pushing them through if she has to. President Beltran is being shepherded down to safety by other loyal military personnel, down to whatever subterranean bunker sits below.

But not Teapard. With no regard for her own safety, she remains behind, making sure everyone else is evacuated down into the stairwell first. Even if this reprieve was fleeting for them, it was a reprieve nonetheless.

Amid this mayhem, Logan blurts out, "General, I can help!"

Teapard turns to respond, faces Logan, and freezes suddenly, eyes wide, face ashen, *looking past him*.

He senses it too—*they're* behind him.

Logan pivots on his ankle warily, one hundred and eighty degrees, and lands shoulder to shoulder with the general, as they both face the five glowering future humans, who have just landed down the hall from them.

Out of the corner of her mouth, eyes still locked on the future humans, Teapard whispers, "Can you do it to them?"

Logan knows just what she means. He whispers back, also keeping his eyes fixed on the future humans, glad that they can't read his mind right now.

"I've tapped into the part of the brain that makes telekinesis possible. So yes, I retrofitted my Mindshot. Of course, I'm just learning how to use it—"

"Yes or no?" she cuts him off in exasperation. "Can you do it again?"

"Yes. I believe so."

"Good. Congratulations. You're a soldier now," Teapard says. "Here's your first order: *stop them*."

Logan nods as Teapard backs away slowly. He takes a deep breath, exhales nervously, and raises his arms outward, taut like a conductor before his orchestra.

The five future humans are about to rip the helmets off Logan's and Teapard's heads and then kill them both. After which, they would kill the rest of the humans hiding down here.

Normally, five future humans would be more than enough to carry out this morbid task. Five of them together would effortlessly annihilate these two like a tsunami washing over a small beach town. Normally, this would be a routine operation, but the situation right now is not normal. They are weakened and unable to go recharge. Soon, they'll be tapping into their strength reserves, which is why the future humans are pleased with their good fortune. Even though they cannot hear the thoughts of Teapard and Logan, the general and scientist are unarmed, with no reinforcements in sight. So they'll simply kill these two, effectively cutting off the head of the snake.

They don't even flinch when Logan holds out his arms—they think nothing of it. Except that it is a perplexing gesture. But what is more perplexing is to suddenly feel lassoed, as if by an unseen rope. Then they are jerked toward each other, whiplash fast, coiled tightly by an invisible winch that ratchets them into a tight bundle—like a bound bouquet of future human flowers. They can no longer move. Something or *somebody* is not letting them separate. That's when they take renewed interest in Dr. Logan, still with his arms outstretched, concentrating tremendously. *On them.* Trembling as he does so.

Could it be? Him? Dr. Logan? He's doing this? Holding us with his mind. But how?

They can't worry about the how right now. They must break free of Logan's mind vice and retaliate with full might.

The future humans begin straining to free themselves.

Logan can feel himself losing his mind grip—like one would if holding onto a sack of potatoes that dangles over the side of a building. After a while, one's hands would tremble, the bag would glide incrementally along sweaty palms, and finally, the bag would slip free.

He'd trapped the future humans with his mind by simply thinking it, but Logan can't do much more than that. He wants to finish them, crush them, kill them, but all he can do is hold them. But for how long? They are fighting back, pushing, using all their own mind powers to break free. Undoubtedly, they would easily have been able to do so on most occasions, but in their weakened state, they need to muster all they have left—which isn't much. Yet, they are still prying free.

Logan is losing them. He doesn't know what to do. He hadn't considered alternatives beyond this point.

Stinging sweat drips into his eyes from his reddened forehead, where veins protrude.

This is too much...I can't...hold them.

Finally, Teapard sidles up, next to Logan.

"Sorry it took me so long," she says and then raises an MP4 carbine, equipped with twin drum C-MAGS, to her eye level. "Needed to go get the right hardware."

She squeezes the carbine's hair trigger, emptying both magazines, spewing scorching flame upon the five bundled future humans. One hundred piercing, hot metal rounds shred them to bits. When the magazines click empty, all that's left of the five future humans is a chunky red stew in a clump of flesh and marrow.

When Logan finally releases them from their levitated state, they drop into a dead cluster where their heft splats onto the floor, sounding like many pounds of moist ground beef being dropped.

Spent, Logan falls to his knees, gasping for air, palms on the floor, chest heaving. He pulls his hands away when the cascading puddle of future human blood reaches his outstretched fingertips that are flat on the linoleum.

Teapard puts her hand on his shoulder. "So, you can do that too?" she asks.

An exhausted Logan nods, unable to look up. "Yeah, I can do that too," he says tiredly.

"I don't suppose you can whip up a bunch more of those, custom fit with telekinesis?" she asks.

Still panting, Logan looks up at her. Her face is grim as she says, "You've just become the tip of the spear to our counteroffensive."

CHAPTER TWENTY

Peter felt it—five more minds went mute all at once. *How is this happening? How? How much more badly can this mission go? Neanderthals beating Cro-Magnons.*

But they can't think about that right now. They have more pressing worries. Peter had hoped to simply march the Voyagers back to the vessel by their own accord. He'd wanted to preserve his already limited strength to use for the journey home. Except that now he'd made an extreme example of Josh the rabble-rouser. He'd had to do it of course, but the result was he now had ninety-nine thousand nine hundred and ninety-nine unwilling and perhaps even hostile Voyagers.

This meant Peter and his comrades would have to take them by force.

None of the Voyagers dared speak. Not after what they just saw happen to Josh. The damage was done. Unwilling and uncooperative Voyagers was a possible scenario the GWO had considered when Operation Noah's Ark was planned. Bringing them back forcibly was, of course, considered a last resort. Unfortunately, they had arrived at that final option now.

Peter nods to the other future humans begrudgingly.

Time is of the essence, he tells them. *Use only what energy you need. Nothing more. This is far from over.*

The others nod, then move off outside quickly, one by one taking a staggered position, spacing themselves out every few hundred yards, leading all the way back to the vessel outside.

They are getting set for the mind relay system.

Then, Peter looks up at the ceiling, over the dormitory, holds up both hands, palm sides facing upward, and unleashes two cobalt-blue energy blasts from them, into the ceiling. Puncturing a gargantuan, gaping hole in their wake. There's practically no roof left.

There are screams of panic, as blasted-out roof residue rains down.

Peter turns back to the Voyagers and looks them over coolly. They begin to weep and tremble. Peter watches them stoically, waiting for the others outside to get set in position, ready to receive the voyagers. Once they're ready, all the Voyagers levitate in unison. They all shriek and squirm in horror.

Peter begins to move the terrified Voyagers-turned-prisoners, in bundles of one hundred, up and out of the building through the lacerated rooftop.

This is frightening, and the screaming only worsens as they rainbow out through the roof, toward the next future human stationed a few hundred yards away just outside the main building, ready to receive the relay.

By the time Logan, Teapard, and a patrol of fifteen fully armed Special Forces arrive in the hallway just outside the dormitory in silence, half of the Voyagers have already been levitated out through the gaping hole in the roof of the building. They'd heard the blast moments before, as they approached, but weren't sure what had happened until just now. They see only one future human, arms outstretched, levitating them out. He's still wearing the ornate sash, so they know that's Peter.

"They're being sent to the ship," Teapard concludes in a whisper. "We can't let that happen."

Logan turns to Teapard and nods. "I can save those people!" he whispers urgently. "I can stop him!"

Teapard shakes her head and clutches his arm. "No. Let's think about this for a second. We take out that Clammy, he drops those people, and then what? It'd turn into a rain storm of falling dead Voyagers," she tells him softly. "You need to bring *the people* down first," Teapard orders, again quietly.

"What about *him*?" Logan asks, pointing at Peter.

"If I were a betting woman, based on how weak the five dead Clammies downstairs seemed before we wasted them, I'd wager that Clammy is dog-tired too," Teapard declares.

"Without nourishment from the sustenance chamber, yes," Logan concurs. "There probably isn't a lot left in his tank at this point."

"That's what I'm counting on," Teapard says. "You need to get those people safely on the ground."

Logan watches Peter send more petrified Voyagers out—most sobbing, some trying to wriggle free, others going limp in defeat.

Logan's breathing quickens. His mouth dries up. He never, in his wildest dreams, ever imagined that this is what he'd be doing with his invention. *This.*

Teapard must sense Logan's trepidation, because she suddenly takes his shoulders with both hands, whips him around, and looks him square in the eyes. "Don't do that. Don't think about the consequences. That's all mind mush," she tells him. "Think about execution—about how you're going to get them down. That's it."

Logan stares blankly, not at her, but through her for a moment. He then perks up as if downing a triple shot of espresso.

"I know how to do this! How to get them down," he whispers, almost too loudly.

Teapard immediately cups his mouth and yanks Logan back out of sight.

Peter looks over his shoulder. From his vantage point, the hallway in the distance is empty. Yet he's sure he heard something just now, but sees nothing from whence the sound came. He continues gliding the last third of the Voyagers out through the huge hole in the ceiling, using all his mind energy to do so.

He hopes the noise was nothing. He fears it wasn't.

Back around the corner, just out of sight, Logan has just finished revealing his idea to Teapard.

She's dubious. "You sure that'll work?"

"Yes, but only if we get there first," Logan tells her urgently. "And only if you can kill one more Clammy."

Teapard scoffs. "Can we kill one more Clammy? Do humans evolve into freaky-looking bastards that can move shit with their minds and read our thoughts?"

With that, the entire team moves off. After all, they have a new target zone.

The team moves like prowling leopards in the African savannah and reaches the same set of crates that Canoga and his ill-fated kill team had operated from. His body— along with the bodies of the rest of the team—is baking in the desert sun, uncared for. This sickens Teapard and the group but strengthens their resolve.

A future human emerges from the vessel. This is one of the two guards from inside. He stops and looks upward, seemingly waiting for something. A simple craning of the head reveals just what he's waiting for.

Off in the distance, the last of the Voyagers have arched out of Hangar One and are gliding toward their position.

Logan whispers, "It's a relay system. Peter moves the Voyagers out of the hangar, right? After that, guy number two takes them, then passes them to guy number three, who passes them to guy number four, until they end up here, with this guy. Number five."

Logan points to the lone future human outside the spacecraft.

"Clearly, this is the guy that's going to move them into the vessel once they're relayed here. I bet guy number six is inside the vessel and he will place them all in their seats."

"It works like a cell tower then?" Teapard asks. "When you drive away from the range of one tower, your call gets relayed to next one?"

"Exactly, and if you want to prevent even one Voyager from being taken aboard that ship, we need to replace tower number five..." Logan motions to the lone future human. "...with me."

Teapard nods. She whips around to the fire-team behind her, who dutifully await orders. She places her right arm diagonally across her chest.

The lone future human, the one Logan has christened Number Five, floats in place just outside the vessel and sees the extremely large group of present-day humans, airborne, already relayed to the second man, on the way to the third, then the fourth. He can't see any of his comrades below them, they're obscured behind buildings, but he knows they're there, each taking the relay at their turn. So he exhales a lungful, ready for when his moment comes.

That's the last thought he has. He never heard the silenced round that split his head open.

The kill-team moves in fast.

After the bloody future human's skull was littered all over the desert sand, the Special Forces team was quick to move out and secure the body, dragging it from sight, and then ducking back into hiding. Logan was impressed at how fast and efficiently they operated.

Teapard then nods to him. "You're up," she tells him. "But stay out of sight, in case a Clammy sees you."

Logan nods. He peeks out and sees the Voyagers are about to be relayed to him.

What if I can't hold them? What if that many people is too much for me? After all, a short while ago, I couldn't even move a coffee mug with my mind. Now, all the sudden, I'm expected to grab hold of those poor people and set them down on the ground. With my mind.

Whether he can or can't, he'll know soon enough. The fourth future human, whom Logan can't see, has now taken the relay and begins sending the group over to him.

Now that the Voyagers are gone and outside of Hangar One, surely being relayed to the ship, Peter decides to investigate the earlier noise but finds nothing. Then, he wonders about the five-man kill team he sent down below and why he can't hear them anymore. He shudders, knowing they must be—*boom*—Peter suddenly perks up again. One more mind has gone silent.

This can't be. It just can't be.

Peter is already greatly exhausted after having sent off the Voyagers. He desperately needs five minutes in a sustenance chamber—*now*. He's running on fumes. But Peter can't think about how tired he is. He must push on. He must head back to the ship. He must leave immediately.

It's Logan's turn. When he sees so many people above him, airborne, floating toward him, he's terrified; he's suddenly consumed with anxiety and doubt, bordering on panic. Those people are all depending on him to get them safely onto the ground. His breathing quickens.

Can I do this? There's so many of them...

He focuses on how he's always gotten over huge obstacles—one small step at a time. Logan ignores the enormity of the task and concentrates on bringing down small groups. He closes his eyes and concentrates. The first group of Voyagers, the one in front of the incoming pack, begins to descend slowly. Logan brings them to Earth. Within moments, they gently touch down onto the soles of their feet.

The moment they do so, a group of soldiers emerges from hiding and redirects the frightened Voyagers around and behind the future human vessel, trying to keep them out of sight.

The team leader whispers to them as they go, "Run. Right now. That way. Go! Run right out off the base and keep going. Go! Now!"

It becomes a mass exodus. These instructions and this process get repeated with each set of Voyagers as they touch down onto the ground and are all redirected off the base.

Logan continues on, with his eyes still shut, deep in concentration, sweat dripping down his visibly veined forehead.

He just keeps lowering the Voyagers to safety.

Betty knew something was amiss. The future human repairing the hull of the ship had finished his work. Gone was the gaping hole created by the twin blasts earlier courtesy of the United States Special Forces, which meant the ship was ready to travel. The sustenance chambers nearby, however, were still in pieces. Those they couldn't repair—not here in this century. They'd need to get back to the fifty-first to repair them with spare parts only available in their time.

The Repairman, having expended so much energy patching up the ship, was not looking good. His chest was heaving and the color had drained further from his already colorless body. All of the Repairman's movements were labored, as he looked over his work.

But that's not what intrigues Betty. Her interest is instead primed on the other future human, one of the two left behind by Peter to guard the ship, as he floats over to the Repairman to confer about something. Since she is no longer wearing her Mindshot helmet, Betty can't hear what they are saying. The second future human guard left the vessel earlier and had not yet returned. Betty suspects *that's* what these two are discussing, as they seem to constantly gesture to the entrance.

Finally, the Repairman shakes his head—clearly objecting to something the guard wants to do. So, the guard heads for the entrance and stops just shy of the entryway. He seems to be listening for something—*or someone*. Betty realizes he's probing with his mind, trying to hear thoughts outside. Then it occurs to her: what if the other guard, the one who left earlier and hadn't returned, what if he had been killed?

Why would that be? she wonders.

Betty is certain this guard is wondering the same thing. She then watches as he leans out of the entrance tentatively to get a better look outside.

The guard hoped to see his compatriot, latching onto the final relay of levitated Voyagers. He'd hoped to see the Voyagers now working their way to him so he can then bring them into the vessel, as planned. He'd hoped to strap them in and once and for all leave this forsaken place.

Instead, for reasons he cannot fathom, he sees a twenty-first-century human, Dr. Logan of all people, standing before the incoming Voyagers, and, most shocking of all, it seems Dr. Logan is setting them down on the ground *and freeing them.* The Voyagers are scattering off, under the direction of armed soldiers, away from the vessel. They are escaping off the base and out into the surrounding desert out to the area where the future humans know the rest of the twenty-first-century military personnel had retreated to and are lying low, several miles away.

The mission is falling apart.

How is it possible that a present-day human has accessed telekinetic ability? The guard wonders where his other compatriots are. No time for that, he has to act alone. He can't just stand around and see the mission ruined. The guard concludes that if he could salvage a handful of these Voyagers, take even a few of them back, it would at the least be a minor victory for the mission. And perhaps he would receive worldwide adulation upon his return, which as a member of a totally egalitarian society, he isn't supposed to covet or even desire, but for reasons he cannot understand, he *does* covet this. He wants adulation for some reason, for just himself, despite knowing he shouldn't. Regardless or perhaps because of this, he decides he will go out there and kill Dr. Logan and his telekinetic ability and reclaim what he can of their prize.

Logan has his eyes shut when he hears the gunfire.

He tries to ignore it but can't because the Voyagers are now screaming in panic. His eyes shoot open and he turns in the direction of the vessel. There he sees Special Forces gunning down a future human that had just emerged from the ship.

It is classic ambush technique. The future human never had a chance and never even knew the well-trained Special Forces were there, *waiting*, just outside the ship's entrance, ready to mow down anybody coming out of the vessel. The remaining Voyagers, still being lowered to the ground by Logan, had screamed at the sight of a future human but seem relieved now that he has been killed. There are only a few hundred more left in the air ready to be brought down.

Logan shuts his eyes again and gets back to it.

Peter hears the gunfire. It came from the direction of the vessel. Worse yet, a moment after the gunfire, *one more* of his comrades went silent.

As they rush off to battle, they do so knowing they've greatly underestimated the humans of this era. They will no longer make that mistake.

CHAPTER TWENTY-ONE

Finally, the last of the Voyagers are set on the ground and run free. Logan opens his eyes and exhales, as if he's been holding his breath this entire time. He watches as the troops guide the final Voyagers off the base, rushing them madly into the safety of the desert. He is about to smile—Logan is about to feel good about what he'd just accomplished.

But then, he sees Betty *floating* out of the vessel.

Moments earlier, while still strapped to the chair, Betty caught glimpses of the carnage outside the craft. Snapshots. The remaining guard had been shot down the moment he exited the ship. A star-field of blood sprayed past the entrance. The Repairman instantly turned his attention to her and unbuckled her straps telekinetically. She screamed as he levitated her, so he slammed her against a chair to shut her up. With no regard for potential whiplash, he thrust Betty toward the entrance of the vessel, mercilessly fast, bringing her to an abrupt halt at the threshold, holding her floating there.

This is the first time, since they were separated that Betty and Logan see each other. He's about a hundred yards away, but might as well be a mile away.

Logan goes ashen at the sight of Betty floating helplessly there at the entrance. All around her, there are commandos taking positions, weapons on the ready, all looking for a kill-shot on the future human hiding behind Betty, still holding her in his mind-grasp. For her part, despite being fearful, Betty tries to smile, seemingly to put Logan at ease, but she can't. Impossible. Tears spring into her eyes instead.

Logan immediately knows why the future human is holding her there, vulnerably, at the entrance to the ship.

She's just become a human shield.

Peter reunites with his other three comrades—four future humans total, not counting the Repairman still on the vessel, which would make it five. But that's it. When fully nourished, five healthy future humans could easily put down an entire twenty-first-century army with absolute ease.

But now, in their weakened state, the battlefield has been evened.

The setting sun is just making contact with the horizon, as the Voyagers foot-race west. They scramble to safety along the road that leads away from the base. They were told to keep running no matter what they saw and no matter what they heard—but suddenly, they have to stop. They have to stop when they look up at the brilliant fireball of the sun and see the silhouettes emerging before it. Silhouettes that ripple from heat waves that arise from the scorching desert sands.

They aren't sure what these silhouettes are at first. Then, they hear a familiar sound.

Chopchopchopchopchopchop.

Is that? They listen. *It is!* Helicopter blades, spinning.

They squint into the sun, focus, and see materializing into view, the full might of the American military. Jets and helicopters, coming right at them. These magnificent machines soar over their heads. Whip past. The white noise of the screaming aircraft is deafening yet exhilarating. And then racing by on the ground, hell-bent, all around them, are rumbling tanks and Humvees, backlit by a crown of orange and purple haze—all barreling back into the base.

The Voyagers cheer and then continue to run toward dusk.

Teapard had just called in the final attack. The Clammies have been adequately weakened, she hopes.

Victory would be now. Or it would be never.

Rage overtakes fear.

Emboldened by his newfound use of telekinetics, Logan marches toward the vessel, fully intent on freeing Betty from the future human's mind-vice.

Even if it means killing the son of a bitch, he thinks to himself. He's mere moments from lashing out and lowering Betty to him when...

Peter and the four other future humans descend like an avalanche of stones, from seemingly nowhere, blocking Logan's path, landing with a resounding jolt, the ground shuddering on impact. The five future humans take up offensive positions around the vessel. This is their Alamo. This is Custer's last stand for them. Nothing more to lose, and so they unload fire, lay waste. Peter and the three other future humans are ferocious, single-minded in their intent to kill.

And a massacre ensues.

Commandos, officers, and soldiers alike are tragically slammed with repeated orbs of energy, horrifically disintegrating them into mere microscopic particles.

Everyone not being slaughtered by cleavers of raw, intense light scrambles for cover.

Pandemonium abounds. Return gunfire does too, but the future humans are ready for that as well. Energy spheres staccato one after the other from their palms, dizzyingly fast, like machine guns of lightning.

Buildings explode, rupture, and collapse. Repeated impacts send stucco, wood, and steel raining everywhere. Dust balls surge. Cover won't be cover for long. It's all being destroyed—everything in sight. It's shock and awe and the Blitz, all rolled together—and then some.

General Teapard is hunched down, taking cover behind a corrugated-metal military warehouse, knowing she won't hold out there much longer, as the entire building is systematically being shredded apart by incoming light-fire around her.

It now dawns on her, to her horror, that present-day humans may be moments from being completely eviscerated.

The instant the future human counterassault begins, Logan is propelled back several feet by one of the many ground-shaking blasts.

His ears still ring, as he shakes off disorientation and staggers up onto his feet. Tries to anyway. His equilibrium is off, and he stumbles back down to his knees. Can't let this stop him. He's needed in this battle, so he faces the attacking future humans, ready to use his Mindshot with telekinesis. He closes his eyes, outstretches his arms, and tries to corral them. Waits. Waits. Nothing happens.

Peter and company continue to annihilate all.

Something must be wrong with the Mindshot.

Logan palms his scalp, feels his head. The Mindshot helmet isn't on there. Logan turns, frantic, surveys, and finds it a few feet away, where it must've fallen when it dislodged moments ago.

Through the haze and blur of battle, he makes eye contact with Peter, who—despite not having a mouth—seems to be smiling somehow. Even though Peter and the remaining future humans are preoccupied, continuing their unflinching relentless onslaught, lashing out with radiant globules of death in all directions, the fallen Mindshot helmet somehow levitates. And it floats right toward Peter. Logan knows if Peter gets that helmet, it's over. Advantage: future humans. Logan and all the rest of them will be killed or captured before another helmet can be wired for telekinesis.

Which is the moment, at long last, that the cavalry arrives.

Apache attack helicopters, F-22 Raptors, and M1A2 tanks discharge their payloads.

Then an AC-130U gunship roars past overhead, blasting the future humans, who are painted by ground forces with laser designators.

This is a virtual light-storm of twenty-first-century retaliation, cascading in on them from all directions with fury—crosshairs squarely on Peter and the other three future humans.

Peter and his cohorts hastily redirect fire onto the incoming ground assault and skyward. No reprieve from the offensive. All erupts into pure bedlam.

Luckily for Logan, this causes another thing to happen.

Attention elsewhere, Peter can't help but release the Mindshot helmet from midair, where it falls straight down to the ground. Logan sees this and wastes no time. His legs and arms pump in a full sprint for it.

Peter whips over and sees Logan racing for his Mindshot. So while keeping one hand pumping orb-rounds at the American counterattack, he uses his other hand to blast a shock wave right at Logan.

Thwoomp!

Peter misses—barely. Sand plumes in Logan's wake, making him tumble and fall, but he gets back up. Relentless, he keeps racing toward his fallen helmet. Peter fires and misses again. Pounds sand. Logan sprints right through the sand burst cloud. Even though Peter's distracted by the circling Apache overhead, he now has a clear shot on Logan. This time, he is intent on taking him down—until Teapard trots up and unloads her M4 on him.

She fires fast; her finger never eases off the trigger, yet she only manages to pepper Peter in the arm. He recoils in pain. She curses to herself, clearly having aimed for a head kill and missed.

Shoulda kept up with target practice! she thinks and then re-aims, looking for a new shot.

But by now, Peter has spun to Teapard, and despite being wounded and enraged, he bangs off light spheres at her—blindly, angrily. Seeing this, Teapard ducks to safety behind a building that bears the brunt of impact.

Logan knows what she's done. Teapard has covered him, giving him the precious seconds he needs to recover his Mindshot helmet.

"Get that helmet, Doctor!" she calls out, already moving to a new cover position. "And get back in this fight!"

Logan obliges.

As if diving into a pool of water, Logan goes airborne. He is horizontal, his arms extended outward. He lands, clutches the helmet, and somersaults head over ankles. He slaps the helmet onto his head, just as he rolls to his feet, facing Peter and the future humans, with not a moment to spare.

The American military is starting to take heavy losses. No matter what they heaved at the future humans, their projectiles were repelled and countered by the future human's lethal energy blasts. Choppers blow apart, engulfed in flame. Tanks buckle, splinter, and explode.

All may be lost, that is until Logan stretches his arms outward like da Vinci's Vitruvian Man and a moment later, slaps his palms together quickly.

Swoompf!

Peter and the other three are suddenly corralled together against their will—by an unseen force—and held together, as if abruptly ensnared by a fast-tightening noose. All four are bunched, courtesy of the unseen telekinetic force emitting from Logan's mind.

Better still, the future humans can no longer discharge their cannon spheres of light at the military. They're forced to abort.

Peter looks over, locks with Logan, and knows immediately what's happened—Logan's got them entangled, rendering them vulnerable to retaliatory strikes.

"Bravo, Doctor, Peter spews. *But you **can't** hold us.*

To his horror, Logan can suddenly feel his helmet begin to collapse slowly in onto his head.

Peter and the others stare at Logan, all four focusing their energy to constrict Logan's helmet and implode his head.

The pain Logan feels—the pressure to his head—it's unbearable. Logan pushes back, resisting what they're trying to do. He trembles and looks over his shoulder, expecting somebody, *hoping* somebody will step up and shoot them down. He waits and holds them in his mind grip. He trembles and waits some more.

But nobody comes. And they keep compressing the Mindshot helmet on his head.

*If only you'd seen what it's like to live worry-free, as we do, in the future. With no war **like this**,* Peter says straining still to crush Logan's head. *No strife of any kind. If you could only see the world, as it becomes, perhaps you would understand what we're fighting to preserve. Why this mission was so **important**.*

Logan manages to loosen the imploding helmet, alleviating the pressure some, never once releasing the group of future humans. They're locked in a stalemate for the time being.

"If *you're* what we humans evolve into," Logan manages to say, still straining to hold them, "then I'm sure I speak for all seven billion people on this planet right now when I say, we want no part of this evolutionary path."

In response, Logan's helmet begins to constrict again, more forcibly than before. His head is literally in a vice, skull moments from splintering.

"If you kill me," Logan says, "then our line...in space-time will be severed. And you will surely vanish."

That's true. Without you, I don't exist, Peter says with labored speech. *Except that I no longer need you. An heir to the Logan line has already been conceived. So the bloodline will continue, whether you live or die.*

Logan doesn't understand what Peter means. He loses focus and finally releases the future humans from his mind grip. Inertia sends Logan staggering backward, where he falls. He looks up, just as all four future humans turn their resolute gazes onto him. He expects to die right there, but they don't move.

Why aren't they finishing me? Logan wonders. Then it occurs to him. *They're exhausted.*

Waging this battle has cost the future humans their precious strength reserves, and it's like they're now waiting for backup.

But from who? Logan wonders.

Then the Repairman exits the spacecraft to join the fray—pushing aggressively right past Betty, who still floats in her precarious human-shield position. He raises his hands, about to strike Logan, only Betty's not going to let him.

By pure instinct, Betty reaches out with her legs, just like in her days as a high school wrestler. She scissor wraps the repairman's neck, yanks him back to her, and twists. It's so shocking for the future human, to be grabbed like that so forcefully, one can almost hear his muted and startled cry for help.

Peter and the other three turn to see what's happened, finding Betty twisting the weakened repairman in a head-lock with her legs, contorting her body, using all her brute strength to try to snap his neck, while he struggles futilely to break free.

It's all the distraction that's needed.

Logan thinks fast—he knows corralling them together won't work; they'll just break free again. Then, it occurs to him why they're staying together en masse, in a cluster, in a group—*they're combining their collective strength.* They're fortifying themselves as a team.

Of course! **Together**, *they're stronger.*

Logan opts for a different tactic—divide and conquer. He brings up both arms, forty-five degrees, hands together, palms only an inch apart. With his fingers taut, pointed directly *at* the future humans, he then quickly outstretches his arms away from his body, straight out like Christ on the cross. This sends an unseen shock wave that flows from him to them like a tsunami. It slams into and disperses the future humans in all different directions. Scatters them airborne, and when they land, they crater the desert surface on impact.

Chin to neck, eyes shut, head sunken into his shoulders, and fingers spread apart, Logan next holds each future human where he lands, *away from each other*, making them more vulnerable. Peter tries to rise. Logan holds him down.

You're not getting up. Not this time.

He has faith that backup will come this time.

And then it does.

Under Teapard's orders, air-support and ground assault have doubled back, to deliver one final, definitive strike, honing in on individual targets this time. Each remaining future human gets obliterated. Each one of them is blasted and pulverized and shot and drilled and burned. Everything the military can unload on them, they do. None of them can escape this decisive raging onslaught of blinding annihilation, courtesy of US firepower.

And their death is delivered definitively.

Except, that is, for the Repairman, who is still gagging and twisting in Betty's thigh-grasp. She squeezes further, no mercy; she constricts with all her might. Even when the Repairman releases her from her levitated state, and she falls next to him, she still doesn't let go. It's as if pent-up animalistic rage consumes her. Finally, with an audible crack, she snaps the Repairman's neck and he goes limp.

Gasping, she exhales, "All state. High school wrestling."

With that, the vehement violence has ended.

Teapard orders a cease fire, and her team of commandos clears the five enemy bodies. She wants to assure herself they're all dead.

After checking, the commandos discover that Peter is still alive.

CHAPTER TWENTY-TWO

Not much life is left in Peter. He's mortally wounded but still gasping for final breaths. The beating and barrage of gunfire inflicted onto him are undoubtedly terminal. Even an advanced human race can only take so much. He is weakened, and gurgling blood spills from the countless fissures, gashes, and wounds all over his body. Barely keeping heavy eyelids from closing, Peter looks up at the commando team towering over him—training their weapons down on him.

He's going to die any moment now—that's painfully obvious. But before he dies, there's one last thing he must say. Barley able to move his blood-drenched head, he searches around feebly. Moments later, he finds who he's looking for. At the foot of the vessel, Logan stands embracing Betty tightly. Peter watches them, as they weep in relief, happy to be in each other's arms again.

Peter has never known love like that. So now, at the moment of his death, he's consumed by a whole new emotion—*envy*.

After a few more moments, he says, *Congratulations.*

Logan and Betty part and turn to Peter, who lies supine at the feet of armed commandos.

To you both.

Betty and Logan exchange looks, wipe tears, purse their lips, and walk toward Peter.

Surprised? You shouldn't be. I do still have emotions, Dr. Logan. And you are my family, Peter says groggily.

Logan fights a mixture of emotions—confusion, sadness, anger.

Peter continues, *So truly, I am happy for you both—**and your unborn child.***

Logan turns to Betty and reads it in her tear-soaked eyes. Cacophonies of new emotions devour Logan—joy, anxiety, fear. He doesn't know whether to laugh or cry. He does both.

"I was going to tell you," Betty manages and then hugs Logan again. "But later."

*Bringing life into this world...*Peter says, after Logan and Betty part. *Take it from me; it's a gift.*

The fleeting moment where Logan felt sympathy for the fallen future human vanishes instantly, when he next says, *But you're all still going to die.*

The commandos blaze forward upon hearing this, fully expecting Peter to lash out telekinetically. They're about to finish him, pound rounds into Peter, but Logan holds up his hands, waves them off.

"Wait! Don't shoot," Logan pleads. "He can't kill us even if he tried. Not anymore."

The strike team ticks over to Teapard for orders. She nods, and the team holds their fire, yet keeps their sights squarely on the fallen future human, ready to strike in case he makes any false moves.

"Isn't that right?" Logan asks.

Regrettably for me, you are correct, Peter replies, not having budged. *I don't have much strength remaining, and it would be imprudent to use up what miniscule reserves I have left attempting to kill any more of you.*

Peter's eyes then narrow, seemingly into the shape of a smile.

*But I won't have to. This is just the beginning. I'll leave that to the **second wave.***

Logan blinks. *Second wave?*

Peter then informs them about the Global World Order for the first time. A brief history lesson about the future ensues, with enough details to cause alarm and dismay.

At the end of it, Peter says, *Did you really believe that the GWO would leave the very survival of the future human race to only one vessel? No, we've always had a contingency plan in place—a second wave—in the event of this very **unfortunate** outcome. An armada of time-traveling vessels, equipped with lethal fifty-first-century armaments, is being constructed. It will take time, but time is on **our** side. They will come one day, and they will complete this mission.*

Just then, General Teapard hears something. A few other soldiers hear it too. There is now a low rumbling noise coming from the vessel.

Which is why all I have to do now...is activate the distress signal inside the vessel, Peter says.

The following happens fast.

In one final surge of strength, a bloody Peter levitates straight up into the air, simultaneously releasing a concentric shockwave that ripples outward, like when a stone impacts water. This propels everyone that towered over him—commandos, Teapard, Logan, and Betty, everyone—several feet backward and onto his or her back.

Peter floats away from them, in spastic ebbs, and flows toward the vessel, which is pulsating and churning. Alive. Peter is bloodied, and slow, and weak, but gives it all to his arduous escape. He clearly anticipates reaching the vessel and getting inside before the victims of his shock wave recover and retaliate. It's a desperate and frantic act to be sure.

Logan sits up now and instantly tosses both hands forward, in Peter's direction, fingers curled in *a grip position.*

This causes Peter to freeze in midair, moments from entering the vessel. Holding Peter helplessly in place, Logan calmly marches over to him and gets in his face.

"What happens when you send the distress signal?" he snarls at Peter, angry.

The second wave will mobilize, of course. They will come, and they will kill you all.

Peter strains to get past Logan.

"No. I don't think you're going to hit any distress signal, pal," Logan tells him.

With his newfound telekinetic ability, and without hesitation, Logan snaps Peter's neck, bending it forty-five degrees. Peter drops down to the ground, a dust cloud in his wake. His black eyes, staring up at Logan–which is the last thing they see before fading to gray.

The Special Forces team, now back on their feet, move in, skillfully, confirming with a check of his pulse, what is obvious.

Peter, the last of the future humans, is at last dead.

"Gotta hand it to the son of a bitch," Teapard says after a while, exhaling in relief that he's dead. "He was still trying to win, right up to the end."

Logan looks around. "I think the vessel is running," Logan suddenly realizes.

"Yeah, I heard it turn on a few moments ago. One way to find out for sure." She turns to her men and shouts, "On my six. Let's move!"

She heads up the gangway under the gantry and marches into the belly of the ship.

The vessel's interior is eerily quiet—just the sound of shuffling soldiers, taking up defensive positions throughout the yawning spacecraft. Logan marches straight for the alcove that Peter identified as the cockpit. There, the sounds of the humming ship's engines are most prevalent. Something is on and running.

"My best guess is the distress signal he was coming for is on this panel somewhere. It's all powered up, but clearly he wasn't close enough in his weakened state to activate the signal."

"Good. Then make sure not to hit it," Teapard says. "We wouldn't want more of his Clammy buddies showing up."

Logan approaches Teapard and whispers, "General, don't you think they will? Eventually, when this Global

World Order he was talking about doesn't hear from Peter, don't you think they'll come either way?" Logan asks, gingerly.

"Of course," Teapard admits with a sigh. "It's what I would do. If my mission team didn't get back at a pre-designated time, I'd assume they were dead, and I'd send another one—bigger and badder than the first. It's only a matter of time."

CHAPTER TWENTY-THREE

Like miners surfacing from the deep darkness of an underground shaft, President Beltran, Kyle, and all the other nonmilitary personnel who were ushered into hiding during the final future human offensive emerge. They adjust their eyes to daylight, then lay them for the first time on the carnage that is the battlefield.

Decimation. All around.

No place to avert one's eyes and give them respite from the carnage. Both present-day humans and future humans.

An aerial view from a hovering Apache reveals orange/white sand bathed blood red. Buildings and a bevy of vehicles, dilapidated and smoldering. This is why there are tears of joy and relief, but no euphoric celebratory outbursts. This is all much too sobering.

Word has quickly spread that although this event has ended in the defeat of the future humans, a second wave is preparing to come. And nobody knows when.

Under orders of General Teapard, all the Mindshot helmets are removed and placed in what's become a rather sizeable pile of head gear near the vessel, which still rumbles, idling in place, waiting to take off.

Logan and Betty take this momentary reprieve to cherish the beginning of the life they created a few hours prior, even as people all around them process destruction and death. Despite both wishing they'd learned about Betty's pregnancy in a less volatile setting, they're elated about it nonetheless. For them, this moment is a mixed potpourri of emotions. A few days ago, each thought they'd never see the other again; now, they're nine months away from becoming parents.

"How're you feeling?" Logan asks, ignoring the soldiers racing by to secure the base.

"Fine. Totally. I mean, normally right now, I wouldn't even know I was, you know, pregnant." Betty shrugs.

Logan speaks softly, placing his forehead to hers. "I can't tell you how happy I am. It's strange...had it not been for all this..." He gestures to the spacecraft. "...we wouldn't be standing here about to become a family."

"I know. It is strange. This is probably the best thing to come out of you inventing your damn Mindshot." She laughs softly.

Logan nods, places his head against her forehead again, and smiles. "Absolutely."

Their gentle moment is interrupted when President Beltran and General Teapard step up to the couple.

"Sorry to interrupt, folks," President Beltran says, "but there's a lot to discuss."

Logan takes a deep breath and exhales a moment later. He manages a smile over to Betty, telling her in that fleeting moment that he wishes they both had regular nine-to-five jobs and that they lived in some small town somewhere, far away from all this insanity.

But now that nobody is wearing a Mindshot helmet, she has to interpret this the old-fashioned way, with just looks.

It seems she does. Betty smiles back, nodding. She understands he's not hers entirely yet and that their life together will have to wait just a little longer.

Logan turns to the president. "What can I do for you, Mr. President?" Logan asks, placing his arm around Betty, squeezing her shoulder tightly.

"Thank you, Doctor. We have a question. This may be too much to ask, especially considering all you've done already..." Logan doesn't know if he likes the sound of this, but listens on. "The general has debriefed me, and as much as I hate to say it, this isn't over. Thankfully, their distress signal wasn't sent. They have no reason to believe Noah's Ark isn't progressing as planned, but soon, they'll suspect it's not. A second wave will come, and we can't sit around waiting for that to happen. We have to take the battle to them, preemptively, before they bring it back to us."

Logan laughs. "I'm sorry, but the only way you're going to do that is if you got inside that vessel and traveled forward in time to the fifty-first century!"

He chortles again. But Beltran and Teapard aren't laughing.

Logan shifts. "Holy shit. That *is* what you're planning."

Teapard says, "I intend to use that vessel as a Trojan horse. Load it up with all we got militarily, sneak up on them three thousand years in the future, and unleash."

Logan and Betty weigh what that means—and can't fathom it.

"Which means, we need somebody to teach us to fly that vessel," General Teapard adds. "And since all the Clammies are dead, that leaves us with you to figure it out."

They all head inside the still humming spacecraft.

Logan, Beltran, Teapard, Betty, and a slew of support staff and security detail stand before the alcove that is the cockpit. Near them, the destroyed sustenance chambers still lie in ruin.

Teapard nods with a smile. Her plan worked.

Logan notices this and nods back. "Let's bear in mind, other than those sustenance chambers, their diagnostics wands, and the distress signal, this whole vehicle is technology free. It's powered only with the mind."

Logan passes his hands over the panel of protruding veins, deferentially. Clearly, this is the brain-thrust of the whole ship. "That said, within this one section of the craft, they've designed some sort of propulsion system, a concept beyond anything we can fathom right now."

"Except that we don't need to know *why* it works," General Teapard interjects, "just *how* it works."

"Best I can tell, this panel right here is somehow *attuned to telekinetic thought*. They've come up with a way to send thoughts into this nerve-center interface—if you will—which receives them, processes them somehow, and those thoughts in turn manifest and become this craft's necessary fuel slash electromotive force...and I suppose space-time guidance as well."

Betty goes full journalist. "Which means, what was once done filling a tank with gas and by punching coordinates into a computer and determining complex flight patterns with fancy charts and GPS is now done by just... *thinking it*?"

"Yeah." Logan smiles. "Pretty much."

"Well, son," Beltran tells Logan, placing his arm on his shoulder in fatherly fashion. "Since you're pretty handy with that Mindshot invention of yours, think you can give it a try? See if you can, you know, pilot this ship with your mind?"

Logan puts on his Mindshot helmet, still rigged to give him telekinetic power. He faces the control panel and cracks his neck.

"We were fortunate that Peter seems to have activated the craft before being killed," Logan says, mostly to himself, getting his thoughts in order. "Hopefully that means that all I need to do is make it go."

"And back?" Betty says.

All heads turn to her, and she tries to cover, feign professionalism.

"You'll be able to *get back*, of course?"

Logan turns to her and nods, worry in his eyes suddenly. "And back, yes. Of course," Logan says and then turns back to the vein-like control panel. "If I can get there, hypothetically, I should be able to reverse it all and get back."

Doubt is only now dawning on Logan.

Betty swallows and her eyelids flutter. She doesn't like how that sounds. It's only now occurring to her too and to all gathered that if Logan can tap into this ship's nerve center, this may end up becoming a one-way trip.

Even though Betty insisted on staying aboard as the pool reporter, General Teapard regrets allowing it. She is clearly distracting Logan. Personal emotions are starting to bubble between them.

"Look, let's focus on one thing at a time, shall we?" General Teapard says. "We may not be from the fifty-first century, but we're still pretty smart...for a bunch of twenty-first century monkeys."

Chuckles break the tension in the ship.

"Also, we figured out how to kick Goliath's ass," adds President Beltran, sensing Betty's concern as well. "I'm sure we can figure out how to get everyone home."

Logan knows Betty is worried—he can hear her with his Mindshot helmet. Betty's private thoughts flow to him like a running faucet.

*I've lost him once. Am I going to lose him again? I can't do this. I have to leave. I should get up and leave. I have my **child** to think about! What am I doing here? But I **love this man**... God help me. I have to keep it together. Keep it together, Betty...*

Logan turns back to her and discreetly nods to her. He flips his eyes up to his Mindshot helmet, telling her in that one look: *I can hear you. Don't worry. We'll be fine.*

Betty realizes Logan is the only one wearing the Mindshot and can hear her thoughts. She laughs out loud. Everyone looks at her again, puzzled.

Betty sends Logan another thought.

I'm sorry. This is bigger than all of us. Please, don't worry about me. You need to focus.

Logan nods and turns back to the control panel. He focuses, shutting out everything else.

As he normally does with any challenge, rather than keying in on the whole enormity of the task, Logan zeroes in on the smallest component of the conundrum. He then moves on to the next small detail, and so forth—micro rather than macro. Right now, all he wants to do is access the control panel, which gets him thinking.

Over the past centuries, human advancement has always occurred for one primary reason: to make daily life easier. From the discovery of fire, to the invention of the wheel, to indoor plumbing, all the way to the Internet, humans are always trying to make their day-to-day as comfortable and as uncomplicated as possible. In the twenty-first century, computer technology is fast moving to be more and more user-friendly—touch a screen, swipe a screen, drag and drop—it's all designed to be simple. Most important, one doesn't need to know *what* the technology is inside that computer that makes the machine run, one *only needs to know how to access it*. This is why Logan is betting that, even three thousand years in the future, humans will have continued their obsession to simplify any and everything in their lives.

Logan is betting that in using his recalibrated Mindshot helmet, he'll be able to telekinetically access that control panel by simply thinking about it, because he's theorizing that future humans would've wanted it to function exactly that way—for their own comfort.

The question now is: is it as simple as thinking, *Control Panel, on?* It seems silly, but he goes for it–he thinks this—and it works.

The moment he thinks, *Control Panel, on*—the circulatory system that makes up the control panel suddenly lights up and throbs, glowing radiantly in emerald green. Some sort of liquid pumps through its complex pattern of capillaries, like the human bloodstream. It's as if the entire spacecraft is suddenly alive.

A moment after powering up the control panel—*bzzzrph*—a holographic dome *arises literally all around him*, just as occurred with the three-dimensional archival videos. Logan is fully encased in a virtual, three-hundred-and-sixty-degree holographic shell, wherein he has a complete view of the military base and surrounding desert. Logan can now literally see in front of him, behind him, above, below, to the side...everywhere. All he has to do is turn and look, and whatever is there, he sees. It's as if he's standing atop the roof of the vessel, like a hiker at the summit of Everest; Logan has a complete circular view of the area surrounding the vessel.

He smiles, awestruck. "Wow."

The vessel begins to hum louder. Its main engines have been accessed and are firing up—except, there's no combustion-based ignition—nothing mechanical.

Logan doesn't understand how it works, but it doesn't matter. It's the same way an automobile driver just needs to know where the gas and brakes are located. He has control of the ship. Without taking his eyes off the pulsating control panel, Logan says to everyone gathered, "I'd take a seat if I were you."

After concerned head turns, they all move into the plush chairs meant for the Voyagers. *Click, clack, click*—they strap on their seat belts and turn to watch Logan.

"Let's take her for a little spin around the block," Logan says, never losing focus.

The ship rises, albeit unceremoniously. It ascends and sputters, then drops, only to waft up again. Logan tries not to be distracted by his inauspicious piloting debut; instead, he keeps his mind on making the ship rise.

User friendly, user friendly, he keeps thinking. *Fly...up... go up...stay up...*

Finally, after a few more fits and starts, the gargantuan vessel soars.

The people gathered outside aren't sure what's happening, and with eyes locked on the spacecraft, they back away fearfully.

Everyone in the chairs holds tightly to the armrests and looks on tensely, not saying a word. Most are wondering to themselves why they didn't get off this damn ship when they could. Logan can hear all their doubtful thoughts, but he tunes them out. He's got more important things to do—like banking the ship around.

Let's see if I can do that.

It was easier to accomplish than he thought. Intuitive actually. He simply looks into the three-hundred-sixty-degree-holographic view, toward the heading he wants to go, and the ship turns, pivots, and banks in that direction.

Logan laughs again—giddy. "This is awesome," he says. "Now, let's see what kind of pick-up-and-go this baby has."

A moment later, he leans forward, as you would on a Segway, peers into the vastness of the open desert spread out before him, and thinks, *Accelerate.*

Zero to sixty is a baby's crawl for this vessel. Its impulse power was more zero to Mach six—dead stop to whiplash. The spacecraft projectiles forward at 4,567 miles per hour, yet nobody inside feels the effect of the G-forces. The three-hundred-and-sixty-degree hologram encasing Logan reveals the surroundings are blurring past at dizzying speeds.

Evidently, the interior of the craft is somehow pressurized, eliminating any of the effects of the high rate of travel. Then Logan stops the ship, not on a dime, but on a microscopic pinpoint. Just to see if he could. The ship halts without the sensation of inertia propelling anyone forward, the spacecraft comes to an absolute standstill, one millisecond to the next, with again no effect on anyone inside.

They're out in the middle of the desert, one second to the next. Logan laughs again. Slowly, he turns to the stunned group, who watch him, still entombed in his holographic cocoon, totally bowled over.

"East to west. Check." Logan grins. "How about south to north?"

Before anyone can object, Logan looks upward into the holographic shell he stands in and sees nothing but blue sky over head.

Up, he thinks.

It's a straight vertical shot up into the heavens, faster than humanly imaginable. Blue sky gives way to clouds, to blue skies again, to the Earth's red-glowing atmosphere, to the stillness of outer space, where they now orbit.

Logan looks all around and beholds the elegance of the cosmos. They're more breathtaking than anything he's ever dreamed. Down at his feet, the holographic encasement reveals planet Earth in all her glory, below him. The passengers sit in silence, mesmerized as well, seeing in sheer captivation what only few humans before them have.

Finally, Teapard breaks the noiselessness. "Well, that settles that," she says with a grin. "We can definitely fly this baby."

CHAPTER TWENTY-FOUR

Logan lands the spacecraft, gently, at exactly the same spot on the base from which he lifted it off. Upon setting her down, he exhales with a ceremonious smile, then steps away from the alcove that is the cockpit. The moment he does so, the holographic viewing dome vanishes. Logan pauses, curious. He steps back into the alcove and swoosh, the dome reappears. Out, it vanishes. In, it reappears.

Logan heads over to the president and the general, who have been in hushed conversation this whole time, clearly stupefied by what they've just experienced, as are all the other passengers, including and especially Betty. She embraces Logan tightly. They part after a few moments, and with his arm still draped over her shoulder, he turns to the group.

General Teapard steps forward and looks Logan in the eyes. "We need to talk. Alone."

The general's plush office is filled with dark wood; medals, commendations, trophies, and weaponry adorn the walls.

Logan plops down onto one of the leather couches, and gets comfortable, as President Beltran and General Teapard take seats across from him in stiff chairs.

"I guess I should begin training your pilots immediately, huh, General?" Logan asks. "It's not that difficult to figure out, once you get the hang of it."

"Dr. Logan, we have the best pilots in the world, I have no doubts you can train the whole lot of them to fly that vessel, just as you did."

"Great." Logan nods.

"So what I'm about to ask you will seem unnecessary at first." Teapard leans forward. "But is absolutely vital to the success of this mission."

"And to our very survival," Beltran adds somberly.

Logan looks from Teapard to Beltran and back. *Where are they going with this?*

"You invented the single most important piece of hardware, arguably ever, in the history of mankind," Teapard says.

Logan shifts uncomfortably in his seat. "My original ambitions ended with me being a billionaire laying on some tropical beach, not with me irrevocably altering the course of human evolution," Logan says, his good mood vanishing. "Just tell me—what are you both driving at?"

"Because you lived and breathed the Mindshot practically your entire life, you have a unique perspective on its use and abilities," Teapard says, calmly.

Logan shrugs. "And?"

"And because of that, we'd need you on this mission to the future," Teapard finally says.

Logan goes taut. "General, are you suggesting I not only have to train your pilots, but I have to go along with them?" Logan asks, incredulously. "*Into the future?*"

"That's exactly what I'm asking you to consider."

"Absolutely not," Logan says without hesitation. "I'm not a soldier. So no, I am not going on some half-cocked suicide mission into the future."

"Is that what you think it is?" Beltran shoots a look to his general and back to Logan. "A suicide mission?"

"Yes!" Logan blurts out but then reconsiders. "I mean maybe. I...I don't know. Seems like it is, doesn't it? You don't know what it's like three thousand years from now. None of us do. Other than that we evolve into a bunch of freaks. I mean, what are you planning to do? Land on Earth in the year fifty-whatever and race out, blasting away. In case you've forgotten, they can move crap with their minds. It'll be like our troops coming off the Higgins boats at Normandy. We'd get slaughtered."

Teapard frowns and straightens up. "As I recall, we ultimately won that war."

"Big difference between Nazis and future humans," Logan spouts back.

"Which is why we need you on this mission," Beltran says calmly, sensing the sudden tension between Dr. Logan and General Teapard. "You're uniquely qualified to learn their technology while pushing ours beyond its limits."

"Besides, it's not all rockets and ramparts. We're planning diplomacy first; isn't that right, Mr. President?" Teapard sighs.

"That's right. A peace delegation will engage first. Attempt negotiations. See if we can't settle this thing diplomatically, without bloodshed."

"And if that doesn't work? Then what?" Logan asks. "War?"

"As a last resort, yes. War," Beltran concedes, soberly.

"War is a losing proposition against them. You know that, right? Tactically speaking," Logan asks them both.

"You leave that part to me." Teapard's tone is clipped and gruff.

Logan stands up and paces. Caged animals seem more relaxed when they pace. "Look, even if I wanted to go, I'm about to become a father. I can't just leave my child. I can't leave Betty. It's not about me and about my own ambitions any more. I'm going to be a father. I'm sure you of all people understand that, Mr. President."

Logan has never felt this emotional but holds back his tears. Yet glossy eyes betray him.

"I certainly do." President Beltran smiles sadly. "Which is why I'm going to go on the mission, as well."

Logan is stunned.

"As a father, if I have a chance to save my children, even if it means risking my life...if I have that chance to personally assure their safety, their lives, their futures, I'll do it." Beltran stands and moves toward Logan slowly. "So, let's say you stay here, become a father. Wonderful. It's amazing. There's nothing like the birth of your child...watching him or her grow up..." Beltran seems lost in memory for a moment. "...but if you're anything like me, or any father worth his salt, you will also want to protect your child at all costs. So yes, you can stay here—that's absolutely your prerogative—but then you're putting your fate and your child's fate in the hands of others who probably won't be able to do the job as well as you. So what we're asking— what I'm personally asking—is that you oversee the mission that can guarantee that your unborn child is born free and safe."

These words percolate in Logan's head.

After several moments, Beltran concludes, "Dr. Logan, the bottom line is we need you and your unique expertise on this mission. I realize that what we're asking is too much, but we wouldn't ask it if it we didn't feel your participation was absolutely critical."

Logan closes his eyes as his head drops toward the floor, knowing this isn't over for him. Far from it.

I'm going on the mission into the future.

There was nothing in that utterance Betty wanted to hear. The words force tears to spring into her eyes—a hybrid of rage and fear. Logan cries as well. He was hoping he wouldn't, but the sight of Betty doing so is too much. They weep together, alone, inside his bungalow on the base. Betty can't even look him in the eyes. She knows he has to go, of course, whether she cares to admit it or not. Right now, as important as it is for the father of her unborn child to be present during pregnancy and birth, she fully comprehends what is at stake here. Perhaps all of humanity needs him more than she does. This only makes her sob more.

She says into his shoulder, "What if you never meet your son?"

He whispers into her hair. "That won't happen."

Betty pulls back and locks her red, wet eyes on Logan. She blinks curiously.

"They want to conduct a time-travel test, a trial run, to make sure we can actually do it," Logan tells her soothingly. "So I gave them my one condition to going along on the mission." He manages a smile.

Betty thinks she knows what that condition is, but Logan's not saying it just yet. He's just smiling at her. So she demands an answer. "What condition? You tell me right now, Norman Logan!"

"They've agreed to travel nine months into the future."

For a moment, they stare at each other, until he swallows her in a sweet embrace.

CHAPTER TWENTY-FIVE

General Teapard stands solemn in her dress blues over dozens of flag-draped caskets.

"Ladies and Gentlemen, I appear to say but a word. This extraordinary war in which we are engaged falls heavily upon all classes of people, but the most heavily upon the soldier. For it has been said, all that a man hath will he give for his life; and while all contribute of their substance, the soldier puts his life at stake, and often yields it up in his country's cause. The highest merit is due to the soldier." Teapard folds the paper she was reading from. "Those words were spoken on March eighteenth, 1864, by Abraham Lincoln. They remain poignant to this day."

After the heart-wrenching service ends, General Teapard assembles what she considers her dream team for the newly christened Operation Finding Hope.

The mission team consists of two hundred people—former NASA astronauts, Special Forces, and a handful of carefully selected politicians, who will be on hand to attempt peace negotiations in the initial stages of arrival during the mission. The core of the mission consists of Logan, Teapard, and Beltran—who had already sworn in the vice president to take command in his absence.

The only nonessential person allowed on the trip is Kyle. The moment Kyle heard about the mission to the future, he insisted on being part of it. He offered to document the whole mission. After all, if they got back alive, his footage of the journey would be recorded for analysis and posterity. Although a glut of international media was now gathered along the perimeter of the base, Teapard was enforcing a strict media blackout. Unless of course, Kyle could become the one and only person to record this mission.

Not going on this voyage would be devastating for Kyle. What more did he have to live for in present day? He was infertile, so staying in the present meant he'd never have a biological family. Going on this mission was what he was meant to do with his life. He knew it and relentlessly insisted on going. So Logan vouched for him, and when Teapard agreed to let him on, Kyle didn't stop hugging Logan for five minutes straight.

Teapard ordered everyone who was going to partake in Operation Finding Hope to come along on the trial voyage through time. Mandatory. No exceptions. She wanted to see if this team was equipped both physically and mentally for the primary mission into the fifty-first century.

Before boarding the ship, they all gathered to rewatch Betty's interview with Peter on a fifty-five-inch plasma erected in the hangar—a refresher course of sorts. They were to pay particular attention to when Peter discussed how time travel works. Peter's face in close up, so large on the TV screen, is off-putting. Despite their disgust in him, they listen to his words closely.

First, they had to travel to Jupiter and in particular the planet's red spot.

During the interview, Peter said, *To travel here, we told the vessel our destination: this year, March, the twenty-fifth day. It processes that command and does the rest in conjunction with the vortex within the Great Red Spot.*

The interview moves on to the contentious part—no more discussions about time travel—so Logan turns it off. He faces the collected ensemble—consisting of Beltran, Teapard, Betty, and the entire motley crew of two hundred personnel that make up the mission team.

"That's it. That's all we have to go on in terms of time travel," Logan says.

Nobody says anything. It's thin. Betty shakes her head in disappointment.

"I'm sorry everybody. I should've asked him more questions about time travel, made him go into more detail. I mean, Christ, that's not remotely enough information for you people to go out there and risk your...risk everything."

"It's not much, I agree," Teapard concedes. "But it's all we have, Miss Suarez."

Betty searches Teapard's face. "Wait. You are going to cancel this mission, right? I mean, you're not still planning on going, are you?"

Betty is on her feet now, fully animated.

"Based on what? On that? On 'we tell the vessel where in time we want it to go' and then we go? Woo-hoo! Off to

Jupiter? Into the frickin' red spot? You're buying that? You can't believe it's that simple, can you?"

Teapard looks over at Logan, whose head is lowered, not daring to make eye contact with Betty. Clearly, her doubts are his. Teapard knows she has to get in front of this.

"When Washington crossed the frozen Delaware—" Teapard begins.

"Oh, please! A history lesson? Now? Really?" Betty interrupts. "What for? So I can hear some inspiring story of triumph and suddenly be swayed into thinking this is a good idea?"

Teapard continues. "...and Washington had no idea if he and his men would sink into the icy waters and drown, or if they'd be slaughtered by the British when reaching the other side," Teapard tells her. "But he carried on and prevailed. In war, you sometimes have to act on very little."

"What's your point? That you can't possibly know what's around every corner?" Betty retorts.

"Exactly my point. Most times, all you have is just your gut. It's not ideal, but if the alternative is defeat—or death—then it's your duty to take that risk...even if you can't be swayed into thinking it's a good idea."

Logan puts his hand on Betty's shoulder and softly turns her to face him.

"Honey...up till now, all their technology has been very user friendly. And I understand it. I do. How it works. It's intuitive for me. As long as I can keep tapping into the vessel with my Mindshot, we'll be fine." She pulls away from his touch. "We need to have a little faith."

"A little faith?" Betty repeats and looks away again from him, tearfully. "I can really use some of that right now."

A little faith indeed.

Both Logan and Betty had an unquenchable thirst for faith suddenly—to the point of feeling marriage was important, even though neither were particularly traditional or religious. But after the turn of events in the last several days and the realization of what was about to happen—the fact they were going to be parents—a bit of religious tradition seemed warranted and sorely needed. Logan even dropped to one knee and proposed the old-fashioned way.

Their wedding ceremony was hastily put together in the chapel, but attended by every single person on the base. Norman Logan and Betty Suarez were married by General Teapard herself with the president of the United States serving as witness.

An elite sampling of Special Forces from every nation in the world volunteered for Operation Finding Hope. Teapard had her pick of the litter—all willing to serve under her.

Even though the vessel was originally going to transport one hundred thousand volunteers into the future making elbowroom not a concern, the mission team was still restricted to a mere two hundred because of all the hardware they were transporting with them. Teapard felt it prudent to make room for several Apache helicopter gunships, some tanks, an AC130 Spectre, and a host of other armored vehicles, as well a mini-armada of remote-controlled, fully-armed drones. Not to mention, *guns*—lots of guns, a plethora in all sizes. If war was to come with the future humans on their home turf, Teapard wanted her toys. She wanted them, ready, at her disposal. And so these machines took up considerable space, limiting how many people she could bring.

The other reason for the small number was obvious.

Even if they had brought one hundred thousand fully armed commandos, if they lost the element of surprise, the future humans were too powerful to defeat head-on, regardless of their numbers. Why send any more combatants than was minimally needed? But nobody talked about that. The soundest reason for the low troop count was that they fully intended to level the battlefield and not need a high number of troops. They intended to engage the future humans, mind versus mind.

Logan had subsequently taught Dr. Rosenberg how to rewire the Mindshot electrodes to access and establish a connection with the cerebrospinal nervous system via the pituitary body and the pineal glands. All two hundred helmets—plus fifty spares—were equipped to give their users telekinesis. Logan hastily trained all the soldiers in a crash course on the how-tos of telekinesis. Teapard's plan was: If diplomacy fails, she will dispatch the T-Squad (T for telekinesis). While wearing the new Mindshots, they were to engage, entrap, and subdue future humans via telekinesis, hold them long enough for a second team—a kill squad, be it troops, helicopters, tanks or drones—to swoop in behind the T-Squad and gun the enemy down. This tactic worked during the final battle on the base, and now with soldiers using telekinetic powers rather than just one lowly scientist, it was sure work again.

Logan didn't like it but went along anyway. He couldn't think of anything better. Whatever CliffsNotes-like telekinesis training Logan gave in haste would have to suffice, as Teapard ordered they all depart on the trial run immediately.

Initially, she'd wanted only to travel forward in time a few days, but Logan insisted on seeing the birth of his son in nine months' time, and thanks to that stubborn arrangement she made with him, everything was accelerated. Teapard's concern was, while the mission's time through space and back will be immediate, here on Earth the nine months will pass in real time. What if in those nine months, the future humans returned? Subsequently, Teapard wanted their away window to be as short as possible. A counter argument was made that the distress signal was never sent. The Telethians waiting in the future had no reason to suspect anything was wrong. And even if they did, future humans wouldn't come back to this exact time. Strategically speaking, they'd most likely come back *earlier in time*, to a day before this time, when their arrival had never happened and present-day humans were unaware of who they were and what they intended. Therefore, the away-window length argument was a wash.

Teapard reluctantly agreed to make the return-date of the trial run nine months into the future, so Norman Logan could meet his son.

Logan takes his place at the alcove, again wearing his Mindshot helmet. Upon stepping forward, he is immediately encased once again in the familiar holographic dome, giving him the full virtual view of all his surroundings in every imaginable direction.

He then quietly searches the hologram, behind him and to his right, in the direction he just left Betty standing outside the ship. She is still there in the exact same spot of their good-byes, which weren't joyful ones. Betty was convinced she wouldn't see Logan again. He tried everything to raise her spirits, but nothing worked. She didn't want Logan to go. Yet, she knew he would—he had to. Their good-bye embrace was held the entire time the final remnants of the mission-party boarded. When they finally parted, no words were spoken.

She watched as Logan moved up the walkway at the gantry. She watched as the ship's outer doors shut, sealing hermetically. She couldn't move, as if roots had sprung from the soles of her shoes, planting her there, watching the ship, waiting for her husband to lift off.

Logan takes a deep breath, soaks in one last eyeful of his beautiful Betty, while gently rubbing his wedding band with his left thumb. Moments later, Logan returns his focus on the ship's control console.

"Here we go," Logan announces.

The mission team behind him shifts in their seats, as if that will ready them more adequately. Kyle raises the HD video camera and begins rolling, just as Logan looks straight up, into the holographic dome—nothing overhead but deep blue sky, as far heavenward as he can see.

Betty watches, as the ship rises—fast, so very fast—straight up into the brilliant blue. She squints, trying desperately to track it in the sky, but loses sight of the ship quickly. Like a gunshot, that fast, it's already out of the atmosphere.

Earth sits peacefully below, as the vessel comes to a gentle rest into majestic orbit at geospace, just over the glowing atmosphere. Logan can see the blue planet at his feet. He keys in on the United States—New Mexico. Betty is down there, probably looking up into the sky but not able to see them anymore.

God, I hope I'll see her again. Can't think about that now. Stop, he thinks to himself. *Stop!*

He's glad nobody is wearing any of the two hundred and fifty Mindshot helmets that were sealed up in nearby containers, ready for use. Logan is thankful at this moment nobody can hear what he's thinking. Logan values his private thoughts of doubt.

And fear.

This is the portion of the mission that he—and everyone else—is uncertain and concerned about.

Right now, this very moment, Logan does not know what will happen next, when he loudly utters the words, "Take us nine months into the future."

Logan holds his breath, fully anticipating something extraordinary to happen, but nothing does. They're still orbiting exactly as they were. The passengers exchange puzzled looks. Logan exhales.

He's perplexed. Time to try again. "And...go," Logan says. "Now! Go! To the future. Go!"

Then, it occurs to him why nothing's happening. He smiles.

Logan next closes his eyes and thinks, *Nine months from today. Go.*

That's all he thinks. He repeats this in his mind over and over. He sends these thoughts into the ethers. Somehow, this will work. Logan knows it will—he feels it. Somehow, these humans of the future have made this possible. This is how he will trigger the ship to go, on its own, taking them where they need to go. Logan can't explain why this will happen, but he knows that it will. He can literally feel it, as if he were becoming *part* of the vessel—*connecting to it.* He's felt something similar whenever he's given a rousing lecture to a large group and can literally feel when he's connected with the audience. He can *feel* their thoughts circling back to him...as he engages them... as if he were linking to them all...because it is reciprocal... like an exchange of intimacy. When that happened, the crowd always hung on his every word—in synchronous harmony. That's what Logan is feeling right now. Because he's now sensing his mind is *linking* with the vessel somehow. The ship is pairing up with his brain.

As if it were literally downloading his thoughts.

Suddenly, the control panel of veins before him lights up more brilliantly than before, still in a glowing tint of green. Once again, Logan sees solid liquid of some sort flow within this circulatory system, bubbling like a fevered bloodstream.

Only this time around, it spreads beyond the control panel—outward.

Capillaries all throughout the ship, that nobody knew were even there, unexpectedly illuminate. They branch out all over the superstructure of the ship, spider-webbing in all directions—and all around them. An intricate pattern mazes from floor to ceiling, wall to wall, all phosphorescent green, throbbing from the liquid within. One doesn't feel they're inside a futuristic interstellar spacecraft but rather inside the belly of an alien beast. Just as they all stare, mesmerized by the complex entanglement of green-glowing webbing spreading all around them, and they forget momentarily where they were, the ship reminds them, when it abruptly bolts forward, into the depths of outer space.

Nobody feels anything in terms of G-Forces, but they know they're careening through space, incalculably fast, they can see it on Logan's holographic view. Distant stars distort horizontally as they blur hastily past, on their way through the galaxy.

And then *the moon*—there it is now, up close.

They take in its details galore, craters, rocks, and barren landscape, only seen prior in NASA images from the Apollo missions. Yet, there it is before them, Earth's only moon, racing past. A fly-by this rapid gives Logan and the passengers no time to revel in it. So before they can have a good look, the moon is behind them, shrinking smaller and smaller.

They continue farther on through the Milky Way. Deep space is all around them—nebulae in the far distance and quasars above. There are multicolored swirling gas clouds in every direction. Despite the blazing speed, they manage to catch fleeting glimpses of glorious, Hand-of-God-type views.

Everywhere Logan looks within the holographic view of the ship's exterior, reveals one magnificent heavenly body after another. A streaking comet horizontals past. Grand pillars of gas and dust are being eaten away by the brilliant light from nearby bright stars. Breathtaking. Nobody says a word.

They watch magnificent outer space move past them. Kyle videos, but catches himself occasionally letting the camera dip as he takes to observing the journey with his own eyes. Now up ahead, there's no doubt what they're heading toward. Unreal, not just because of what it is, but also because *they're already arriving there*, leaving no doubts as to the hyperspeed they're traveling.

Mars, as it is known to be, red, glowing like an intersection stoplight. Even as they whiz past the fourth planet from the sun, not once slowing down, Logan still gets a good look at the flat northern hemisphere and can even make out a few impact craters. Down in the southern hemisphere, he sees mostly mountains and highlands. The border separating the two areas contains mesas, knobs, and flat-floored valleys with cliff walls that look about a mile deep. But just as he soaks in the stark Martian topography, the vessel moves past the red planet.

And onward.

Then they move into the main asteroid belt. Some scientists have suggested this field of asteroids is densely populated and would be difficult to navigate—perilous to any vessel that enters. But as Logan discovers, these colossal stones, spinning in the belt, are actually spaced quite far apart. The asteroids are spread over such a large volume that it would be highly improbable to crash into one, without carefully aiming and intentionally doing so. Nonetheless, there are hundreds of thousands of asteroids visible all around them as they pass through the belt, and just as quickly as they enter, they shoot out of it.

Moving fast, continuing deeper into space, and toward their final destination.

Jupiter.

She's massive. Especially, as they get closer to her, where Logan can now see in striking detail the churning gaseous and liquid matter that composes the planet.

The ship makes a sharp beeline for the great spot, not slowing down. Closer and closer, they move right to the planet until they slam into the atmosphere—made up of rotating cloud layers several miles deep, resembling syrupy cotton balls. Periodic flashes of lightning convulse all around the spacecraft from every direction. Each of these unnerving electrical discharges looks a thousand times more powerful than a lightning strike on Earth.

The vessel descends into the vortex that is the Great Red Spot and comes to a dead stop dead center in this hellish storm. It's like they've been dropped into a metropolis of vexed reddish-brown clouds, stretching upward like skyscrapers, twisting furiously all around and over them.

Logan and the passengers feel like they're entombed in a vast chamber of atmospheric horrors, vulnerable to an unforgiving maelstrom that seems to now close in on them with relentless ferocity, like the walls of a trash compactor, only made of pulsating lightning clouds.

Is this where the ship has brought us? Can this be right? Or could this be some fail-safe the future humans put in place, a booby-trap of sorts they're now springing on us?

This is the first time Logan feels arrant fear. Gone is his euphoria of space travel—until he notices something peculiar.

The storm in Jupiter's red spot, which is known to spin counterclockwise, changes direction. Here, inside of the whirlpool, where the vessel now floats helplessly, the direction of the contortion is now shifting into a *clockwise circulation, just around them*, sharply altering the wind velocities and forcing the cloud patterns to squeeze inward, tightening, closing in on them. Something is happening, almost as if the storm has...*recognized* the vessel. Giving the ship all its raging attention.

Logan then watches as an immense portion of the twisting turbulent Jupiter clouds splinter into five grisly appendages that resemble a grasping hand of wrathful weather. The hand reaches out to the vessel like it wants to grab the ship, like this gigantic hand from hell wants to take hold of the spacecraft and crush it. But instead, five bolts of sharpened lightning shoot out from each extremity, like sabers, slamming right onto the vessel, encasing it fully—digesting it.

Suddenly, every vein inside the ship extending out from the control panel dispersing throughout the ship begins to tremble. The green matter inside boils. It begins to seethe.

And then, an explosion consumes the ship.

CHAPTER TWENTY-SIX

Earth: Nine months later

Screaming. Straining. Red-faced. Sweaty.

Betty bolts upright and jerks forward inside the base's military infirmary. Her pregnancy has not gone well. She attributes it mostly to the stress and worry she took on in Logan's absence. Despite doctors strongly advising her to relax—at one point late in her term, even forcing her into mandatory bed rest—she still burdened herself with concern for Logan's safety. Betty tried working, she tried exercising, she tried everything to get her mind off Logan, but nothing worked. The nine months of waiting seemed like an eternity. Now, she's giving birth—induced by doctors—and it's not going well.

The OBGYN barks orders through his surgical mask. "The cord's tangled around the baby's neck," the doctor announces. "We have to conduct an emergency cesarean!"

Betty rears back, spent and weeping. "He said he'd be back by now—"

281

"Please, Mrs. Logan," a nurse pleads. "We need you to remain calm. For your baby."

But Betty can't be consoled and the doctors realize they will need to fully sedate her, simply to proceed with the delivery of the child. The pain she's experiencing, the anxiety—

"Why isn't he back? Something's happened out there." Those are the last words she says just before she succumbs to sedation.

Focus. She can't get her eyes to focus. There is a fuzzy image of a man standing over her. She squints, tries to clear up her vision, tries to make out who this man is. Finally, Betty's view sharpens *on her husband.*

Logan looks down at her, smiling warmly. "How are you feeling?"

Is it a dream? Please, she prays, *tell me it's not.* "Norman?" she asks delicately. He nods. "I'm back."

Logan motions out the window, just off to the side of Betty's hospital bed. Parked outside is the future human vessel.

Logan bends down and embraces her tightly, saying in a gentle whisper, "You didn't think I'd miss the birth of our son, did you?"

Betty pulls away and gasps, realizing she has yet to meet her baby—her son. The cesarean was performed once she was sedated. She's only now waking from her medicated slumber.

Logan moves toward the door as a smiling nurse wheels in a bassinet. Inside, bundled tightly in a blue-and-red thin-striped cloth with a beanie warming his head, is their newborn child.

Logan reaches in, cradles the baby's head, and lovingly lifts his son out, bringing him up to his lips for a kiss on the forehead. He delivers the infant to his mother's waiting arms. Betty takes him, nestles him into her arms, and weeps.

Her son—*their* son.

"He's so beautiful." Betty cries joyfully. She's never known love until this very moment—not this kind of pure, unadulterated love. The love for your child—only a parent can truly understand how deeply profound this exact moment is.

A rush of emotions also gushes from Logan, who is unable to fight them off any longer. Between the interplanetary voyage to Jupiter, the tumultuous lightning storm in the red spot, which lurched him forward through time, bringing him back home safely, and now this, the greatest of all, the birth of a son. A son...Logan cannot maintain his faculties in order anymore. He breaks down, hugs his family—*his family*. He now has one, which also means, he now has more to lose.

"*Henry*," Betty says. "I want to name him Henry. After my father."

Logan wipes his tears, as it now occurs to him. He's already seen his son all grown up in Peter's holographic video from the future. The concept is staggering: He's already had a sneak peek into this baby's future.

"Henry's a great name." Logan nods.

The trial run had been a resounding success. Moments after they thought the ship was about to be consumed by the explosion on Jupiter, they were swept out of the red spot and catapulted back into space, directly toward Earth. They may not understand the machinations of this, why it works, but they do understand now what must be done operationally to travel through time. So Operation Finding Hope is set to commence in earnest immediately, without delay. General Teapard is now absolutely confident they'll reach the fifty-first century. But that's where her confidence wanes. She isn't so sure beyond getting there, what will happen—although she'd never openly admit that. She's found it best to keep her doubts private.

Thank goodness, she thinks, *I'm not wearing a Mindshot.*

She takes comfort in knowing that she's planned as sound a mission as she can, considering the fact she knows not what waits for them in the future. She's allowed everyone to say his or her good-byes and get his or her affairs in order. After all, she can't guarantee their safe return. Thankfully, the group of international soldiers assembled for this mission is in large part made of seasoned veterans, who make this sort of sacrifice routinely on every mission, knowing any given operation could potentially be their last. However, with the exception of Logan, the president, the politicians, and Kyle, they all know what they are sacrificing. This mission has no backup plan. They have no way of sending a distress signal should it go awry. No means to send a search-and-rescue party after them. It is just them, which fills the proceedings with a sense of finality. They all know this might be a kamikaze mission, which is why Teapard is moved almost to tears that every single team member valiantly accepts this profound notion without complaint.

Logan is the only one that Teapard is concerned about, yet he is arguably her most important asset. When she finds him, he's just emerged from the infirmary having spent the last few hours with his newborn and wife. He is seated on the bumper of a parked jeep, absently rotating the Mindshot helmet in his fingertips.

"Congratulations are in order," the general says.

Logan snaps out of what was clearly a daydream daze, his thoughts surely on the enormity of what lies ahead. He smiles, his eyes twinkling as he thinks about his baby. "Thank you, General."

After a few moments of silence, Teapard says, "I never had children, so I can't begin to understand what you're going through right now, but if it's any solace for you, a number of the other men and women taking part in this mission are leaving families behind as well. Including President Beltran."

"You don't have to sell me, General." Logan nods. "I get the enormity of this. It's not like you're forcing me to go. I chose to...but yeah, I'd be lying if I said fatherhood isn't making me question my decision."

More silence, until Logan then flips over the Mindshot helmet and holds it up to Teapard, revealing the intricate labyrinth of electrodes at its base.

"All I ever wanted my entire life was to be a huge success. I dreamt about it, I worked for it, and here it is. This was my crowning achievement," Logan tells her, shaking the helmet.

"But with great success comes great burden," Teapard replies, sage-like. "The more success you attain, the more that is expected of you."

"Now you tell me that." Logan chuckles.

Teapard laughs too. She's been burdened by the high expectations success brings too. As much as she's grateful for all she's achieved and would never complain about any real or perceived burden brought on as a result of good fortune, she understands that you can't take your success, fold, and simply walk off with your winnings, like in a game of cards in Vegas. Once you reach a certain success level, as she and Dr. Logan have, the world expects more. They expect you to top yourself—an odd by-product of success.

"Look, maybe the Mindshot has changed mankind forever, and maybe it hasn't, I don't know, but it's not my crowning achievement. That little baby in there, Henry, *he's* my success; he's my legacy, and I'm going on this mission for him. Not to preserve his future, but to save it."

The first good-bye was detached and unemotional compared to this one.

This time, all the families have come out to see the mission off. Even the first lady and the president's daughter are there. It's as if there is a sense of kismet in the air. Destiny. The future of mankind is now irrevocably tied to this very day and to these very people. But the families also came out for another reason—they expect the mission to return immediately.

Logan stands before Betty, who totes baby Henry snugly. The heartfelt good-bye becomes yet another heartbreaking one. This is too much. What can be said that wasn't said the first time? What more grief and anxiety does one have to withstand? So they focus on their child.

"I don't intend to miss a moment of this child's life," Logan tells Betty softly. "You understand that, right?"

"I do," she tells him, swaddling Henry in a blanket. She wants to focus on him, his future, rather than on this wrenching good-bye.

"Tell it back to me. Tell me why I'm not going to miss a moment of Henry's life."

"Because when you come back, you'll come back to this very second."

"That's right. I'll be gone one whole second. For you, I'll leave and literally be right back, a second later," Logan tells her. "It'll be like I never left."

"No. I get it. I get what you're telling me." Betty seems perturbed; still she repeats, almost by rote, what Logan has said. "While the mission for you may take days, or months, or years, when it's over, and you're ready to return, you'll set the time machine to bring you back to this exact time. You'll be gone only a blink. I get it."

Logan smiles, but when Betty doesn't, he frowns. "Then what's the problem?"

"You're presuming you will come back." Her voice wavers a bit. "What if you're captured in the future? What if you're—" She can't even finish that sentence.

"Betty, please—"

"No, what if a second later, you don't reappear? What if two, three, four seconds go by? Minutes? Hours? Days?

Months?" Betty is crying yet again. "What if, for whatever reason, you can't come back to us, Norman?"

"Betty, I will come back. I promise."

"No. Don't. You can't promise that. And that's my problem." Betty clears her throat and regains her composure somewhat. "Please, don't make a promise you may not be able to keep, no matter how much you want to keep it."

Logan is smart enough not to say anything else. He embraces his wife and child again. She's right. As always.

What he hasn't told her is that he hides behind a veneer of optimism. The thought of being away from her, and his newborn son, is excruciating beyond any emotional pain he's ever endured. Even though for Betty and Henry, he'll only be gone a second or two, for Logan, the duration of the mission will play out in real time, which means he will literally be apart from his new family for however long the mission takes. This is why Logan has to force himself to remember that, despite the lengthy separation, and even if the mission drags on for any unforeseen reason, and despite the fact that he will return quite possibly a bit older, he can take solace in knowing that he still won't miss one moment with his new family. Logan wants to be there for the first smile and his son's coos and laughs. He wants to wipe away his son's tears and see him sit up and crawl—everything. He wants to be there.

But he has also considered the worst-case scenario. Even before Betty brought it up. What if he never comes back? What if this is the last time he will ever see his family again? Logan holds his family close.

He is once again the last person to board the vessel.

As during the trial run, Betty watches the ship rise, only this time, she readies a smile, grasping onto hope. If the mission goes well, one second from now, Logan will return.

But...

One second after the ship disappears into the rich blue sky, it has not yet returned.

Two seconds. Three. Four. Nothing. No sign of the vessel.

As baby Henry begins to cry, Betty does too.

Even though this is the second time taking this exact journey through space, following the same exact course, it is no less breathtaking. However, by the time they plummet into Jupiter's atmosphere and settle into the great spot, the mission team completes their final checks—weapons hot, Mindshot helmets on, everyone is focused, ready for the real thing.

Mission is a go.

As the cumulonimbus red-typhoon clouds collapse onto the vessel, it forms once again into a monstrous fiver-finger claw. Everyone knows what to expect. Hellacious lightning spears again shoot out of the five cloud limbs, engulfing the vessel with a net of scalding amperage. In response, the circulatory system within the vessel again illuminates and pulses in an immense spider web of green.

And as happened during the trial run, the quintuplet of lightning bolts rip out from the intracloud storm; ensnare the vessel in a cocoon of enormous atmospheric, high-voltage, electrical sparks; and then draw the spacecraft back, like an archer would an arrow. Moments later, a powerful explosion erupts, but the huge blast is actually the lightning concentrating in a cluster to literally *propel the vessel out of the Great Red Spot*, like it were on a catapult–out, through Jupiter's atmosphere and back into space.

Logan and the others know what happens next. They'll zip through the asteroid belt, past Mars, past the moon, and back to Earth—only when they touch down, it'll be the fifty-first century, not the twenty-first, just where Logan's thought-transferences commanded the vessel to travel.

The mission team is readying themselves for this, as they enter the asteroid belt, expecting to move out of it in a moment. But then, as the huge stones tumble end over end all around them, the ship begins to slow down. Logan perks up as they slow down.

Then the ship grinds to a dead stop in the middle of the asteroid belt.

"Why are we stopping?" General Teapard asks tensely from her seat behind Logan.

"I don't know," Logan responds, just as perplexed by this unsettling development, which obviously did not occur during the trial run. The three former NASA astronauts confer, but they're also perplexed. Nobody knows what's happening.

Then they see a colossal asteroid dead ahead, drifting right toward them.

The sheer magnitude of its size is not apparent initially. But as this asteroid continues to move, closer and closer, they gasp. All of them do. The asteroid is gargantuan, oblong in shape, the size of a small moon, it seems. And it is still moving horrifically right at them.

"Um, I'm sure you've noticed the very large asteroid coming right at us, Doctor Logan," Teapard says as evenly as she can.

Logan has noticed something else too. That immense asteroid is the only one—out of the thousands out here—that isn't tumbling. It isn't spinning end over end. Instead, it's moving on a direct, deliberate path right toward them. He cocks his head curiously, eyes locked on the incoming asteroid.

Teapard shouts, "Move the ship, Doctor! We're moments from impacting that asteroid!"

"I don't think that's an asteroid," Logan says, his scientific curiosity taking over.

Teapard's forehead furrows intensely. *What does he mean that's not a—*

Scant milliseconds later, she notices the same thing Logan has.

That asteroid isn't drifting aimlessly—it's *navigating purposefully.*

All eyes are now on the jumbo asteroid, as it changes course, an odd sight indeed to behold. It ascends, moving right over their vessel, casting an obliterating black shadow over them entirely, plunging them into darkness, as it towers overhead, dwarfing the vessel.

Then, it stops.

Bizarre to see what appears to be a colossal asteroid come to a willful and abrupt halt. Holding there.

A moment later, what appears to be a bomb-bay door of some sort, on the underbelly of the asteroid, opens, directly over their vessel. And when the doors open, they all peer beyond the jagged rock of the asteroid's exterior inside it and see steel and metal and...*lights*.

There are no doubts that this is a *man-made* entryway.

Then, Logan and the others feel their spacecraft being pulled upward, as if being drawn up there by some magnetic force. Logan processes this, fast as he can. Only logical conclusion: the asteroid, which clearly isn't a real asteroid, is using its own gravity to pull their vessel up into it.

"We must be getting pulled up by a gravity tractor," Logan announces.

As he says this, everything from the control panel, to the network reticulation spread all over the vessel goes dark. As if the power were switched off. Not by Logan, but by whoever now has ahold of them. The 3-D hologram also flickers off, like pulsating fluorescent bulbs, enveloping them in darkness. They can no longer see what's happening outside. They've been rendered blind. Teapard's training and instincts compel her to react.

"Not sure what's happening out there, Ladies and Gentlemen, but keep your heads on swivel," she tells the mission team. "We've been captured."

CHAPTER TWENTY-SEVEN

All the passengers sit in darkness, save for the flashlights and halogen emergency lights that have been turned on. Shafts of light oscillate, cutting into pitch-black as they listen intently for sound, any sound, unable to see what's happening. Just outside, they sense what's happening to their disabled vessel, even if they can't see it. They've stopped rising, and they seem to have been set down on a solid surface. The vessel rattles when it settles. Next, they hear what sounds like metallic doors closing with a loud clang.

"We're inside the asteroid," Teapard whispers.

They listen. It's now quiet out there, except for the faint sound of...*movement*. Just below the craft's gantry they hear boots, lots of them. Shuffling.

Then—*click, click, click*—the unmistakable sound of rounds being chambered into automatic weapons.

No doubts now, there is an armed presence outside.

Thwoomp! Thwoomp!

Two resounding metallic impacts pound right onto the door of the vessel, followed quickly by *brrrrzzzzz* sounds like drilling, like something is boring into the door of the ship.

Teapard whispers, "They're about to breach."

"We should put on our pressurized suits!" one of the NASA astronauts barks. "No telling if we can breathe that air—"

Whatever attached to the door is now straining to pry it off.

"Too late for that now." Teapard never takes her eyes off that door as she clutches her MP4 tightly and racks a round into the chamber. "They're already in."

The door rips clean off. It lands flat, clanks loudly, and reveals solid ground of some sort out there. The pried-off door spins where it lands, like a dizzying top. The entire mission team braces, takes cover, switches the safeties off on their weapons, and waits, ready to see who—or what—comes through that now open doorway.

Logan realizes immediately that wherever they are is pressurized and perfectly acclimated for human breathing. Had it not been, their lungs would have imploded instantly and they would've all gagged and choked to death.

All eyes—tense and fearful—watch the door.

Just beyond the door, they can make out that they're inside what appears to be a very large empty hangar—steel walls in the distance, built solid with rivets, girders, and traditional support beams. It seems familiar, yet there are unique details—computer panels on the far walls and perplexing fixtures throughout—that suggest this is some sort of man-made *advanced* construction.

From outside, a man's voice calls out in perfect American English, maybe Midwestern.

"This space station is insulated, so your mind powers are completely useless in here," the male says, booming loudly. "We have disabled your ship. There is no escape. You are now our prisoners. Come out immediately."

Teapard looks over to President Beltran and whispers, "Whoever that is must think we're Clammies."

"Or maybe those are Clammies setting a trap to get us to come out."

"Thought of that as well." Teapard nods. "One way to find out."

She turns to the door and calls out, "My name is General Anne Teapard. United States Army. We have commandeered this vessel from a hostile enemy."

She waits for a reaction and is met with silence, so Teapard adds, "My mission team and I are from the year 2013."

After a long pause, the booming voice bellows back, "General Teapard, you and your team are to disembark immediately."

"I'm afraid I can't do that!" Teapard shouts back. "Not without some kind of assurance as to our safety."

"If you are who you say you are, then you and your team have nothing to fear," the man replies. "Come out, but leave your weapons inside. Understood?"

"To whom am I speaking?" General Teapard asks.

"You'll find out soon enough," the voice booms. "For now, exit the spacecraft. No weapons."

"You can't ask us to leave our weapons!"

"I'm not asking; I'm ordering. Last time I say it, *leave the weapons. Exit the spacecraft.*"

Teapard turns to Beltran. She exhales. "I don't know if we have a choice, Mr. President."

"You may be right," he responds.

"But we have no idea who or what we're talking to or even where we are," she adds.

"Seems to me, General, this has just become a diplomatic mission," Beltran tells her.

Beltran then motions to the group of very nervous men and women, a baker's dozen of them—the politicians. "You'll come out with me. Make first contact and negotiate."

Teapard doesn't like this. She looks over her mission team and takes solace in the fact that they still dutifully cling to their weapons.

As Teapard and Beltran discuss/whisper what the next step is, Logan has quietly been inching away from the group, craning for a better look out the door, at whoever is out there. And when he sees what he sees, he's stunned. Is that an optical illusion? A deep-space mirage?

No—he knows what he just saw. That *has to be* real. Logan grins and raises his hands up in the air as if in surrender.

By the time Teapard sees the movement in her peripheral, it's too late. Logan has already moved out through the forced-open entryway, hands still held high.

"Logan! No!" she cries out, but he's gone, already outside the vessel.

Teapard can't believe that of all people, Logan just went on out there casually. Everyone remains planted, stunned by the sudden turn of events.

Then, they hear muffled voices just outside the ship. Beltran and Teapard lean to listen, but they can't make out what's being said. Is that arguing? No, it sounds like a calm conversation.

"Defensive positions. Be ready for anything," Teapard orders in a tense whisper.

Minutes go by. One, two. Several more. Maybe fifteen minutes total. The muffled voices carry on the entire time outside. Nobody knows what to do next. Nobody moves. The soldiers and Special Forces await orders deferentially, as they look to Teapard and to Beltran. But they don't know what to do either.

After a long wait, Logan bounces back on board, up the walkway, pokes his head into the ship, and he's smiling big!

"Everyone, you have to come out here and see this," Logan says. "Leave your weapons in here. We won't need them. Trust me."

With that, before anyone can object, Logan turns and heads back out again. The mission team is speechless. What is happening? Who is Logan talking to? Who's out there? Nobody moves at first. Not until Teapard nods hesitantly. They all begin to disarm, laying their weapons down or leaning them against the seats. Empty-handed now, they all shuffle warily to the exit.

Beltran steps out of the vessel first and does a double take. He finds Logan, standing there, with a huge grin on his face, among a *small company of soldiers*. About *one hundred and fifty human soldiers*! Traditional humans.

Humans who look just like them.

Their uniforms are an advanced, futuristic mixture of NASA flight suits and conventional, battle-dress uniform, but there's no mistaking it, under all that garb are humans who physically look and sound exactly like them.

Logan crosses his arms nobly, as General Teapard sidles up next to Beltran in dismay, "Mr. President, General, *meet the Exiles.*"

One of the soldiers—a captain according to the stripes on his arm—steps forward. He's in his forties and ruggedly handsome, with a hint of gray in the temples. The moment he speaks, they recognize him as the owner of the bellowing voice they'd been hearing.

"My God, President Beltran. I recognize you from the history books. *It is you,*" the captain says in awe. He then looks at General Teapard and smiles even broader. "And you really are General Teapard. Your missions are still studied in field manuals to this day, ma'am. I'm Captain Robert Miller. Welcome aboard the *USS Earth.*"

Captain Miller gives them both a hearty salute. Beltran and then Teapard gingerly salute Captain Miller in return, glancing warily at Logan.

Captain Miller keeps grinning. "Wow. Okay. This is amazing. President Beltran and General Teapard, from the twenty-first century, on board my ship."

Captain Miller chuckles, only now noticing the confusion on the faces of not only Beltran but the entire mission team, as they exit the vessel into what is indeed a huge, arching hangar.

So he loudly asks, "Guess you're all wondering where you are?"

Everyone's perplexed and anxious to know what's happening. Captain Miller removes his helmet and casually rests his foot on the gangway to the vessel, draping his elbow over his knee and says, "The year is 5035. As Dr. Logan here mentioned, we're the Exiles. Exiles from Earth."

"Exiles from Earth?" Beltran waves the whole thing off. "There's peace on Earth in this century. Why are there exiles from peace?"

"The question you should be asking, sir, is," Logan interjects, "why don't the Exiles in the fifty-first century look like the Utopians?"

Beltran tries to make sense of this. "*Utopians?*"

"Sorry. *Homo telethians.* The Clammies, Mr. President," Logan clarifies, while smiling at Teapard.

"I love that, by the way, General. Clammies. Wish I'd thought of that," Miller says. "Anyway, we called them Utopians after they tried to create, well, a Utopia."

Miller strolls up to Beltran with his hands folded casually on his lower back and nods. "Let me guess, sir. They fed you the whole world-peace-has-finally-been-attained story?" Miller asks.

"I take it that wasn't true." Beltran shakes his head.

"Oh, they got peace. It's just *how* they got it that is a lie," Miller responds.

"They lied about everything," Logan adds. "Even about not altering space-time. It was a lie when they claimed they'd figured out a loophole in space-time and that they weren't affecting the future by interacting with the past. They were."

"So the future changed?" Beltran asks.

"Yes and no," Miller tells him. "Yes, it changed, but nobody knows about it. They simply rewrote the history books and altered *our own* past. Whoosh, as if it never happened."

Beltran shakes his head now, angry at having believed the Clammies to begin with. Maybe, had he been more cynical, had he been more cautious and less interested in his own political future, perhaps this all could have been avoided.

Miller can sense Beltran's disenchantment and says, "Sir, don't beat yourself up. Humans have always lied since the beginning of time. Nothing's changed today. Even the really smart ones in this century lie. So, yeah, they managed to get peace all right, but it's only peace if you go along with the rules they've set in place. You only have peace if you comply fully with what they've *deemed as righteous*," Miller says the last three words, while doing the quotes gesture with his fingers.

"You still haven't answered why you people don't look like *them*. Why you haven't..."

"Evolved?" Miller asks dryly.

The president nods. "Exactly."

Logan steps forward, nodding to Miller. "Allow me, please, to explain, Captain. Since the Mindshot has a lot to do with it."

"Go right ahead."

"Thank you, and please stop me if I get anything wrong." Logan turns back to the throng and begins to move among them as he tells the story.

"In the future, not too far from our own, pessimism abounds. Culture has been denigrated. War is rampant. People all over the globe are tired of bloodshed. People wanted a savior, but instead of one, they get many."

"The Global World Order?" Beltran asks.

"That's right. We all heard the story from Peter just before he died. What Peter couldn't—or perhaps didn't want to—tell us was that in order to attain peace, the GWO had to fundamentally transform the world first."

Logan glances over to Captain Miller, who nods. Logan exhales, before releasing the heavy burden of the next part. "And that's when the GWO introduced the concept of *advanced evolution*."

"Advanced evolution? What the hell is that?" Teapard asks.

"Exactly as it sounds, I'm afraid." Logan motions to the Exiles. "Mr. President, the answer to the question of why these fifty-first century humans look like you and I and why the ones who traveled through time appeared as they did is a simple one. *The Utopians intentionally chose to evolve into* Homo telethians."

"They chose to evolve into that? Why would they do that?"

301

"Equality," Logan reveals. "In order to achieve world peace and live in Utopia, the GWO determined everyone had to be equal. People had to look the same, think the same, be the same—exactly the same. This meant, of course, that we all had to be superior beings–nobody inferior or weaker than the other. The invention of the Mindshot made that possible."

"Are you saying they reached *Singularity*?" Teapard asks.

"I'm afraid so. Thanks to the Mindshot," Logan tells her, not proud of this.

Logan had read a lot about Singularity—particularly the work of futurist Raymond Kurzweil, whom he'd met once and greatly admired. Kurzweil maintained that Singularity is the point in the future when technology progresses so rapidly that a singular milestone of learning will be reached, pushing average humans to their intellectual limit, rendering them unable to keep up with the influx of new information. That singular and profound moment would have a disruptive impact on everyday human life, forcing everyone to become smarter simply to keep up with the relentless inundation of accelerated learning; Singularity alters human intelligence forever, giving them the capacity to keep up—like getting more storage on your hard drive. This will be aided by a combination of three important technologies from the twenty-first century: genetic engineering, nanotechnology, and robotics.

The average human will be overwhelmed, unable to consume it all, and will die off to be ultimately replaced by cybernetically augmented humans, who then become the new dominant forms of sentient life on the Earth. Singularity triggers the next stage of emergent evolution. The same way humans evolved from *Homo habilis* to *Homo erectus*, people will become *Homo telethian.*

Singularity was made possible with Logan's invention of the Mindshot. In thinking about this, the ramifications of it, Logan's mouth dries, but he continues with a mouthful of cotton.

"I'm afraid advanced evolution was intentionally set in motion," Logan continues, "wherein we were all to evolve purposely into smarter humans, humans able to speak through their thoughts, able to move any and all items with their minds. This is when they began to implant Mindshots directly into the brains of newborn babies."

Logan chokes up with the idea of somebody implanting a Mindshot chip into his own newborn son's head.

Sensing Logan's discomfort, Captain Miller now chimes in. "Thing is, in order for this notion of equality for all to function properly, *it had to be mandated.* It had to be, because it was too insane a premise. We may all be born equal, but we obviously don't turn out equal. *That's natural human life, but **they** wanted to **subvert human nature**, which meant* in order to achieve equality, the GWO issued a directive that every single newborn, from everywhere on the planet, have that Mindshot implanted. No exceptions. They wanted this for everyone, because they knew eventually implants wouldn't be necessary. They knew that eventually, through intentional advanced evolution, all humans would be born not only smarter, but with thought-transference being an ability as natural as blinking."

Miller has their attention now.

"But that was only the beginning. Soon, they started passing laws that they felt would assure equality and fairness for all. There were a couple of key laws the GWO passed that were instrumental to sparking the evolution into *Homo telethians*. The Animal Rights Act of 2535 was the first. It declared that every animal on Earth had equal rights to humans, so the killing of an animal of any kind, no matter if it was a cow or a pig or a chicken, even to eat, was now illegal. Crazy, I know, but they did it. With the signing of that law, the entire planet became vegetarian, *because it was only fair.*"

Logan adds, "Soon, humans that no longer ate meat began to evolve."

"But it wasn't until the Global World Order passed the Return to Nature Act of 2606 that human life was altered even further and more significantly." Miller can barely mask his disgust. "The Return to Nature Act of 2606 made it illegal for any human on Earth to grow and harvest food. The GWO, in their infinite wisdom, determined that compassion had to extend to *all* living entities on Earth, and since plants are living, breathing organisms, they should be afforded the same equal rights as humans and animals. The passage of that quaint little law meant that human beings could no longer eat vegetables or fruits. This meant humans had to find other ways of attaining sustenance, but truth be told, this law was now possible and could only be passed because of new emerging technology that had been developed to fill in the obvious vacuum created by outlawing the killing of animals and now the harvesting of plants."

"Sustenance chambers," Teapard says, her voice dripping with disgust.

"That's right." Miller nods. "And if I may say so, ma'am, brilliant play in starving them to gain advantage. Simple, but effective."

"All of this led to them evolving the way they are, with no mouths and gaunt? As freaks?" Beltran asks with disgust.

"Affirmative, sir, but there's more."

He explains further that to maintain world peace and oversee equality for all, the GWO determined it was best for all humans also to live together, everyone subsisting next to everyone else in the same place. This was the final step in assuring the eradication of national identity and adherence to a one-world citizenship. The entire planet's population was eventually mandated to leave the global suburbs if you will, their homelands, and move to centralized urban areas. The GWO selected what was once Europe and the Middle East as the area all humans were to live. To accommodate the influx, these areas were first completely torn down, dismantled city by city, brick by brick, until any and all remnants of old were wiped away. Rebuilt overtop of what were cities like Paris and Rome and Baghdad were modern gleaming metropolises, able to lodge seven billion humans. Everyone now lived happily in concentrated, densely packed global cities, filled with sleek high-rises and urban sprawl under the promised welfare of the GWO. As for the remainder of the globe, North and South America, Asia, and anywhere else the GWO determined was uninhabitable, these areas were abandoned and left to reclamation by nature.

Once proud nations, cities, and towns stood empty and uncared for. They fell into disrepair and ultimately succumbed to the will of the environment. They were, in due course, lost under miles of thick wilderness, forest, and jungle overgrowth. Within a millennium, only a fraction of the Earth was populated by humans, while the rest of it, the United States included, returned to looking as it did in the day of the dinosaurs. Once this egalitarian society was firmly entrenched and adhered to by all, no citizen on Earth felt different than another. No human being felt better or worse than any other. It was utopia manifested. Equality of outcome is assured.

And this is was how world peace was finally achieved.

CHAPTER TWENTY-EIGHT

Captain Miller sees that he's stunned the newcomers, so he attempts a smile.

"Luckily, there were those back then who felt just as you do now. There were those who rejected these barbaric mandates and tried to stop them, but the GWO insisted on compliance, promising *they* had our best interests at heart. We knew they didn't. How? Because those that refused to comply were hunted down and killed."

Gasps all around.

"Hard to fathom, I know, but it's true. Those *peace-seeking* Utopians set out to eliminate dissenters. This was for the sake and good of *the people*, of course." Captain Miller can barely mask his sarcasm. "Anyway, *Anthony Logan* led this inquisition. He used advanced mind control, and rounded up millions of dissidents world wide. Then you had two choices—join or die. Luckily, millions were able to escape. That was almost a millennium ago. Those exiles and their descendants have been living in this space-station, in secret, ever since."

Logan steps over, motioning to the space station they stand in.

"The Exiles built this technological marvel, the *USS Earth*, to look just like an ordinary asteroid on the outside. Disguising it to blend in within the main belt, undetectable to the Utopians."

"They'd have to land on every single asteroid out here to find us. Which would take them about, oh, forever." Miller barks a laugh and then turns sober. "Meanwhile, the humans who remained back on Earth, willingly or not, eventually succumbed to the GWO. You saw what they one day evolved into."

"But," Logan adds, "the Utopians never expected that they'd become extinct. With all their advanced thinking and supreme knowledge, the Utopians never anticipated—in all their human tweaking and advanced evolution—that they'd go sterile."

"Because they are *still fallible* human beings." Teapard nods. "Even *they* make mistakes."

Miller laughs out loud. "Yeah, much to their elitist-minded horror! So, what do they do next? Freaky freaks can't make babies and can't find us, so they come up with the next best thing—this elaborate time-travel plan back to *your time*. Operation Noah's Ark, to be led by Peter Logan himself. We, of course, did all we could to disrupt this operation."

Being a student of military campaigns in history, Teapard knows just what he means. "Sabotage?"

Miller grins. "That's right, ma'am. We were able to blow up a bunch of their prototype vessels, setting them back," he says and then shakes his head in frustration, looking up at the captured spacecraft. "But then they built this behemoth underground where we couldn't get to it. We slowed them down but couldn't stop them. By the time they launched the mission, we weren't in a position to take action."

Logan jumps back in. "Which is when, earlier today, the Exiles saw the Utopians enter the quantum portal in Jupiter's red spot and knew they were traveling through time to us."

"Exactly. It was the break we were looking for," Miller adds. "The Clammies knew we were out here somewhere watching them. They know we have the means to insulate ourselves from their mind-powers, yet, they still risked big anyway—something they don't ever do—and jumped back in time with one of the GWO's own aboard. This told us the GWO was desperate. That they were running out of time. We knew if they went into the red spot, they'd have to come back out of the red spot—so we waited. And out came this ship again. Only...low and behold, *you people* were on board instead of them."

"Just a moment, please, and maybe this is the politician in me..." Beltran pipes up. "...but couldn't that have been your opportunity to negotiate a peace settlement with them? In order to come back to Earth? Couldn't you have gone back to repopulate it for them?"

"Right. You're working on the assumption, sir, that they would have allowed us to come back and live on Earth. Or, for that matter, that they would've allowed the humans from *your* time to do so," Miller says.

Beltran frowns. "What are you getting at?"

Logan jumps in and looks Beltran in the eyes. "Mr. President, had the Utopians succeeded in bringing our Voyagers back from the twenty-first century, according to Captain Miller, they would not have been introduced into the population, as they promised, and allowed to live freely."

Beltran asks, "What would they have done with them then?"

"The plan was to *harvest their bodies* for their reproductive abilities," Miller says matter-of-factly. "Strip them clean. Once they pulled out what they needed, your Voyagers would've been killed off and discarded."

"Then, afterward, in some laboratory, with all the reproductive DNA they needed, they would've kept making humans," Logan adds, "making more like them. That's why they needed to travel back to our time, because they gave up on looking for the Exiles. They had to, given they couldn't find them and Telethian extinction was eminent."

Miller then smiles, proudly. "Which is why here on the *USS Earth*, we staunchly protect our most sacred and valued commodity. The one thing we have—" Miller nods to the platoon, as he says, "and they desperately want."

The soldiers part like the Red Sea to reveal a group of children of all ages.

The children race in from a doorway to the hangar, all laughing and carrying on, happily. The children surround the mission team gleefully, all talking at once, joyful, as kids usually are.

Following the children out, are *the pregnant women*—the exiled wives and girlfriends of the exiled men. Some of these women are farther along in their pregnancy than others.

But it's evident that children are *being raised*. And children are being born, cheerfully, on this mega space station.

Miller motions to all of the children. He speaks above the din of children's laughter and talking. "These children only know about the actual planet Earth from books and videos, but look at them; they're happy. Happy, because they're kids, and kids don't know any better. Eventually, though, these children will grow up and learn the truth—about what we're fighting for and why...just as happened with me."

Miller smiles a bittersweet smile as everyone cocks their heads curiously at him.

"That's right. I was born and raised on this space station, just as my parents, grandparents, and great-grandparents were before me. But each generation hopes that theirs is the last born in exile. We're no different. We all hope and dream of the day the Utopians are all finally dead and extinct so we can at long last return to Earth and go home."

Logan desperately wishes that Betty were here right now. Her journalistic juices would be boiling over. Hell, he wishes his son were here. What a thing to see. Logan turns to the president and Teapard.

"So, here's what it comes down to," he says. "If we can figure out how to overthrow and eliminate the Utopians, declare renewed independence, and bring these people safely back to Earth, to live as individuals, where they are all free to pursue life, liberty, and happiness...*if we can do this, then by God, we will absolutely save the future of mankind.*"

EPILOGUE

These were not aliens.

They were indeed humans filled with envy, wrath, greed, and pride. With which centuries of humans before them were also burdened. In their hubris, however, these humans viewed the word *hope* as the underlying issue shackling all of mankind.

In their view, as long as man *hoped* for something, there could never be peace. They concluded that no matter how content a human being was, he or she would stubbornly hold onto an instinctive longing for something else, for something better. No matter their station in life, humans always hoped to reach some other greater plateau.

Humans are always hoping. They *always* are.

So, the Utopians wanted to do away with hope. Eliminate it. They wanted to establish a world wanting for nothing, not needing hope, and establish absolute peace.

This is why they defined hope. Hope was labeled and stamped as a specific want. Methodically, hope became a clear and attainable milestone, the notion being that once that tangible marker was reached, definitively, the word *hope* would no longer be relevant, as there would be nothing further to long for. Everything would have been accomplished. Once there was no need to be hopeful for anything, man would not only be created equal, but at long last, *become* equal *in outcome* too.

However, what Norman Logan and the rest of the mission team saw the moment they met the Exiles was that hope is, simply put, the quest for the very survival of mankind.

Hope is the idea that even in the face of the endless indescribable horrors of life, mankind must live on.

These Exiles, to Logan, were the true definition of hope.

Hope is what every human that has ever lived, and ever shall, will ever need to get through just a single day.

Humans will always hope for that better tomorrow, which will perhaps remain just out of reach, indefinitely, beyond the horizon, but that hope will always be there as a shining beacon of optimism.

To be continued in book 2:
Within Mindshot

ACKNOWLEDGMENTS

I must confess my exposure to sci-fi comes mostly from movies. Seminal sci-fi movies like the original Star Wars series and *ET* and *Close Encounters* influenced my love of the genre primarily and were the types of sci-fi stories I've always gravitated toward ever since I was very young. *Star Wars* came out when I was seven years old, and it got me interested in movies. *ET* came out when I was twelve and made me want to be a director. If you can consider *Back to the Future* a sci-fi story (I was fifteen when that came out), then that movie also had a huge impact on me, as well. I was influenced by those great movies that came out in the seventies and eighties and wanted to pay homage to that era.

So essentially, with *Mindshot*, I wrote the kind of sci-fi novel I'd want to read—a fast read—on a beach, or on an airplane, or at bedtime. I wanted to write something that was pure escapist, and exciting fun, just like all those great movies that inspired me.

Many thanks go to the wonderful people who read the manuscript beforehand and gave me comments and encouragement.

In particular, I want to thank:

Jon Molerio

Vicky Eguia

And of course, Roni Menendez

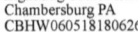